ahōti

A Novel

A Story of Tamar

Praise for *Ahoti*

As an author of biblical fiction, I know the amount of research and work that goes into crafting a story like this. Miriam Feinberg Vamosh and Eva Marie Everson comprise the perfect team.

Jerry B. Jenkins
Writer of the *Left Behind* series and *The Chosen* novels

Evocative, illuminating, beautiful, tragic, and triumphant at once. *Ahoti* is the story of Tamar we only thought we knew— a tale of faith and hardship written in breathtaking detail.

Tosca Lee
New York Times best-selling author of *Iscariot*
and *The Legend of Sheba*

In a compelling melding of Jewish history, folklore, and biblical truth, the tragic story of King David's daughter, Tamar, leaps off the page and shouts a redemptive cry for every woman silenced by her circumstance. A masterpiece of fiction based on solid historical documentation, Ahoti: *A Story of Tamar*, is a biblically accurate and believable story about one of the most unfairly treated women in the Bible. The authors have successfully related Tamar's tragic tale without villainizing David or the ancient culture in which he ruled by presenting a strong woman's response to a lifetime of adversity. Today's reader will find an example of hard-won redemption for the past and hope for an unexpectedly hopeful future.

Mesu Andrews
Best-selling author of *In Feast or Famine*

I was privileged to have the opportunity to discover, annotate, and publish the ancient text *Words of Gad the Seer*. Now I feel even more privileged, when Ms. Feinberg Vamosh and Mrs. Everson share part of the book with the whole world. This story of Tamar is for women by nature, and it is almost unbelievable that it was told thousands of years ago.

Prof. Meir Bar-Ilan, Professor Emeritus
Former chair, Talmud Department, Bar-Ilan University, Israel
Author, among many other works, of *Words of Gad the Seer*
(Scotts Valley, CA: CreateSpace Publishing, 2016),
Some Jewish Women in Antiquity
(Atlanta: Scholars Press, 1998)

Fans of Biblical historical fiction will fall in love with Vamosh & Everson's *Ahoti*. This story is filled with heartache and healing in a beautifully crafted tale of pain, loss, and redemption. A compelling historical novel that answers the question, "What happened to Tamar?" The authors bring well-known historical figures to life through this familiar tale of woe with an unexpected twist. From the splendor of David's palace in Jerusalem, to the lowly streets of Abel, to the haven and confinement of Geshur, and back again, Tamar finds herself on a journey she never knew was waiting for her. Vamosh & Everson grant Tamar not only a well-crafted story that ultimately results in a new name, but also a woven tapestry of God's redemption they can wrap around their personal struggles.

Jenifer Jennings
Biblical historical fiction author

ahōti

A Novel

A Story of Tamar

Miriam Feinberg Vamosh
Eva Marie Everson

Raven

PARACLETE PRESS
BREWSTER, MASSACHUSETTS

2024 First Printing

Ahoti: *A Story of Tamar*

Copyright © 2024 by Miriam Feinberg Vamosh and Eva Marie Everson

ISBN 978-1-64060-898-6

The Paraclete Press name and the Raven name and logo are trademarks of Paraclete Press.

Library of Congress Cataloging-in-Publication Data
Names: Vamosh, Miriam Feinberg, author. | Everson, Eva Marie, author.
Title: Ahoti : a story of Tamar / a novel by Miriam Feinberg Vamosh & Eva
    Marie Everson.
Other titles: Words of Gad the Seer.
Description: Brewster, Massachusetts : Paraclete Press, [2024]
Identifiers: LCCN 2023046875 (print) | LCCN 2023046876 (ebook) | ISBN
    9781640608986 (trade paperback) | ISBN 9781640609006 (pdf) | ISBN
    9781640608993 (epub)
Subjects: LCSH: Tamar (Daughter of David)--Fiction. | BISAC: FICTION /
    Jewish | FICTION / Women | LCGFT: Bible fiction. | Christian fiction. |
    Novels.
Classification: LCC PS3622.A55624 A74 2024 (print) | LCC PS3622.A55624
    (ebook) | DDC 813/.6--dc23/eng/20231120
LC record available at https://lccn.loc.gov/2023046875
LC ebook record available at https://lccn.loc.gov/2023046876

10 9 8 7 6 5 4 3 2 1

Published by Paraclete Press
Brewster, Massachusetts
www.paracletepress.com

Printed in the United States of America

Dedicated to the memory of
Lucy W. Feinberg
1948–2018

"Two lights are not twin-born, yet shine as one;

Two voices sing no duplicate of tone;

Yet in the song two lives are strangely blent,

As if a double soul gave it one vent."

—Louisa May Alcott

Dedicated to the Memory of

Gary W Feinberg

1948-2018

Glossary of Hebrew Terms

Ahi – my brother

Ahōt – sister

Ahōti – my sister

argaman – a shade of purple

Avi – my father

beit sohar – prison

Biti – my daughter

Chileab – Like (resembling) the father

Duda'im – Mandrake

Hahozeh – lit. "the seer" but also the form used
              when addressing such a person

Lo Valo – certainly not!

tamarim – date palms

Yakirati – my darling

Geshur
961 BCE

On the day they came for me, I had earlier dreamed I was walking through the pungent fir copse of my youth, high in the mountains near Jerusalem, seeking the nuts I once gave out to strengthen weak hearts. The crisp, comforting aroma of pine resin filled the air from flickering torches like the ones that kept the night at bay in the palaces where I grew up.

But this had been no mere dream.

I opened my eyes and looked over at Mother, her form the vaguest outline in the still-dark room. She had sat up on her mat and stared straight ahead.

"Mother . . . *Mother!*"

But she couldn't hear me over the clamor that intruded into the night. Creaking wheels, clanking armor, the shouts of men that even the stout stone walls of our confinement could not keep out. That aroma—resin from a thousand torches that lit the path of my brother's army from where they marched to the walls of Geshur. That mighty army of King Solomon, come to fetch me.

Cracks of gray light now filtered in through the slats of the locked door as I scrambled to Mother's sleeping mat and clasped her to me. We sat, wordless in the knowing. She held me to her breast, her chin resting atop my head. "Now, we wait," she said above the din. She disengaged from our embrace and rose. As if this day were no different from any other, she rolled away her sleeping mat and blanket, and motioned me to do the same. The guard would be in soon with a jug of water along with bread, olives, and figs.

But there was no sustenance that day. I paced, while Mother kept mostly to the cushioned bench against the wall and watched me, her eyes wary, occasionally looking away toward some distant place I could never go.

The cracks in the door grew bright as the day wore on, then gray again with dusk. Finally, the door rattled as the heavy wooden key turned the lock.

Manas, the man who had kept us under lock and key, pushed open the door in one swift, rough move. His small black eyes roved the chamber, landing everywhere but on us. His jaw clenched and unclenched repeatedly as if he were about to say something, until he stepped aside.

He was not alone.

The man who stepped heavily over the threshold after him looked vaguely familiar. Taller than any man I had ever seen. A silver mane spilled from beneath his helmet, still shot through with the copper strands that bound him to the mountain folk of southern Judah where my father had first reigned. It was a trait he shared with King David, my brother Absalom, and me, once, before white had wiped away the russet that recalled a tie to family and homeland.

Broad pink scars beat paths through the warrior's grit-caked beard. One emerged from the tangle and ran up his cheek, spanning the place where an eye had once been, and disappeared under his helmet. I would never forget that wound. I had treated it myself. Though I could not save the eye, I had saved his life.

"Mother," I said with a calm I didn't fully feel. She had sprung from her seat like a panther when the key turned the lock and had stepped in front of me as if that was all that was needed to shield me from the stranger. Love flooded through me to dissolve the fear.

"It's Benaiah. Benaiah, son of Jehoiaha. Do you remember him?" I spoke softly. Perhaps it was I who could shield her, repeating a name from her past that would calm her and diffuse the danger in this moment.

She might remember. Benaiah had been with my father from the days of the desert. His valiant spirit and loyalty had rightly earned the title by which he was known far and wide in Judah. They had taken him through a hundred battles against men and gods. I struggled to pull a memory deep from the well of the past, from before the time of my disgrace. And hers.

"Mother, Benaiah is the man who returned from Moab at the head of his men—thousands and thousands of them—marching through the streets of Jerusalem to present the smashed altar hearths of the abominable Chemosh to the king. What a glorious day that was! Remember?"

I couldn't see her expression, but when her shoulders relaxed, relief flooded Benaiah's battle-torn face.

"*Bat Hamelech!*" he said then.

My childhood title, my native language. Those two words seemed to fell the walls of our prison as if a battering ram had smashed into them.

Tamar . . . my name. *Bat Hamelech* . . . my title, because I was the daughter of the late king of Israel. And now . . . I stood before the man who had been sent to return me to Jerusalem after nearly two decades of hiding. Now, I would be taken to see my brother, the newly crowned king.

And my fate—whether I lived or whether I died—lay completely in his hands.

Jerusalem
17 years earlier

The milk thistles' royal heads were gone now. Weeks ago, before the rains stopped, they had risen tall on their stalks, lording their beauty over all the other herbs in my spring garden. But it was now, gray and withered, that they called to me, ready to offer up their precious seeds. My turmeric plants no longer had rivals; they no longer needed to shy away among their leaves. Their time had, at last, come to show off their fuchsia blossoms. The caper flowers had unfurled, their violet stamens proudly announcing that they, too, were ready for harvest.

And here now had come my favorite time of day—when I, the healer, strolled among the furrows and offered my thanks for these healing beauties.

But then, as if on the wings of a flitting butterfly, I no longer walked between the rows. No, I drifted just above them. This happened sometimes in my visions, and it was good for the healing. I welcomed it.

The floating would stop when I reached the garden wall. There it would always be, this wall, forcing itself between the women of the palace and the world beyond. This wall, the one constant in my life.

I opened my basket, stretched out my hand, ready to pinch off the heads of the thistles growing along it. *But what is this? . . .* The thistles were pulling away.

No. As the distance grew, I realized not they, but I pulled away. I continued to float until the wall disappeared. Below me, where the city's dwellings should cluster shoulder to shoulder, was nothingness. I clawed at the air, which stole my breath. Then, just as panic threatened to rise, the sash around my midriff caught on the cliff edge, spiraling and spinning me as I plunged until . . .

I jerked. A dream. Another dream. I forced my eyes open and shook my head free of it, determined to steady my breathing and thinking that perhaps today—this morning, in fact—I'd take the story to the seer. Gad would know what it meant. For I, healer and diviner of the dreams of others, could not interpret it.

"Mara." I looked up, acknowledging my servant's presence, kneeling next to my bed, as she did every morning. Wordlessly, she handed me my cup. The clay was cool in my hands. It brought calm, but the pomegranate juice it held burned as I swallowed, which told me that I'd been screaming again. Ah, so this was why Mara peered at me under knit brows, lower lip caged behind her teeth. Gratitude coursed through me that she was no ordinary servant, but something closer to an ally, to the mother of whom I had been robbed, in the world of women I inhabited.

Behind her lay my robe, the bright orange-, blue-, and green-dyed strips woven among the wool's natural blacks, browns, and beige. Bright, even against the vermilion walls of my room. Cradled in the colorful cloth, gleaming against it, was my special pendant, hanging from its intricately twisted gold chain. The sweet scent of tiny, fresh-cut, blushing spikenard flowers Mara had placed in my slippers wafted across the room. Seeing these only meant one thing—

"The king has sent for you, my lady," Mara said, answering the question I had not yet opened my mouth to ask. Ah, my thoughts have always been too easy to read, over the years, for Mara.

I did not ask her why my father called for me. Every day brought new tasks, many of them requiring my ceremonial robe. And today? For a prince, perhaps? A visiting dignitary? Or perhaps I had been called to help with an ailing servant. This was what I did, and that was what I wore. I would find out soon enough.

My visit to Gad the Seer would have to wait.

After splashing my face with water from the bronze laver in the corner that Mara filled, I stood and raised my arms, ready to be dressed. The garment floated down to my ankles as she draped it over my tunic, seemingly lighter than air, belying the nature of the wool from which it was woven. I took courage from the magical geometric patterns I myself had embroidered into the sleeves and flounced hem. The supple cloth swayed like a blossom in the breeze, the inner red and the outer purple turning into alternating stripes. I remembered, as I always did when donning the garment, the day my father announced he was commissioning it for me. He hadn't even waited until we were alone but proclaimed it proudly before all my brothers gathered in the audience hall.

Mara looped the sash around my waist. I pulled aside the curtain over the niche where I kept my healing herbs and picked up the little linen bags, each one filled with a different herb or mixture, then tucked them into the folds of the sash. As Mara tightened it, I had another memory of my father: the day he had paraded his friend Hushai, grandly robed, before me around the courtyard. "You'll have a robe more beautiful than Hushai's, and certainly richer by far than Joseph's," he'd boasted, and then told me I'd be a healer.

My father did not see me shiver at the vision that came that very moment, a vision of that fine garment's golden threads, unraveled, and the magnificently woven, multicolored wool torn and filthy. Of course, being only *the ahot* to my brothers, my father neither saw nor sensed my trembling. He generally ignored anything of significance in my life. He never tested my knowledge of the sacred stories the way he did my brothers, so how could he have known Joseph's robe would mean anything at all to me?

But I knew all the stories, thanks to the seer, and I knew that Joseph's robe spelled doom. That robe had been Joseph's downfall, the seer told me on the day he first taught me the story. Joseph's robe, given to him in love by his father, had taken him into the depths of a pit. And so, I knew, my robe would drag me into a place blacker and deeper than Joseph's ever was. But would there—could there—be redemption?

"Princess, none of that now." Mara broke through my darkness, her stern voice belied by the gentle way she'd turned and steered me with one hand toward my dressing table, holding out my beloved glass pendant in the other. This, I would not appear without. Given to me by my mother after she had persuaded the king to make me the court healer, back when I was too young even to know what it meant, it told our story. Tiny, glinting, rough-cut carnelians flanked a single smooth, great white bead, gleaming in splendor like a full moon on a clear winter night above the palace. Mother said it would remind me of her faraway roots and the worship she had put aside when she came to Judah to marry my father. A tiny, twisted thread of blue glass coiled around one end, and green glass at the other. There was none other like it anywhere in Judah, she told me. It was a treasure handed down from her mother; no one was sure where it had come from. But Mother had said it was my own version of the thread of blue in the hem of the garments only the men in Judah wore, and the healing powers of the warm, blue lake near her old home in Geshur.

Mara never ceased to remind me that the azure and the iridescence in the glass, together with the golden threads in my garment, were the exact color of my eyes—the blue-gold of my left, and the green-gold of my right.

She told me as soon as I was old enough to hear it, that more than simply my skills would persuade people of my powers. No, those two different eyes, as if coming from two realms of another world, would convince even the most cynical.

Finally, in the center of the bead was a bright red iris against a golden corona. "The eye of God, protecting you," Mother said, "and those you worked to heal."

As I sat at my dressing table, I bowed my head so Mara could slip the pendant around my neck. It nestled against the richly embroidered symbols on the breast of my robe, radiating its strange but familiar warmth while the gold chain lay cool on my neck. Lifting the bronze mirror, I watched as Mara dressed my hair.

"I don't want to go," I confessed, as if Mara did not already know. Her face betrayed nothing as she went about her task. "You were there during my last royal audience. You stood behind me. Don't pretend you can't remember that princeling from some horrid little border town whose favor my father sought, standing right next to the throne."

I took Mara's nod as a sign of encouragement, although I was surprised she didn't cut me off to remind me of some important lesson I should take away from the encounter, as she always did. So, I ventured even further. "Don't you remember his cruel little rat's eyes and the stench of garlic and burnt oil that reached us all the way across the great audience hall?"

The comb Mara wielded pulled a little too hard at my tangled curls. I had gone too far. But I couldn't help it. The words tumbled out as easily as they did in my visions.

"Fine, Mara, you've told me before. It was my mother's fate and it will be mine. I know better than to expect love. Besides, what good is love, as you've told me so many times."

"My princess," Mara said firmly, "if love were important, you would never have been born."

"And that you've told me as well . . . countless times since my mother was sent back to my grandfather in Geshur. But who in Judah has not heard the fate of Father's first wife, Michal? She *loved* the king at first, so much that she put his life ahead of everything else. And yet look how she despised him at the end, how he toyed with her and how she was reduced to tending to her sister Merav's children for the rest of her life." I paused, allowing my words to reach their target. "And so, without love, how like Michal's life might mine become—"

"Snippets of gossip carried home like trinkets from the market." Mara was the only person, besides the king and my brothers, who could interrupt me, and she had done so again. "Mindless nothings that you hear from the kitchens and storerooms while tending your herbs are not the way for our court healer—and sister of the king's heir—to decide her future." She added another sharp twist to my hair.

"Then what should?" I asked, as if for the first time.

"You've seen fifteen summers already, Tamar. Since childhood you've chafed at your life like a muzzled donkey on the threshing floor, because you want to get out. Now is the time."

Only Mara could compare me to a donkey and get away with it. I couldn't hide a smile, although I needn't have tried—Mara ignored it. "You are a beauty and the daughter of a beauty, who, until she married your father, stood to inherit a realm much older and greater than Judah. And though the moon god does not rule here as he does at home, and some disparage you because your mother was from foreign stock, never forget that your mother was the daughter of a great kingdom.

"And even when your father appoints Amnon, his eldest, as his successor, as he certainly will, even though the two of you have different mothers, you'll find a place of strength because you are his sister. His *ahot*. You will take the authority for healing your father granted you and transform it into a position no woman but you could hope to have—overseeing all the vast property and possessions that your father, whom God has shown favor to, will pass on to Amnon."

Mara's lips were pursed as usual, but her brows flitted briefly upward, and the smile that never failed to encourage me lit up her eyes. "You will soon learn to control even the expressions that you so poorly conceal now. And your power will multiply all the more when you are the wife of a great man. No one will be able to touch you."

Mara's final words floated down with the veil she placed over my head and arranged around my shoulders. I saw in my reflection that a few of the fat red curls I had inherited from my father had escaped despite her best efforts. No matter, I liked it that way. When her mood was good, Mara would remind me that my mother wore her raven hair much the same way.

At Mara's signal I gazed up to focus on the plaster flowers blooming along the line where the wall met the ceiling as she applied the cobalt blue kohl below my eyes. When I obediently lowered my lids, she carefully coated them too.

I refused to open my eyes, although the delicate work was finished. "I woke with a troubling dream this morning, and I need the counsel of the seer. I will go to him before the throne room," I announced as if my mere words, simply because I had uttered them, were enough to carry out my will. I had to go. I must. Even Mara's ministrations, the power of my robe of office, the pendant and protective kohl had not dispelled the wisps of my dream.

"We won't reach Gad's apartments until the second step in the sun staircase is in shadow, Princess. There's no time even for your meal," Mara shot back. She was right, of course. As king, my father could not be kept waiting once he had called for me, no matter the cause, whether for matters of the palace or for the pleasure of seeing his only daughter.

As if on cue, my bedroom door opened, and the aroma of the freshly baked bread wafted in momentarily, then disappeared. I suspected Mara had shooed off the kitchen maid with my breakfast tray.

I opened my eyes. "All right," I said.

I was ready now to see my father.

I was ready to see the king.

The perpetual dusk of my room gave way to blinding morning light as I stepped over the threshold into the women's courtyard. Once I shielded my eyes from the glare, vague, shifting outlines morphed into a cluster of women. They sheltered in the short shadows cast by the colonnade of *tamarim* planted as saplings by

my mother to celebrate the name she had chosen for me. Like every
morning but Shabbat, here these women sat on woven straw mats,
legs tucked under their robes, fingers flashing as they whirled their
spindles, turning wool into thread. As soon as they spotted me, they
stood to offer a murmured greeting.

"Blessed be your hands," I greeted them in return. They didn't
bother making space for me on their mats—my ceremonial robes
clearly signaled I would not join them as I often did when the sick or
my herbs did not call for care. At Mara's signal, they set aside their
tools and fanned out behind me as we moved from our courtyard
to the main palace plaza. The women's courtyard fell silent, a rarity;
as the day wore on it filled with talk, lively or languorous, baby
squalls, and the squeals of playing or quarreling children. The gentle
strumming of a lyre often flowed in the background.

Still, the noise that greeted us in the outer plaza buzzed like a
town square in comparison. The courtiers' self-important droning
had already abandoned all pretense of decorum and deteriorated
into market-stall shouting as they tried to drown each other out.
They mixed unwillingly with supplicants from near and far, all
waiting for their turn before the king. But, when they saw me, they
fell silent, and inclined their heads. Voices arched over the wall.

At the slave market, the day's bidding had already begun—
although the king had brought so many Ammonite slaves back
with him from his war in the east that the calls were desultory
and punctuated by silence; prices were low. I had seen the slaves
paraded before the city gate where my brothers and I had stood
to welcome our father back from across the Jordan at the head of
his exhausted army. There were hundreds of them—Ammonites,
mixed with mercenary Arameans, encrusted with dirt and defeat.
And the king knew just where to put them to work—from dawn to
dark, hammering out swords and shields as once they had done for
themselves in their homeland.

The throne room seemed as crowded as the courtyard, but there,
the courtiers' chatter hardly rose above a whisper, conscious as they

were of the king's presence and his top officials poised at the bottom of the staircase to the podium. The throng parted for me and my ladies, and we approached the far end of the room. The king, seated on his massive gilt throne, smiled when he saw me and raised his arms toward me in welcome. His newest wife, Bathsheba, tall and bejeweled, stood nearby. Their son, my little half-brother Solomon, squirmed in the arms of his nurse alongside them. Absently, she cupped his head with a calming hand but kept her eyes on me.

The king pushed himself up with difficulty, hands braced on the beautifully carved, recessed armrests of his throne. I had not been this close in his presence since his return from Ammon, and I wondered whether he had been wounded, and they had feared to tell me. Then I realized why he was unsteady on his feet.

My father David. His kingdom had flourished in size and strength. Delegations of supplicants from Jerusalem to the Great Sea, the Negev, and the lands across the Sea of Chinneroth waited for days to be in his presence. None of this was enough, nor were the captured shields and spears adorning the walls behind the throne. No. He tottered as he stood to greet me, because atop his unruly russet curls the weight of the Ammonite King Malcam's massive crown had unbalanced him.

The unwanted feeling crept over me again, and I worked to hide it as Mara endlessly urged me to practice. Queen Michal had described that same feeling to me one day in the women's courtyard, the sense she could not overcome when she saw my father prancing before the Ark on its way to Jerusalem.

"Daughter!" he called warmly, the servant behind him raising one unobtrusive hand to support the colossal, captured crown and keep it from toppling off. My father's voice bounded across the room, rippling against the cavernous sky-blue ceiling and down the long double rows of cedar columns, startling even courtiers used to their master's sudden outbursts. "Here you are," he added. "And in the robes of office I gave you. How clever my daughter, as if she knew what I would command."

"Come, my daughter." My father—my king—beckoned me forward to climb the staircase and stand beside him, next to the throne.

Moving closer, I saw his closest advisors at the foot of the podium, and for a moment this cheered me: Gad the Seer—my protector—and the prophet Nathan. I acknowledged their bows with a nod as I climbed the staircase to face the king.

Finally, he lowered his voice and half-turned away from our audience. It wouldn't do for hostile ears to know his message and mission for me. "Jonadab came to see me yesterday." Jonadab, the ne'er-do-well son of my father's brother, Shimeah. "He and your brother Amnon are closer than sons of the same mother, and so I trust what he told me."

Those two? Amnon, that beast of a man, with goose fat dribbling unnoticed from his tangled beard at every banquet and an already considerable paunch overhanging the broad sash of his robe. And Jonadab, his closest companion, right alongside him, as usual. When wine overcame them, they threw dripping dumplings at each other as they had when we were children while our nurses looked the other way. What did anything about those two ruffians have to do with me?

No, I knew. Amnon had probably been stricken with some disease, dubbed mysterious by my father's physicians but doubtless brought on by too much fatty meat and peppered beer. And the doctors had probably already been to see him and informed the king, as usual, that the malady would simply run its course. But our father had faith, both in God and the gift given to me—to understand the healing qualities of herbs and spices. So now it was my turn.

Confirmation came immediately. "I want you to go to your brother. Summon all of your skills and conduct the most potent *birya* ritual you have ever performed to heal him."

Averting my eyes sometimes hid what I was thinking. But my heart had fallen, dropping just as I had from my dream-cliff that morning. And of course, the king saw it in my face. "Why do you resist, *biti?* Everyone knows that no one draws forth the power of the ancient ritual like you do. Entire families gather to watch you knead and bake the sacred bread and feed it to the sick. Would you have your healing powers work for everyone else, in every palace and hovel, and not accept the task for which God chose you when it comes to healing your own brother?"

My father's impetuousness was known and feared farther and wider than my healing skills. But when it came to his firstborn and heir, he was meticulous and clear-sighted.

So then, how to evert the edict?

"Let's not give the physicians cause for anger and insult, which would impair their own skills, Father. Let their advice be heeded for a few more days. Perhaps they are right. Perhaps my brother's health will return on its own."

I might as well not have spoken. The king had already beckoned Gad and Nathan to the podium. The two older men, both at his side from the beginning, never afraid to deliver God's blessing or God's curse—sometimes in the same breath. But they also knew when to be silent, because my father was God's chosen.

Little Solomon was now quiet in his nurse's arms, his great eyes taking in everything. Bathsheba's possessive hand still rested on the boy, as it did whenever I saw them. That, as much as anything, must have been proof enough for Nathan of God's favor.

As for Gad, he had watched David choose pestilence on his people as punishment for his own sin, and then had seen David persuade God directly, not bothering to go through the seer, to lift the pestilence. Gad, after all, was a mere messenger, unable to influence the king even as much as Nathan with his parables.

These wise men knew precisely how to help me. But they could not . . . or would not.

They inclined their gray heads as they approached, keeping them bowed as they stood alongside him.

"What does the Lord God tell you?" David asked them. "Shall we wait and test the skills of the physicians further, as Princess Tamar suggests? Or should she use the skills which with the Lord has blessed her?"

So he *had* heard me after all.

The two prophets turned aside, knit their bushy brows and stroked their beards as if deep in thought. Then they murmured to each other as if their answer was not foregone. The all-knowing prophet and the all-knowing seer. Gad, especially, had been like a father to me, so my disappointment was all the greater.

As I realized I had run out of options, my thoughts turned to Absalom, my brother, offspring of the same mother. I had never told Mara what Absalom knew all too well, that Amnon was like a scorpion quietly biding its time beneath a colorful tapestry. I saw it, felt it, at the last banquet when Amnon looked in my direction and then shared a coarse laugh with his men. Absalom had been seated far from me, among our brothers who caroused near the king, his long red curls plastered to his neck with sweaty camaraderie, all abstaining from the wine as Nazirites must. But when that fiendish laughter pealed out, Absalom's eyes locked on mine for a moment, and in them I read an ominous message. And as we filed out of the room when the banquet was over, he moved alongside me and whispered, "Never find yourself alone with him, *ahoti.*"

There was no need to say the name. *Amnon.*

Gad and Nathan concluded their consultation and announced their decision. David's eyes shone at the verdict. He raised his arms waist high, palms upward, one hand toward me and one toward the prophets.

"So there we have it," was all he had to say. My audience with my father—*my king*—was over.

The prophet and the seer descended the podium first, then Mara and my ladies approached to accompany me; it was my turn to bow and turn away.

Nathan strode ahead, but Gad waited at the bottom of the staircase. He fell in beside me as we left the room through the wide, respectful swath the courtiers had once again cleared for us. He looked at me expectantly. Mara laid a gentle hand on my arm and almost imperceptibly tilted her head toward the seer.

"He's waiting. Ask him," she murmured.

But as anxious as I had been to consult Gad this morning, I had nothing to say to him now, and he could tell me nothing I did not now already know. The dream, of course, portended disaster. Oddly, though, I was more at peace than I had been since I opened my eyes that morning.

Somehow, I vowed, I would not fall off that cliff; I would not lose my garden.

I had yet to collect the flour, water, and wine for the ancient *birya* healing ritual, but, to collect my thoughts, I slowed my pace as if already in procession of the sacred ingredients. Mara and my ladies followed suit. Once again, we crossed the main palace square, this time heading to the storerooms. As soon as the attendant at the door caught a glimpse of us, he disappeared, but was back by the time we had crossed the gleaming expanse. One hand grasped the heavy key that opened the room to which only I had access. The fingertips of the other grasped an oil lamp. He unlocked the door, handed me the lamp with care, and stepped aside. The flame of the floating wick flickered and hissed in protest as the olive oil sloshed against its basin. But it did its work, relieving the blackness enough for me to spot the table near the door, piled with stacks of bowls, lids, and trays. I took a vessel and filled it with flour from the waist-high storage jar opposite the table. I set the full bowl on a tray and covered it with a lid. Then I dipped into the salt jar and set aside the amount I'd need for the *birya* dough. Next, I placed the water jug on the tray, still full after my last visit, thanks to the cool darkness of the room. And finally, the amphora, heavy with wine, the reddish hue of the pottery glowing with healing promise in the lamplight.

I opened the door, placed the lamp on the tray, picked it up and exited the chamber. At my nod, the attendant took back the lamp. Mara motioned to one of the women to carry the tray for me. She raised both hands, fingers spread in warning—wordless and unnecessary—not to touch the contents.

Meanwhile, my cluster of women had attracted enough attention for the courtyard to fall silent as we left the storeroom and made our way to Amnon's apartments. I had never expected to be there. I glanced around quickly to get my bearings and hold fast to my confidence. Unlike my courtyard, shaded by its two colonnades of stately date palms, the crown prince's courtyard had almost no shade; squat stone pillars created a stunted portico fronting the rooms. Amnon's men lounged in front of the doorways, stealing what shade they could, playing rowdy games of Senet. The guard, whose presence revealed which door was Amnon's, snapped straight and banged his lance on the stone floor. The din quieted gradually, as the guard's abrupt movement caught the attention of one after the other, and they followed his eyes to the courtyard doorway. Some of them knocked over their wine flasks, swiping at their mouths awkwardly with a forearm as they struggled to stand when they saw me.

I ignored their stares and glanced around to determine if the fire to bake the *birya* was ready, properly tended and prepared for the ceremony, to ensure its healing power. My eyes widened when I saw the large flat stone, already set among coals glowing perfectly for quick baking. Waiting for me.

I stepped across the threshold to Amnon's room and moved aside so Mara and my ladies could enter and line up along the back wall. The odors of the sickroom fought a losing battle against the sprigs of lavender and rosemary that had been scattered about, dipped in the olive oil burning in the lamps. Sunbeams speared the room through the row of small windows around the top of the walls. This chamber was larger than mine, but still, only a few paces would bring me alongside the bed where the crown prince reclined among magnificent, embroidered bedclothes.

Since childhood, this was the closest I had ever been to my brother, the future king of Israel.

Certainly, closer than Absalom would have ever wanted me to be—a thought I pushed away to fix my attention on the sick man. He already reclined; good, I wouldn't need to tell him to lie down after the *birya*, to await the dreams whose meaning I might interpret to heal him.

A man stepped from the shadows into another beam of sunlight, snatching my attention. *Jonadab*. Of course, the cousin would be there; the two of them were rarely apart. He would want to witness every step of the ceremony.

"*Bat David.*" It was not Amnon who spoke first, but Jonadab. He bowed, but his eyes never left mine, as if making a mockery of that most basic of courtly gestures. I inclined my head slightly in acknowledgment, choosing to ignore that he had not used my title, but rather addressed me as he would any other woman, as the father's daughter. *Bat David*. I found my bearings as I turned back to Amnon and delivered my greeting of encouragement, my first words to all who sought my healing. "May the Lord restore your health and may I be His humble servant in so doing."

"Come closer, *ahoti*," a gravelly voice commanded from among the bedclothes. I forced myself not to step back from the fetid chill that came with the voice from the prince's bed, but neither did I obey his command to approach. Unbidden, the cliff edge from my dream appeared, then dissipated as strength from the impending ritual and my skills pushed away suspicion. "Indeed, I will, *achi*, but now it is time for the kneading of the flour," I said. "As I begin, let's both direct our hearts toward your healing."

I turned away and gestured to Mara to bring me the tray with the sacred ingredients and knelt before them. I poured out my prayers with the water onto the small pyramid of flour. The sandy brown granules that coated my hands soon disappeared into dough, which sprang to life in my fingers. I added more water, pressed and pulled and pressed some more. My veil slipped over my eyes with my movements and I stopped only to push it away with the back of a flour-coated hand. My beloved eye pendant performed its work, swaying back and forth with the kneading and flattening. A glance told me that Amnon and his cousin were both fixed on it.

In a single motion I swept up the flat loaf, rose from my haunches, and made for the door. Jonadab, alert now, got there before me and blocked my exit.

But it was his master's voice I heard. "Don't leave." This time, the tone was dark.

"But I must bake the *birya* myself. And thanks to the excellent fire I found your men had prepared, I'll be back with the loaves in no time. You wouldn't want a coal fire in here, filling your chamber with smoke as well as shadows, would you?" I said, as lightly as I could.

I couldn't see Amnon's face, but after the briefest hesitation Jonadab had been waved aside, and I was out in the courtyard.

The baking stone emitted a satisfied sizzle when I placed the pliant loaves on it. The tiny air holes that appeared on the top told me when to turn them over, and soon—too soon—dark brown patches indicated that they were perfectly baked. The serving women who had all followed Mara out of the room, now followed us dutifully in our return and took up their places along the wall.

Mara set the tray with the warm *birya* on the table near the door and placed the sacred wine amphora next to it. She stepped aside for me to pick up the tray. My pace was truly ceremonial now, heel to toe, heel to toe, covering the distance to my brother's bed, slowly as if I walked in total darkness. The rustling of my robe became the room's only sound; the air felt close. I knelt next to Amnon's bed and set the tray on the floor at my side.

Then, without preamble, "Everyone *out*," Amnon barked. I jerked as the women scattered like chicks in a courtyard chased by children. I lowered my eyes, attempting to hide the lurking feeling that something had gone very wrong. This was it, then: the moment Absalom had warned me against. Surely, he had wanted nothing more than to protect me. Why had I not heeded him? The dread crept closer at Amnon's next words, directed at Jonadab.

"You, too, cousin."

All my senses heightened. But, I reminded myself, they always were when I began the *birya* ceremony. Jonadab's sinister, satisfied snort as he closed the door behind him echoed as loud as a thousand drums. He feared no one because of the power of his master—who at that time I had no inkling was anyone other than Amnon.

We were now alone. I could perform the *birya*. I would do my part as my father had required and then I would leave, never to return. Never to linger this close to my half-brother. I would do this because this is what healers do. What they—I—had prepared for.

Yet nothing in all my training could have prepared me for Amnon's next words.

"Come. Lie with me, my sister."

I knew instantly that I'd never forget the words, which slithered forth as Amnon rose from his pillows, leaned on one elbow, and grabbed my wrist. The *birya* had given me horrific visions before, but never about my own fate.

I had, indeed, fallen over the edge of my dream cliff. The air that rushed up to meet me filled with the lie that brought me here. Sickness feigned. But not like the one about which Michal had whispered to me while she, too, had gripped my wrist as her life— and a baby who would never draw his first breath—slipped from her body. That feint came out of love for my father, and it made a mockery of my brother's next words to me.

"I love you."

Horrified, I could only whisper, "No."

"What? I can't hear you." The words dripped with contempt, and with a breathiness that I would one day come to recognize for what it was—a man's unbridled lust. But even then, having never known a man, I saw what lay ahead. I had heard enough stories during those sunny courtyard mornings, tales of woe that the women spun into their thread and wove into the cloth at their looms. A woman, it was said, could only save herself from ruin if she screamed, and even then, only if anyone nearby chose to hear. I couldn't remember the last time I had screamed. Perhaps in some childhood game. But if I did scream now, no one—*no one*—would be permitted to save me.

The scent of Amnon's perfumed, mangy beard, mixed with his fetid breath, filled my nostrils. The salt and metal of my own blood seeped into my mouth as he clamped his hand over it and my teeth sank into my tongue. I wanted desperately to cry out, but the look in his eyes condemned me to silence. When I shut my own against them, he slid his hand away.

"Don't do this, Amnon. Don't force me," I whispered. "Amnon, you are my brother. Such a thing is not done in Israel." I called him twice by name as I did when I summoned out illnesses. Could this not distract the evil that had possessed him?

But he had called me "sister" when he yanked me onto the bed, and my muted plea seemed only to inflame him further. He pinned my hands behind my back with one beefy hand.

"We share only a father," he said through clenched teeth, as he pawed aside my robe and grasped my precious healing pendant by its golden chain, twisting it around my neck and holding it behind my back to keep me pinned down. Fingers of dank air now touched my bare legs; my arms strained in his grip. I could not give up so easily, but what did I have left? Perhaps our sibling ties would save me after all? Would it not be better to be married to my brother than to endure what was coming and be shamed forever? "Then let's go together to the king," I said, my voice a beggar's whisper as I continued to try to escape him, "and seek his blessing on a proper union. That's the way . . . royal blood reigns . . . in Egypt. He will not . . . refuse you."

But Amnon's brutish mind was not as clouded as I had hoped. "First, I'm your brother and I'm forbidden to you. Then suddenly you're my destined sister-wife?" His jeer fouled the air further and I turned my face aside.

Capture his vanity, save your life, the courtyard women would sometimes say cryptically behind a cupped hand. And so I tried again. "Prince Amnon," I said, turning back to look at him, my voice attempting to emerge calmly. "Remember who you are." I managed to push up farther on the bed, but he yanked me back to my submission and I cried out before my next words poured out of me. "Will your men know that the heir to the throne of Israel had to use a mean trick to lure your younger sister, a virgin, to your chamber to lie with her?"

But the man was done talking. His tiny black eyes glazed over as he fumbled with his own clothing, his weight pressing harder than before. He arched, dug at me, stabbed, his hand coming over my mouth again when I cried out in the agony of flesh tearing flesh. Before he collapsed, he sank his teeth into my breast. Searing pain daggered through me as a roaring in my ears swallowed all other sound. I reached for the heavy, blessed blackness, to pull it down and wrap myself in it forever. But only ephemeral wisps were left. The air was cold, but my body burned and oozed. The black haze turned to red.

When I opened my eyes, he stood over me and we were no longer alone.

The manservant peered out from behind him, his eyes sidling as he calculated the market value of grinding my shame through the busy palace rumor mill.

Amnon's eyes were colder than the air as they swept over me. I summoned dignity from some deep learned place and whipped my robe closed.

Through a crooked sneer, he spit out two words. "Get up."

The prince glanced over his shoulder at his gawking servant, then raised his bearded chin in my direction. The other man tried to settle his features back into that mask that servants wear, but my blessing and my curse were to see emotions surge from others like

living creatures. And, sure enough, the man's reluctance to touch me
seeped out from behind his rigid face like oil from a cracked pitcher.
But, by then, I was more woman than princess to him; his fear of
Amnon overcame his reluctance to manhandle the king's daughter.

Amnon turned his back on me. The servant grabbed my arm and
pulled me off the bed. He picked up my slippers, thrust them into
my hands, and bundled me toward the door. In a single move he
opened it, pushed me over the threshold. A slam, then the slide of
the bolt. I was locked out of my old world forever.

Mara rose from among the women immediately. She must have
taken in the meaning of my crumpled robe, my veil around my
shoulders exposing my disheveled hair, and my cheeks, ruddy with
the shame of it all. She placed herself in front of me, shielding from
others the smudges of kohl she had so carefully applied to my eyes
a lifetime ago, now against my burning cheeks. But I pushed past
her. I had died and there were rites for the dead. I knew them all. I
rushed for the brazier where I had baked the bread for the birya; its
coals still glowed under a coat of ashes. I knelt, thrust both hands
into the hot ash and left them there.

"*Tamar!*" It was Mara, shouting my name, a thing not done in
public or private. Startled, I pulled my cupped hands from the
brazier. The blisters already reddened on my wrists, yet there was
no pain. These were the hands of another. I lifted my full palms to
my bowed head and laid the ashes on my hair.

There was still one more ritual to perform. I stood, grabbed the
edge of my beloved robe of many colors and miracles in both ash-
dusted hands and pulled at it, gritting my teeth with the effort. It
had not been made to tear this way, but tear it did. I watched as the
healing herbs I had nurtured in my garden, lovingly harvested and
placed inside my sash that morning, fluttered down and scattered,
spoiled and worthless on the dusty stone pavement.

Mara's arm hovered around my waist behind me, nearly
touching, as she shepherded me to the courtyard door. Behind her,
the women followed. A wail pierced the transfixed silence in the

courtyard—the cry of women mourning when the dead were brought out for burial. But this cry was not from mourners I did not know. Faces I could not see. It was my own, and I was the one who had died.

I took my place in front of my little troupe of women, Mara directly behind me as always, for the walk back through the palace to my apartments. I held my head high, my tattered robe clutched around my aching body with throbbing fists. But why pretend? Wasn't I invisible now? Plundered, like a newly purchased slave walking behind her master to an unknown home? Who looked twice at such a creature? No, as we moved through dim walkways and glaring, sun-drenched courtyards, servants and courtiers made way for us. And the look they gave me—some sorrowful but most insolent—told me they knew. Somehow, malevolent rumor had winged its way through the palace ahead of me. Nursemaids placed their hands on the backs of their little charges, turned their heads away, and buried them in their robes.

Would this dismal parade ever end? The blood roared in my ears and my heart pounded. I listed and the stone pavement rose up. But before it could strike, a tall form detached itself from the shadows, grabbed my bruised shoulders and propped me against a wall. The women stepped aside quickly in recognition of the man.

As if he had been waiting for me, my big brother Absalom, my protector, stared into my eyes. "Has Aminon been with you?"

Aminon? The strange way he said our brother's name sparked a memory. It allowed me to flee just a little longer from that moment when my own words would first acknowledge my disaster. That little extra syllable was the mean-spirited diminutive that we'd tacked on to the middle of Amnon's name when we'd tease him as children—little allies in cruelty. Stubby, rotund, his upper lip already darkened by a sprouting mustache, he would quiver at the insult and we would laugh at him.

"Tamar?" Absalom still held me by the shoulders, his whispered question now a violent hiss. "Tamar! Has he been with you?"

"He forced me." I no longer recognized my own voice; all my strength had been choked out of it. It was thin as a silken thread, pleading.

"What do you mean, he forced you? I told you never to be alone with him. You know how he is. You should have known this would happen." He shook me by my shoulders. "Didn't you scream? Didn't anyone hear?" With each question came another shake that brought new pain coursing through me; I couldn't bear even his touch. "Right in the heart of the palace," he said then, these last words in the litany of accusations not a question.

And in that moment, I knew. He had already framed the story. My heart sank further into the ranging depths of my anguish. I writhed out of his grasp and stepped to one side. My brother knew Amnon. As did our father. So why had Amnon been allowed to send Mara and the serving women out of the room? And why was Absalom waiting for me so near our brother's chamber?

My thoughts crashed like rocks through a swirling torrent. There must be an explanation. My father must have been sure my healing powers would protect me from Amnon . . . yes, that was it. Amnon would recover, he would succeed our father as he should. The kingdom would continue to flourish, all thanks to my healing powers. And, he'd make Amnon pay.

Again, "He forced me," I eked out. I was screaming within, drowning, but the words that emerged grew softer and softer until my mouth still formed them, but there was no sound at all. "He forced me. He forced me. He forced me."

Absalom wrapped his arms around my aching shoulders as he cut me off with a finger to my lips, his eyes locked on mine even as I jerked from his sudden movement. "Shhhh. We must think this through. He's your brother, after all, heir to the throne our father has fought so hard for." His own tone had grown oddly urgent. "You'll never be able to avenge this outrage. Even if you are questioned by the priests—who love you—and they find that, though you did not scream, the fault is not yours, what good can happen next? The best you can do is keep it quiet." He squeezed me closer to himself as he dipped his lips close to my ear. "Humiliation is not death, now, is it? Perhaps we can save your honor and give you to one of the princes from afar whom our father has been considering and he will take you away as his wife."

Absalom released me as suddenly as he had gathered me, then stepped out of the shadows and gestured to Mara. "Send word. We're going to the king."

Absalom linked my fingers in his within the folds of his own robe, locked our forearms, and rushed me through the manicured palace grounds. I could do nothing more than keep up with him or find myself dragged, incomprehensibly, like a leopard's prey from the killing field. I was barely able to hold my torn robe together, hiding the rip I had made. The strange flows from my body had slowed, leaving my skin both tight and cold where viscous fluids stuck to my thighs. When I looked down to steady my feet, I saw red stains on my jeweled slippers as they flashed in and out from beneath my embroidered hem. I could not even look back to see if Mara and the women were still behind us.

The magnificently carved cedar recesses of the audience room loomed ahead. Somehow, I freed my arm from Absalom's unrelenting clutches and turned so my back was to the doorway. I felt my nails rip as I dug my fingers into its polished recesses and clung there, my eyes squeezed shut with the effort.

"Absalom, Absalom, why does it have to be now? And why must I be there with you? I can't bear for anyone else to see my shame, most especially our father. Please, brother, have mercy."

Absalom also turned and faced me. Was he going to relent? Mara caught up to us and stopped short. She seemed poised to sweep me away if he gave in.

"It has to be now, and you must be here, too," he said as he pried my fingers from the doorway, his voice as hollow as a tree fallen dead. "You need not be seen. Keep to the back wall and hide yourself if you must. But you must witness what is said." His balled fist between my shoulders thrust me roughly into shadows alongside the crowd of courtiers and supplicants.

None of the usual murmuring now. Silence reigned as people strained to hear what was being said between the king and each favor-seeker. This could not possibly be the same hall into which I had swept proudly this morning, where my father had greeted me with honor, affection as he could show it, and a special mission. Who was this aching girl whom I seemed to watch from outside myself, barely creeping along the cold, dark wall like a lizard in winter? Invisible forces propelled me forward to where I could hide behind a corner pillar in the front of the chamber and still see the throne on the dais. Absalom, meanwhile, strode, head and shoulders above the crowd, turning every head, as always.

But the throne sat empty. All eyes were directed to the space in front of the dais, and I knew what I would see when I followed them. It was a familiar scene.

The king studied the sacred texts with his inner circle, all of them on the floor. As a child, our father often left the plump pillows and soft rugs that cushioned his throne to sit cross-legged on the stones with a scroll open on his lap, a little knot of nobles encircling him like nomads around a crackling campfire. I had raced around behind the dais with Absalom, our brother Chileab who died so long ago, Amnon, Adonijah, and the others.

Often, our father talked; sometimes, he listened.

There were our prophets—Gad and Nathan—with Zadok, the priest who watched over the Holy Ark in the Great Courtyard of David's palace. Abiathar, who officiated at the altar in the Tabernacle at Gibeon, sat nearby, as did the king's chief minister, Ira the Yairite. My pain began to increase, drawing a corona around every man and woman in the chamber. Did such a circle of light illuminate me as well? Was I glowing from the inside where a piercing flame ate away at me? I shrank back further. If the priests or the prophets, not to mention my father, caught a glimpse of me, the flame would burst, and I would not be able to hide my shame from them.

Another thought came then, more frightening than the first. Perhaps the rumor had entered the room behind us, before Absalom could even whisper in the king's ear. *Lord, shield me!* For a moment I covered my eyes, believing like a child that this would make me invisible. But the rays of sunlight filtering in through the windows near the ceiling passed over my hiding place, landing in the circle of sages.

At the king's right hand, as always, was Mephibosheth, old King Saul's grandson, who was about the age of my brothers. By the time I knew him, he was already dragging his feet on his oak-wood crutches, so he never shared in our games of chase, hunt, and war. But when we saw him prepare his bow and arrow, we all fell into an admiring little half circle behind him. Mephibosheth could hit the mark, no matter how small or far off, better than any of us. Ah, but did my father know any of this? No. While the king kept Jonathan's son close, he was, of course, only vaguely aware of his archery skills.

Everyone said that the king's first attraction to the son of his beloved friend was that urgent need he had to repent and make things right. And so, after years of exile, Mephibosheth returned to court. Once King David had invited him back, he was at every meal with the king. There my father discovered the boy's sharp mind, steeped in the sacred writings, honed over years spent in exile, much of it bedridden as the doctors tried to straighten broken bones. And, like Mephibosheth, my father knew a thing or two about growing up alone and unwanted. So, of course, there was Mephibosheth again in the ring of scholars on the floor, sitting right next to my father.

The king's eyes lit up when he saw the son who was nothing less than his mirror image approach the scholars. Absalom could delight his father in a way our older brothers never could. Certainly, I could not, no matter what status my skills had given me at court. My throat tightened as he entered the inner circle.

Absalom knelt so David could reach up and rest his hand on the lightly oiled auburn curls that cascaded down his back. He struggled to keep his balance as David then pulled him back and forth by the cheeks, planting noisy kisses on both. Absalom stood again. David's hand slipped from his son's head to his broad, multicolored belt, tucking his fingers into it firmly.

"Come . . . son . . . sit . . . with . . . us," he said, emphasizing each word with a pull on the belt. And then he bellowed to the men in the circle, "What do you think of my boy? The crown prince he is not, but still, what a man he has become, eh? The first wife of my youth named our poor first-born Chileab because everyone said he looked like me. But Absalom here is my spitting image, is he not? And that hasn't done him any harm, no?" At that, the king chuckled.

My brother had heard it all before and remained silent until our father signaled he was finished with the barely concealed bawdiness in which he indulged when none of his wives were present. Then he crouched down and whispered urgently into the king's ear. Along with everyone else I saw my father's ruddy complexion darken. His gray-amber brows knit into a single bushy line over narrowed eyes. His nostrils flared.

No. *No.* The wail rose in my throat but when I pressed my bloodstained hands to my mouth, it retreated on its own, pushed back as I gagged. My fingers still reeked of Amnon. Of his sin.

Silence reigned in the room. Confused silence as priests, prophets, and nobles watched their king's rage take hold. Absalom finished his hushed litany and stood, his back now to me while our father seemed to stare into nothingness, his breathing labored. One final exhale and his face relaxed.

"*Rei'ai*—my friends." His voice was eerily calm. My heart fluttered, knowing—believing—his next words would surely be a shouted order to bring Amnon before him. Instead, he said, "Let us leave our previous discussion for another time. I would like to turn to a different topic of our sacred scriptures, one that will help my people know what to do when a certain disaster strikes their family." David gestured toward the audience. It was all I could do not to run to my father from my hiding place and beg for his understanding.

The king motioned to the servant standing behind him next to a finely carved cedar wood cabinet full of rows of goatskin scrolls. "Bring me . . . that one," he said, pointing at a scroll in the middle row.

David lay the scroll over his crossed knees and ran his finger along the line of closely packed ancient letters. "Yes . . . it's right around here somewhere. Who else has already heard these particular words of God to Moses?" David mumbled. "Myself, and the scribes, obviously. The prophets, the priests . . . I suppose the old village judges. But they really should be heard far and wide. They have always particularly fascinated me." He clucked his tongue.

I waited, barely breathing now. The king seemed to be rambling, but I knew him better. I knew his methods. "How can one find what one is looking for in this sea of words? There should really be a system. Ah . . . finally." His voice, oddly expressionless for my exuberant father, carried to every corner of the silent room. "Listen!

"If there be a damsel that is a virgin betrothed unto a man, and a man find her in the city, and lie with her; then ye shall bring them both out unto the gate of that city, and ye shall stone them with stones that they die: the damsel, because she cried not, being in the city; and the man, because he hath humbled his neighbor's wife; so thou . . . well, and so on . . . . But if the man find the damsel that is betrothed in the field, and the man take hold of her, and lie with her; then the man only that lay with her shall die. But unto the damsel thou shalt do nothing; there is in the damsel no sin worthy of death; for as when a man rises against his neighbor, and slay him, even so is this matter. For he found her in the field; the betrothed damsel cried, and there was none to save her."

He stopped and looked up from the scroll. "Nathan! What do you say? Suppose a rich man found such a woman to his liking, not only merely in the city but in his own household, his very own rooms, and committed the folly of taking her and lying with her. What should be done to *him?*"

My heart beat wildly now beneath the torn fabric of my robe. Was my father about to mete out to Amnon the punishment he deserved? But how could he, when he had committed virtually the same sin described in the holy writings against the woman who was now his favorite wife?

"I would say . . . if that happens . . ." Nathan began softly, cautiously, all scholarly and priestly eyes locked on him. My breath caught. Nathan needed no scroll; he knew it all by heart. He closed his eyes and his voice grew stronger as he recited the ancient words: "*If a man find a damsel that is a virgin, that is not betrothed, and lay hold on her, and lie with her, and they be found; then the man that lay with her shall give unto the damsel's father fifty shekels of silver, and she shall be his wife, because he hath humbled her; he may not put her—*"

"All well and good, *Avi*"—Absalom daringly broke in on the prophet's words. But the interruption was not to engage Nathan in a lively exchange, as had become the usual practice at such sessions. Instead, he kept his eyes locked on the king. "But what if the man and the woman were blood relatives?"

I was surely lost now. My mouth was so dry I could not open it even to gasp. I became more aware now of the number of people within the room. Clustered so close to me. Too close. Why? Why would Absalom bring up this side of things in front of the whole assembly, the people who now held their collective breath. This was no ordinary discussion of scripture, and they knew it. How soon would it be before everyone knew that the virgin in this interminable, horrific, and humiliating tale was none other than the king's own daughter? *Bat David.*

My father gently stroked his carefully coifed beard, as red as his hair and much thicker, as if pondering a reply. His color, which had gone back to normal as he read the sacred words, rose again. His other hand, still resting on the scroll, trembled. I thought I heard him grind his teeth as he always did when he was given advice he did not like. Absalom, this son of his heart, had cornered him.

"In that case . . ." David began, but his voice had uncharacteristically failed him. He cleared his throat and began again. "If this were to come out, the family would be shamed. The girl would lose her value. In that case, the solution is clear. The family must keep the thing quiet. Interrogate no one. Punish no one. Arrangements should be made to sequester the girl, and the man who stole her worth from her family should be watched closely from then on. Things will return to normal."

Now it was the prophet Nathan's face that darkened. Gad and the others knew why. So did I, and who knows how many others in the room. The king was applying the outcome of the sins he had committed in his own household only a few years ago, which Nathan himself had so roundly excoriated, as a guide to the conduct of others, but as if he—and the woman now his wife—had evaded divine punishment.

If the audience to this charade understood the source of the tension in the room, they did not care. After all, had not all ended well for David? Did not the child Solomon play behind the dais as we once had? Did his wife Bathsheba not order everyone around at court with his blessing? *Things would return to normal*, the king had declared. And so the people were pleased. By the time the ripple of satisfaction that had begun in the first row of courtiers reached me in my hiding place behind the pillar, it had become a wave, one that engulfed me in despair. I had become a puppet in a game of chance. A war not between Amnon and me, but between brothers.

What came next was no more than what I should have expected.

Absalom beckoned imperceptibly to me as he turned to leave the throne room. I knew to follow, keeping to the shadows as before, still searching for Mara. Once out of the room, he seized me again roughly by the arm, and I gasped. Even when we reached the portico at the far side of the courtyard and he pulled me around and stood me against the back of a stout column, out of sight and out of earshot, he did not let go.

"It's a ruse, Absalom," I said, my voice shaking. From fear? From anger? From exhaustion? Who could say for sure. "Father will make Amnon pay, I'm sure of it." But hope drained away, the last shreds of my strength pulled with it like twigs in a flooded stream.

My brother's eyes met mine, gentler now. "Our father's anger is worthless to you. What would you expect from a man who has committed his own outrages with eventual impunity? The best thing you can do is forget what happened today and come to live under my roof."

I blinked at Absalom, saying nothing, noting how oddly calm he was as he uttered the words that would decide the rest of my life. I nodded, once. Twice more. Yes, I could trust him. I could trust this brother.

He glanced over his shoulder, then back at me. "I will protect you. You will see."

For Mara, no one was out of earshot where I was concerned. Before I could begin to contemplate what Absalom's plan for me would mean, she had stepped up from behind us, and placed her warm palm on the small of my back. Normally Mara would never show affection for me in public, but this woman—the closest thing to a mother I had since my own mother left the palace—was there for me now.

"My lord," she said sharply, gesticulating wildly like a mother bird flapping her wings to distract a predator from its nesting young. Sure enough, Absalom turned his gaze from me to her. Mara bowed her head but continued speaking, lowering her voice so Absalom had to step away from me and cock his ear in an effort to hear her. Whatever she murmured—I had no idea what it was—caused him to turn on his heel and lope away.

She faced me then, and, with her thumb and forefinger, lifted the edge of her long, broad sleeve to my cheek. Gently, she dabbed at the tears that, until that moment, I had not known stained my cheeks.

"We're going to Gibeon, to Grandmother Nitzevet." Ah, the first kind voice I had heard since leaving my room that morning and the thought of seeing my father's mother again filled me with something akin to hope.

"But Absalom . . ."

"Never mind your brother. Even he cannot prevent you from going to Gibeon to the Tabernacle to make an offering. He is thinking only of himself as usual, and so I doubt it would even occur to him that you'd be able to see Nitzevet while you're there." Mara locked her dark eyes on mine. "But you need to hear her voice." Her next words left me unsure as to their meaning, but I put my faith in what I saw in her eyes. Eyes filled with the wisdom of the past mulled with her clear perception of my agonizing predicament. "Nitzevet has been where you are."

Mara then instructed the serving women to accompany me back to my room, where I was to wait until all preparations were ready for our journey to the northern hilltop shrine. I sent the women to my small courtyard cistern to fill the vessels to bathe me. "Don't bother lighting a fire to heat the water," I told them after I shrugged off their usual ministrations and waved them out.

A collective sigh of relief escaped their lips. They'd been anxious to leave the room. Their faces were impassive . . . but of course, they knew. The palace pulsated with the tale of my shame mere moments after Amnon assaulted me.

But who could have—would have—spread the word so quickly?

By now, Amnon would have come to his senses and begun to fear the consequences. Would he not have sworn Jonadab to silence on pain of his life? Had people in the throne room heard a rumor and deduced what was behind my father's elaborate, angry recitation?

The serving women returned, each carrying a clay jug of water and a bowl with soaked nitre leaves for cleansing. They prepared to bathe me as usual; normally one would pour a little water over my body and the other would dip a sea sponge in the bowl of leaves and cleanse my skin and hair. But not today; I couldn't bear it today.

"Leave me," I ordered. They looked at each other questioningly, then back at me. When I glared at them, they backed out.

I poured the water over the sponge, dipped in the leaves and then scrubbed my body with all my might. The shock of cold water, and even the pain of washing the place dishonored, doused the confusion, grief, and pain that had by then stirred my thoughts into a frenzy.

When Mara returned, the only evidence of my shame that remained was what could not be scrubbed away. She picked up my torn and bloodied robe of office and handed it to a waiting servant.

"I'll deal with this later," she said, as if to herself. She would burn it with her own hands, I was sure.

Then, addressing me again: "Your pendant?"

Instinctively, I put my hand to my chest, where I would always clasp it lovingly with one hand as I treated the sick or listened to their sorrows. *Where was it?* Lost it in my brother's filthy bedding? My hands crept up to my neck. Carefully I picked the chain from the wound it had made around my neck when Amnon had choked me with it and pulled the amulet from where it still hung down my back.

"It's still here," I said, those three simple words giving me strange comfort.

Gently, Mara lifted it off me and tucked it tightly in her belt, giving it a pat for good measure when she was done. Then she eyed me closely until, with a small grunt of satisfaction, she pronounced me ready for the journey.

I wore a dark woolen robe over a sand-colored shift of the same material and a shawl to cover my head and shoulders. These garments remained well camouflaged in the back of my curtained wall niche behind my colorful embroidered tunics. They were there for me to don on my forays from the palace that Mara pretended to know nothing about, when the urge overcame me to scale the hills behind the city to breathe in the heady air of vineyards and olive groves, perfumed with blossoms in the spring and with lavender and hyssop in the fall.

Mara led me through a back corridor and out to the vegetable garden behind the main palace kitchen to the same path I had taken on my secret forays. Two donkeys waited, one for me and one for Mara. I pointed to the bulging saddlebags.

"What are we taking?" I asked, my voice low.

"Flour and oil for Nitzevet," Mara answered. Usually my grandmother relied on contributions from pilgrims to survive, but if they were not generous and her food ran out, she would never send word. We supplied her whenever we could, although I had never understood why this task fell to Mara instead of the palace steward. She was, after all, a member of the royal family, even though she had distanced herself from us.

"And this?" I asked, pointing now to the clay jar of palace wine destined to be offered at the shrine, suspended by stout leather straps from the saddle frame.

"Palace wine for sacrifice at the Tabernacle."

A man I knew as Jalam—a man both deaf and mute—stood between the two donkeys, ready to help us mount. Mara had taken Jalam under her wing after his mother collapsed and died at the cistern under the burden of one too many water skins. Of course, we would need a man to accompany us so we wouldn't attract attention, and Jalam's devotion to Mara for giving him a life would have ensured his silence, even if he *could* speak.

The pungent aroma of woody fleabane flowers, a staple of my herbal healing kit, wafted around us, crushed under the donkeys' hooves as they took us up a path behind the palace that barely broke the brush. The sun had passed its zenith; we would arrive at Gibeon with last light.

At the top of the ridge we turned north and blended in with other travelers plying the street that followed the city wall. We passed through the massive gateway unnoticed; people focused on their journey meant that we merited not even a passing glance.

The crowd thinned once we were out of the gate. Some turned south to Bethlehem, their saddlebags empty of the grapes, pomegranates, and dates that would have bulged from them that morning on the way to market. My shoulders slumped at the strange realization that while they greeted their first customers in the sunbathed streets of Jerusalem, the path of their hardscrabble day clearly set out before them, my own life's path had been lost to a brute among fine pillows and tapestries.

Pain remained my constant companion. Every time my animal stumbled on a rock in the path, the jagged edge tore through me. To ease it, I hooked my left leg over the wooden frame of the overstuffed, goat-hair saddle.

Mara clicked her tongue to urge her animal forward. When it was neck and neck with mine, she allowed it to slow to its usual sluggish pace. "Sit tall, my lady," she said. "You are *bat hamelech*." Mara breathed out the last two words, pausing between them as if announcing my entrance to a roomful of nobles.

Sit tall. Stand tall. Walk tall. *Bat hamelech*.

If ever I ignored Mara's call to end my courtyard games or dawdled when summoned to see my father or his noble comrades . . . or if I poorly scratched my letters onto my practice potsherds, this was her exhortation. And it had irritated me as far back as I could remember. But never before this had those two short words describing my royal station sounded like such a mockery.

Still, habit prevailed; I lifted my head and straightened my shoulders and focused on Jalam as he led my animal and Mara's fell behind.

And then, in the waning light, Gibeon drew so close I could make out the knot of people sieving through the gates before the town guards closed them for the night. Once again Mara urged her donkey alongside mine. She leaned toward me and pulled on my animal's bridle rope to get Jalam's attention. At his questioning look, Mara gestured to the south and up the hill, silhouetted by fiery tongues of the dying sun shooting through pillared clouds of twilight. He nodded and maneuvered my animal in the direction Mara indicated. We made our final climb up a broad path tamped by a thousand pilgrims' feet, onward to the High Place of Gibeon. The sun had disappeared, but another glow replaced it. As we mounted the hill, it grew brighter, accompanied by the crackling of a fire. My mouth watered unwillingly—I had not eaten now in nearly a full day—at the aroma of roasting meat that came from behind a low stone wall separating us from the Tabernacle and the altar. We had arrived at the time of the evening sacrifice. Pilgrims who had come to spend the night peered over the wall at the priests bustling back and forth with wood to keep the fire high.

A row of stout stone rooms stood a stone's throw from the Tabernacle enclosure wall. One doorway framed a tall woman, her eyes fixed on our little road-weary party. Relief flooded out in a sigh—Grandmother Nitzevet, as if she had been waiting for us. We dismounted, and Jalam removed the saddlebags with the provisions and the offering. He set them by the door and led the donkeys away into the darkness.

Mara hung back as I approached my grandmother, my legs weak from hunger and abuse. I let her envelop me in her open arms and tightly wound my own around her, nestling my head in the nearly forgotten place of comfort where neck and shoulder met. I had not seen her for four summers, not since Mara brought me to the High Place to sacrifice and celebrate the onset of my womanhood.

"My sweet," she murmured over and over in the warm lull of a chant leaving me to wonder if, by some miracle, she knew the true reason for my visit.

She broke our embrace, but continued to hold me by my shoulders, our bodies still touching at the waist. Those bright eyes, like two full moons rising beneath her powerful brow from the creased landscape of her cheeks, saw straight into my soul.

Nitzevet turned away and stepped across the high threshold, one palm facing up, trailing behind in invitation, the other hand clinging to a walking stick almost as tall as she. I didn't recall the hobble or the stick from before and wondered—albeit briefly—how she could still serve in the Tabernacle in this condition. But once within her four walls, Nitzevet bat Adael sprang to life. Wordlessly, she unrolled a woven mat in one corner of the room and motioned us to sit. The flickering light from the oil lamps set in two niches on opposite walls illuminated her as she warmed the already baked flatbread over the small brazier that kept out the night chill. She set it before us, together with dishes brimming with golden olive oil and ground chickpeas for dipping the bread, and dishes of fresh dates and dried figs to fortify us. Her next gesture told us to partake.

For as long as I had known her, my grandmother hardly spoke and barely moved when in the company of others, even when that company included her son David. And that was rare. Over the years, I had heard it said that no matter how much my father begged her to live at court, she always refused. Finally, he gave up. In time, it seemed everyone forgot her. Few even knew she had become a Tabernacle servant . . . a recluse.

Still fewer knew why.

Mara, who knew better than to offer to help the old woman serve, squatted beside me at the edge of the mat and eyed me with understanding. "You must wait until tomorrow for your answers," she said. I wondered if, in my exhaustion, I had spoken aloud without realizing it.

Nitzevet tore a small piece from the edge of the flat bread, dipped it in oil, and lifted it to her thin, colorless lips. Her mouth worked hard to maneuver the food around her remaining teeth. The silence in the room was broken only by the sounds of the pilgrims outside that filtered through the door slats. Babies wailed and men and women called to each other as they began to bed down for the night under the open sky. Normal sounds, just beyond the door . . . yet forever out of my reach.

Then finally, a feeling I could recognize rose within me. Hunger. I took advantage of the older woman's slow, methodical chewing to swoop down with my torn pieces of bread on the contents of every dish on the mat until my hunger was satisfied.

After the meal, we waited while Nitzevet won the fight against the frailness of her body, and she stood. We followed suit and waited again while she crossed the small room. She took a rolled sleeping mat and sheepskins from their daytime storage place beneath a scarred, wooden bench against the wall, then motioned to Mara to help her unroll the bedding. After the task had been completed, she gestured to me to lie down. The two women covered me with a warm, redolent woolen skin before lying alongside me.

No more thoughts now. No more pain. I drifted to a blessed place in the darkness.

I woke to my grandmother and Mara's shuffling around the room, the creak of the door opening and closing. Morning? Yet it was so dark. I must have fallen asleep for only a moment. I stretched. My body protested; the deep pain that had come to nest within me, a constant reminder of my degradation, had disappeared. Or at least, it was now disguised by another pain, unfamiliar but simpler to explain, the one that followed hours in the saddle and unaccustomed sleep with only a mat to separate me from a hard-packed dirt floor.

Excited voices came from the courtyard. No, not night.

Mara laid her gentle hand on my shoulder. "It's time for the dawn sacrifice," she whispered. There would be no choosing of a garment, no combing of my hair, *kohl* to apply, or food to wave away. That was yesterday. Unfathomable yesterday.

I stood, wrapped myself in my travel cloak and knelt awkwardly to lace my own sandals. I managed to lift the cover on a small jug in the corner and steal a sip of cold water from the dipper before Nitzevet opened the door.

Dawn softly breathed out the last of its cool air, caressing my face. The courtyard, brightened a little by the eastern sky, thronged with people, all moving in one direction. As they walked, some shouted songs of praise and leaped in a frenzied dance, their rhythmic clapping taken up by everyone around them. Some raised their hands to the sky, streaked with pink and purple clouds, and clapped rhythmically as they sang. And, like us, almost every man and woman carried a vessel containing their offering.

Mara cradled our fine palace wine. Others held a covered dish of flour or a cruse of oil. There were live goats and sheep too, calm in the arms of servants whose masters loudly admonished them to keep the animals safe for these last few steps to the Tabernacle, where the priests could still exclude them for the slightest bruise.

Nitzevet led the way. There was no walking stick now, and none of the stiffness I had seen the previous night. We moved forward with the crowd and joined the singing, an ancient, wordless melody no one could place but that had become part of this ceremony of approaching the sacred.

Finally, it was our turn to behold the Tabernacle tent. In the excitement of my first offering that summer years ago, I hadn't noticed the simplicity of the sacred structure. Signs of its hasty reassembling after its destruction at Nob were obvious—many of its components, even the wooden beams that had once held its fine hangings, silver and gold threads glinting in the first rays of sunlight, lay heaped to one side.

"Stop," a magnificently garbed priest at the entrance ordered, and I dutifully obeyed.

"Not us," my grandmother instructed, propelling me past him into the sacred enclosure, Mara in tow.

"He means them," Mara explained, gesturing to the people behind us. "As a sanctuary servant Nitzevet is welcomed with the homage denied her at home, and she serves proudly in the Tent of Meeting with the other women."

I had only a moment to dwell on Mara's mysterious words when an elderly priest approached us. "Welcome, Tamar, daughter of our king," he said, gesturing toward the Tent of Meeting. My stomach dropped as we moved forward, but not from the sanctity of the moment. I wondered how he knew my identity. Did everyone else? Did they also know my shame?

The magnificent blue, purple, and crimson in its woven walls had faded, some parts threadbare. But even bereft of its Holy Ark, now in the Great Courtyard of the palace where King David alone offered sacrifices, something divine penetrated every fiber of my being . . . something healing . . . loving.

When we stood close to the brazen altar, closer than anyone in the crowd outside could hope to do, Nitzevet began to chant. Unlike the pilgrim's song in the courtyard, this one had words, although I couldn't make them out. Even this early in the day, the priest who took our wine jar from Mara had to navigate a narrow path through heaped jars of flour, wine, and oil already surrounding the brazen altar. Its flame, tended by a cadre of busy functionaries, rapidly consumed the people's gifts.

The brazen altar, where sin offerings were made. Was that why Mara had brought me here? Had I sinned? Then perhaps when Nitzevet heard my story, her counsel would be to leave me here, with her, to expiate my shame. Was this to be the sequestering my father had spoken of yesterday to Absalom? And would that be such a bad thing?

Then, it seemed in no more than a heartbeat, our time in the sacred courtyard came to an end. Despite our special privilege, the priest on duty at the doorway signaled to his superior that we should move on; the line behind us grew long and restless.

Nitzevet bowed her head and paced backward until she reached the doorway; we did the same. We followed her out and waited as she gazed southward into the distance.

"Is she ever going to speak to me?" I mumbled to Mara. "Why are we here? I don't under—"

Mara laid her hand on my forearm as Nitzevet motioned us away from the crowded Tabernacle courtyard. When we stood beside her with our backs to the commotion, her raised arm swept broadly across the landscape to the mountains on the southeastern horizon, still dark against the dawn sky but crowned with a glimmering arc of bronze.

"There. Bethlehem. My home. I was born there, married there. There, your father was born. There . . ."

I hoped for even a wisp of the sense of Nitzevet's wisdom and protection that had surrounded me from the moment we arrived at the Tabernacle. But it was gone. Nitzevet hadn't mysteriously divined the real reason we had sought her out. She was going to go on and on about her past in that way old people do when they have no future to dream of. She would not be able to help me. *What did I have left?*

Her rambling recitation stopped as suddenly as it had started. "Come. We'll talk," she said. We followed as she turned toward her room.

Brushing aside our help, again, she rolled up the sleeping mat, folded away the sheepskin bedding and set out the morning meal. It was almost exactly the same as we had shared the previous night, and in almost the exact darkness, broken now only by cracks of light where the door failed to meet the doorpost and between the rough wooden slats.

Her voice, in the confines of the small room, was warm and low, with the timbre of a young woman. "I sensed you were coming," Nitzevet said. She leaned forward on the mat, her hands clasped. "What has happened? Has your father been killed? No . . . that I would have known. But someone has died." Her eyes now met mine. "Tell me."

Mara placed her hand gently behind my elbow, a sign that I should speak.

I gulped for air and turned myself into a stranger for the telling.

The trembling of the older woman's eyes in their deep sockets was the only sign she took in what I said. From time to time she bent her wrinkled neck and tilted her head toward the cracked plastered walls of her hovel. From time to time she shivered and shook her head as if the earth quaked beneath us.

Finally, she spoke. "And so Absalom has told you your only choice is to go to live with him? That he will take care of you?" Grandmother reiterated my final sentence.

A thought that had come to me on the way to Gibeon as the worst possible outcome now seemed comforting. "Instead, I thought I could come here and live with you, here at the Tabernacle. I've seen my father's passion for the Lord when he sacrifices before the Ark in the Great Courtyard of the palace. Why could I not serve the Lord, too? Here, where I could be like you, unknown to the outside world, and leave my woes behind."

Her lips stretched into a line that reset the folds of her parchment skin, stopping just short of what would have been an unhappy smile. She unclasped her hands and reached across the mat to take my hand in hers. Their dryness sent a light chill through me: my palms were still tender from the day before. She turned my hands in hers, then nodded. She understood. "Let me tell you how I came to serve the Lord here, Granddaughter. Then you can decide," Nitzevet said. "Do you know why I don't live at the palace?" Even though she addressed me, her eyes were on Mara, who responded with a small shake of her head. Nitzevet went on. "The court thrives on the story that King David was a shepherd before he was anointed by the prophet

Samuel. It's the way a future king must learn to protect the weak in the harshest surroundings before fulfilling his royal destiny."

"Grandmother, I know the story. What does it have to do with me?"

"Nothing. And everything. Now you will hear what really brought your father to the desert, and me to this place.

"Your grandfather Jesse was the leader of our people in Bethlehem for many years. He was counselor, mediator, loved by all. Every year I gave birth to a son, your uncles, whom you barely know."

This was true. My uncles had remained in Bethlehem when my father was anointed king. Our new station could have brought each their own palace, land to work and lease to tenants, a life of leisure. But it was said that they stayed in Bethlehem because my father had commanded them to live near the family estate and administer the property. No one ever questioned it, and few in Jerusalem knew them by sight.

"I don't recall ever meeting them, Grandmother."

"That's because of the story I'm going to tell you now," Nitzevet responded in a warning tone that matched Mara's gesture. Her hand came to rest unobtrusively on my knee—no more interruptions.

"I began to see that Jesse was no longer the companion I had come to love. He no longer spoke to me except when necessary. Then, one day, he would no longer take a plate of food from me or let me wrap him in his cloak as I always did on cold days before he left the house. Our household stopped being that of a husband and wife. Your uncles were grown by then, living with their own families. No one knew anything was amiss. And I had no idea why anything should have been.

"Until one day, after I had served the morning meal, your grand-father finally shared his thoughts with me. He said he had become horrified when he suddenly realized the significance of the fact that his own grandmother, Ruth, was descended from Moabites—cursed because they had refused our wandering tribes food and drink as we passed through their country on the way to the land God had promised us. Because of his Moabite ancestry, he said, he had come to believe that he did not deserve the respect our people lavished on him. And most of all, he said, he did not want to taint *me* with his suddenly accursed ancestry."

I sputtered and looked to Mara for help. *Accursed?* Gad had taught me that my great-grandmother Ruth was a hero who, out of love for our people and our God, had taken upon herself to join us. Most important, she had been the mistress of her own fate, just as Gad encouraged me to be. Ruth was the very symbol of righteousness, I was taught, and by her actions had redeemed the sin of her entire people when they turned us away. I tried to catch Mara's eye for permission to speak, despite her admonition to remain silent. But she seemed intent on examining every crack and speck in the tamped earthen floor and did not return my glance.

"Jesse commanded me to leave him that very day," Nitzevet continued with a resigned shrug of her shoulders. "What was I to do? Where was I to go? My shame was almost too great to bear. I could do nothing else but return to the house of my father, Adael, where I lived for three years. Tongues wagged, but that was nothing compared to what was to come. I was alone, day after day, with my sorrow. I sought my help in the Lord as never before. The words of comfort that came to me in those years were the same ones I would someday teach your father to sustain him in his own trials.

"One day, it seemed your grandfather could no longer bear the emptiness of his bed. But it was not me he called to his Moabite-blemished household," Nitzevet said, her tone turning as bitter as wormwood.

"He resolved to take a Canaanite slave woman to produce another heir, whose lineage would not be Israelite, but because the child's mother would not be Israelite, neither would it be in doubt. Before he took the woman, he freed her, because it is our custom that from the moment we liberate slaves, they become one of us. At best, Jesse had concluded, if he ever decided his lineage was untainted after all, the slave would then be free to marry him. At worst she would be a Canaanite married to a Moabite."

"That makes no sense!" I blurted out; not even Mara's restraining hand could stop me then.

Nitzevet's laugh sent a chill through the warm room.

"Think for a moment, Granddaughter, about what had happened to you by this time yesterday. Men take what they want and discard what is no longer useful."

I exhaled heavily, somehow knowing that I had not yet heard the worst part of the story. I tried to put off the inevitable by asking a question. "Grandmother, how do you know all this?"

"I know because the slave your grandfather took, Anat, was a good woman. She told me she felt my anguish and had no desire to take my place, and so she had come to me with a plan. She suggested I go to his bed that very night, disguised as her, the way our foremothers Rachel and Leah and done. At first I laughed. One look at that supple young woman and I could do nothing else. How would Jesse not notice my sagging breasts and wrinkled face? But Anat said he would believe what he wanted to believe, and he would not notice." Her tired eyes widened. "And he didn't."

To practice my healing art, the priests had taught me not only the secrets of men's and women's bodies and the maladies that could be healed by herbs or flowers, but also the illnesses that afflicted the soul. But what had happened to my grandmother was so beyond my experience that I barely understood what she said.

"When I left your grandfather in the darkness that night, your father David already nestled in my womb. And as people began to notice my swelling belly, your uncles, my own sons, branded me an adulteress, for though I was still married to your grandfather, we led separate lives, and no one knew I had been to his bed.

"Your grandfather said nothing in my defense, nothing at all. When your father was born and your uncles saw that he was a redhead, unlike any of them, it further incensed them. But all of your uncles' teeth-gnashing did them no good. Jesse recognized David as his own son and took him in. Even then, they didn't stop. They relegated your father to a sheep pen and the desert. And that, Tamar, is the true story of why he became a shepherd.

"Your father was with me for only seven years before he was sent to the desert. I taught him what I could, and I know he took it to heart, because here in Gibeon I hear people singing the poems— poems I composed for him so long ago."

Nitzevet cleared her throat, and a rhythmic, resonant chant, emerged, every word clear. "*Save me, O God; for the waters are come in even unto the soul. I am sunk in deep mire, where there is no standing; I am weary of my crying; my throat is dried; They that hate me without a cause are more than the hairs of my head; They that would cut me off, being mine enemies wrongfully, are many; should I restore that which I took not away? Mine eyes fail while I wait for my God. I am become a stranger unto my brethren, and an alien unto my mother's children.*"

I nearly gasped. Those were the very words my father chanted by the Ark of the Covenant in the grand courtyard. I had heard them so often I knew them by heart. Evyatar and the other priests who served at the Ark in Jerusalem would stand and watch as David repeated the closing words over and over before finally falling silent, the sign he was going to offer sacrifice. Now, for the first time, I realized what they meant to him.

"I didn't know how to fight once my own sons turned against me. For twenty-eight years I hid my secret. After they took your father to the desert, I had no one and nothing. It was only after the prophet Samuel came to our estate seeking the man that God had chosen as king that everything changed. It was only after he badgered your grandfather, rejecting our other sons one after the other, that Jesse had no choice but to send for David. It was only then that I was vindicated."

Warmth toward my father coursed through me unlike any I had felt in his actual presence during those rare times in my childhood when he placed an affectionate hand on my small head or when he had given me my robe of office.

But before I could voice my new insights, Nitzevet spoke them for me. "So you see, Granddaughter, suffering injustice is in our blood. Your father has done many wrongs, as he sought ways to assuage the wrongs done to him—and he never could. He sent countless people to their deaths. People were relieved if his sentence was mere exile, like your own mother's. He understood better than anyone the demons King Saul had faced because he faced his own. He still does. He faces them in his warfare and womanizing, shouting his victories from the highest hill but then, before the Ark, softly chanting the words I taught him. My own demons I greet in silence, serving God by seeing to the needs of the people who come here to worship."

The pain had returned, deeper than anything left by the ravaging of my body. My poor grandmother. My poor father. A vision came to me unbidden of that time when I stood on the rooftop of the palace in Jerusalem, barely tall enough to see over the parapet, and watched churning winter storm clouds roll in over the city. Before I was whisked back into the palace, I remember imagining that the black clouds would descend and suck me into them, and no one would know where I was. I now stood just as precariously under the dark, billowing sorrows of my family.

A wail, deep and guttural, came out of me as my tears welled up and spilled over. "What will happen to me, Grandmother?"

I expected Nitzevet's own cry of pain to join mine, but instead, her voice remained as passive as it had been throughout her horrific recitation.

She rose with difficulty from across the mat and settled next to me. "You have committed no sin. You have stolen nothing, nor told an untruth, nor harmed any living thing. But . . . you will never be able to restore what another's sin has stolen from you." Her weathered hand cupped my chin and brought my face close to hers. "Go, live at Absalom's house. Stop counting the days and hours from the time of the evil done to you."

This is what I had come to hear? I looked at Mara, whose eyes pleaded with me not to speak—my grandmother was not finished. "Do not forgive and do not forget. But neither should you hide yourself away forever as I have, nor vent your anger on others as your father does. Cloister yourself if you must, but only as long as it takes for you to discover who your true enemies are—and whom you can trust. Do no harm to those who do not seek to harm you." She paused then. "But be watchful." A gnarled finger unfurled and wagged slowly, nearly touching my nose. "When the time comes—and it will—you will know what to do.

"And when all else fails, sing the words I taught your father. I know you've heard them before. They will help you in ways they could never help him. Come, sing with me . . ."

"They that sit in the gate talk of me," we began, our voices in unison, but forming a shaky melody, *"and I am the song of the drunkards. But as for me, let my prayer be unto Thee, O Lord, in an acceptable time."* Our voices grew strong then as our hearts knew the coming lyrics. *"O God, in the abundance of Thy mercy, answer me with the truth of Thy salvation. Deliver me out of the mire, and let me not sink; let me be delivered from them that hate me, and out of the deep waters."*

I had sung with my grandmother, the woman who had borne the future king. When we were done, we finished with a nod, a smile, and an understanding. And so, over and over, I sang the song again and again and again . . . all the way back to the City of David.

And so it was. We moved into Absalom's house as he had commanded, and Nitzevet had urged. Mara watched me constantly, just as she had when I was a toddler and the fever came to steal away children in the night. We told no one of my arrival. We trusted, instead, in the all-invasive power of palace rumor.

The moon waned and waxed until summer melted into fall. My body healed. I had numbered the days, and my regular flow of blood appeared at its appointed time. And when Mara brought me the cloths, her relief was as obvious as her own obsessive counting had been unobtrusive.

I rose long after sunup and spent my days denned by the chambers and hallways of my brother's apartment. Eventually I discovered the quiet of the flat rooftop, where the western breeze caressed me in the afternoons as I stood among the drying figs and dates that carpeted the plaster floor. Before long, I made it my refuge. Looking up to the huddle of the other spacious homes on the slope above, I could just make out a corner of the palace parapets. Sometimes I glimpsed my father as he paced back and forth, pausing between the crenellations to look down on his capital, his people.

Did he ever spot me watching him? If so, he made no show of it.

One day, like an apparition, Gad appeared beside me on the rooftop.

"He's still angry," the older man said as he followed my gaze to where the king stood. "When he sees Amnon at court, he turns his back."

A bitter laugh was all I could force out of my shattered heart. In those days, I did not speak.

Gad brought over two of the rough, three-legged wooden stools that the servants used when they sat selecting the firmest dried fruit for winter storage. The older man eased himself onto one and motioned me to take the other. He embraced my silence companionably as golden sunlight waned behind the towering ridge.

That was all. From then on, the seer came often to sit beside me on the rooftop. To be the companion to my silence.

I had not stopped speaking because Absalom had commanded me to keep silent. No, I had fallen mute because speech, which before that awful day with Amnon had outranked my herb teas and poultices as tools of comfort and relief, had utterly failed to protect me from my half-brother. My rapist. So, I rejected it as a useless affectation. In those first days and months I was as desolate as the hilltop ruins beyond Jerusalem, no longer even picked through by scavengers. Ravaged by one brother, silenced by another, abandoned by my father.

Was it any wonder Mara feared for me?

The Feast of Tabernacles came and went, a joyful convocation near the Gihon Spring a few lanes and a world away. Gad would sometimes pat my arm and point wordlessly until he drew my eyes upward where a cloud had puffed from nothingness in the glaring blue sky, or later, as the heavens filled with storks winging south.

But slowly, on that rooftop, with Gad, something akin to healing began to stir, and I imagined that someday I might speak again.

Winter forced me indoors. As rain and sleet pummeled the walls of Absalom's house, Mara brought me fine lambs' wool that the servant girls spun into thread in my antechamber. In those days, I stood for hours at my loom, the damp draft kept at bay by two glowing braziers. My shuttle sailed back and forth, under and over, as I wove intricate patterns in black and white, each one with meanings even I didn't know. When I tired at the loom, I plucked my lyre as my mother had taught me in childhood, working the strings into intricate melodies that spoke to the depths of my sorrowing soul. Days dissolved into weeks, and then months. I must have slept. I must have dreamed.

I don't remember.

When spring came and the storks once again crossed the sky, I felt an unfamiliar stirring. One morning, like every other, Mara puttered around my room as usual, needlessly arranging and rearranging my meager possessions. A servant came to remove my breakfast tray. But this morning was different.

After the girl had slipped out, I announced, "I will plant a new herb garden. Fruit trees, too."

Mara's raised brow and pursed lips told me an argument was brewing. I couldn't help smiling a little. Her expression reminded me of better days.

If the older woman thought she could quash my idea by voicing doubts about who I thought I could possibly treat, given my confinement in my brother's house, or that the patch of dry earth in my small courtyard, which she had disdainfully dubbed "the field," could yield life . . . then, it was her turn to surprise me.

"Then do it," was all she said.

Mara knew that the first step would be to buy seeds in the market. She turned to the wall niche and brought out the cloak that had once made me invisible to the world into which I secretly escaped from the palace in my old life. She stood behind me and wrapped me in it, ending with a rare, affectionate little squeeze. Then she placed her hands on my shoulders to give her blessing over my seed-seeking expedition.

My undyed, unremarkable black woolen cloak may have made me invisible to other marketgoers, but not to the burly guard at the doorway out of Absalom's house.

"*Bat David,*" he said in a startled voice. He stepped in front of me but stopped short of taking me by the arm. Instead, he said: "My orders are to inform Prince Absalom if you try to leave the house." His kept his tone light, but he clearly intended to stop me if he had to. He knew of my sorrow, as did all the servants in Absalom's house. I saw most of them more frequently than I saw my brother, my keeper. Their sympathetic glances were warmer than any words Absalom had tossed my way on the rare occasions when our paths had crossed.

Servants know the pain of humiliation that never heals.

The man lifted his chin and folded his massive arms across his brawny chest. He stepped forward, away from the door, just enough so that I could slip around him. I skirted him as nonchalantly as I could, opened the door, and stepped into the street without a backward glance.

I was back before the sun reached its zenith, entering the house through the kitchen courtyard. I now had two linen bags full of seeds and roots, which Mara and I planted and watered before sunset on that very day.

Late spring saw the hard, cracked ground in the small courtyard give way to thick clumps of bright green turmeric leaves that by summer had produced towering stacks of flowers so white they glowed in the moonlight. We had to cut back the yellow-topped wild mustard almost every day, and silvery-leaved sage bushes thrived, too. There was even room for the garlic stalks, clustered together in one corner like worshipers at the Tabernacle.

Early one morning, as we were about to harvest the tasty little garlic buds, a servant appeared in the courtyard doorway. "Prince Absalom is here to see you, my lady," she said, her voice trembling.

My brother pushed past her before she had finished announcing him. I barely had time to stand and slap my hands against my tunic to rid them of soil before he stood beside me. Mara moved protectively in my direction, but I signaled her to remain where she was so I could face my brother. It was time.

I watched him as he surveyed my burgeoning garden. He seemed to be waiting for me to greet him first, as etiquette demanded. But I was more used to silence than he. And so I looked at him, waiting.

"I see you have done well with the seeds you sneaked out to bring from the market. If you had only asked, I would have gladly had them brought to you." In those few words of mean praise, Absalom had managed to remind me what I already knew all too well: In this house I was neither a guest nor a protected little sister; I was a prisoner. But I couldn't have hoped for a more perfect opening for the speech I had prepared for when the time came, with my flourishing garden the perfect backdrop.

"As you see, we've created a treasure trove of healing here. I want to—hope to—use it," I said firmly.

"No."

Oh, how much more power that simple word held when he said it.

"I will not have you leave the house. It's for your own protection, *ahoti*. Who knows what Amnon might do if he sees the living proof of his vile act walking among us at court."

"Rumormongers can malign me all they want, but not even the meanest can challenge my reputation as a healer," I retorted. My voice rose at the end. My throat tightened. Next, tears would fall, as they did when I was angry. But he would pounce on them as a sign of weakness. This I would not allow. I drew a breath and exhaled. I was silent long enough that Absalom cocked his head in confusion. I had caught him off guard, and that was good. I plunged ahead. "This will bring honor to your household, and thus I will be able to repay you for your protection these past two years. And it will show the king that you have let bygones be bygones, that Amnon and the succession are in no danger from your revenge."

I was used to people in thrall to my eyes, and Absalom was no different. Now, as always, his gaze shifted constantly from the gold-flecked blue to the bronze-green. But had he glimpsed the fire there, he would have known I was doing this for me, not him. I lowered my lids and hoped he would misinterpret this as a sign that I had accepted my fate. When I looked back up at him, the smug downturn of his mouth told me I was right. I could imagine him picturing his home filling with the high and mighty seeking something only he could provide.

He ruminated in silence and finally said: "So be it."

Within weeks, the parade of the sick in body and soul began to arrive. Absalom had allotted me two servants for the harvest and to prepare the flowers and roots under my exacting directions. I taught them how to infuse sage leaves into tea to comfort laboring mothers, to squeeze the juice from raw garlic to ease breathing and aching heads and to crush fennel to strengthen brittle bones. The air in my chamber was perfumed with healing.

I still rarely left my rooms; now the city came to me in an almost unceasing parade, all that summer. The sick, grateful for my ministrations, seemed to care little about the shameful reason I no longer practiced my art at the palace. Awareness of it faded like the flowers of the field. As they shared their most intimate secrets, I became their healer.

They also regaled me with stories about life beyond my brother's walls. Because of these tales, I gleaned that a plot had been woven in the house where I lived. And I remembered what Grandmother Nitzevet told me about my *true* enemies.

When winter swept in again the muscles of the elderly ached and stiffened, and I was grateful that my little patch of ground had burgeoned with healing plants. The purple heads of the fresh garlic had whitened and dried, and they hung in clusters by their pale green stalks from courtyard columns. Steeped in hot water, they came alive to open even stubbornly clogged nostrils. I set bones broken in inevitable falls in slippery streets and courtyards, and quieted festering sores by washing them with wine and coating them with mustard paste. A few mauve *basha* flowers had come up. The farmers hated them for their stink, but to me, they signaled that I would have more than enough for the tiny dosage needed to still a violent cough.

One day, chatter in my anteroom told me Zilla, one of my most satisfied patients, was on her way in—again. There were days when her shrill voice grated on me, especially as I knew she needed little in the way of my herbal treatments. She was a widow, passing her days in an isolated wing of her eldest son's house, and she needed to hear her own voice, as she often said. So, I listened, because I knew that in the voluminous folds of her garrulousness she carried precious information from her chance encounters. This time, it was her darting eyes that brought me knowledge.

"You'll never guess who I saw on my way in here, huddled with your brother Absalom right out there in a hallway," the woman gurgled, flapping her hand vaguely outward, her moon face glowing with satisfaction.

I pretended to be absorbed in my task of massaging her feet with cleansing granules of salt dipped in olive oil.

"And who might that have been, Auntie?" I said lightly.

Zilla paused. She grabbed the arms of her chair, wiggled her ample hips, and sat up a little straighter. For good measure, she raised her chin, pleased with the drama she must have thought she was creating. "Jonadab, your cousin, who serves your brother, Prince Amnon," she finally said.

Zilla was so filled with self-important gravitas that, amazingly, she seemed to forget what hearing the name Amnon—or Jonadab, for that matter—would do to me. My heart raced. Roaring in my ears drowned out my own words to a whisper spoken from the deepest cave.

"Indeed," I said, pulling in a breath. "How strange." I did not look at her. I wouldn't let her see what her words had done to me. "I wonder what he wanted," I said evenly.

"Now how would I know that, my lady? They spoke in whispers, as those types always do in public. It's not the first time I've seen him here, I'll tell you that. No one I know can figure it out," she finished, her tone as cheerful as if she were sharing news of a healthy birth in the family. She opened her forearms, elbows at her sides, palms up. She was clearly waiting for me to provide the answer that would become grist for her gossip mill.

I hid my disgust by pulling down my tried-and-true veil of silence. By the time I had rinsed away the salve and sprinkled sweet calamus powder over her plump, pale feet, I reasoned that "figure it out" was exactly what I had to do, and exactly how I would do it.

Zilla was my last patient that day. As she started to leave, Mara entered the room, stepping aside to let her pass. She knew the woman well enough to recall that her constant patter was a drain on me. And she also knew better than to ask about her ailment, so she busied herself helping me put my tools and salves away. Nevertheless, one look at my face told her that something more was amiss than a headache brought on by unrelenting jabbering.

"All right, what did she say this time?" Mara's tone said she would brook no evasion, that the pretense of princess and serving woman had long been abandoned within my chamber. I no sooner finished telling her than Mara voiced a plan. "We must bring in Gad. He'll know what's afoot."

"My thoughts exactly. Have him summoned. The servants can tell him I have a new tea that will ease his breathing. He will understand."

"It will be done," Mara said.

"A new tea, eh?" Gad said the next day as he stepped over my threshold. His smile was warm, as always, but it did not reach his eyes, which darted around the room to make sure we were alone. "Here I am. Now, why have you really called me?"

I did not reply. Instead I questioned myself, just as I had been doing since we had sent word to Gad. My reasoning. My entire existence. Was I ready to know what Gad the Seer might tell me?

He settled himself in the patient's chair facing me.

"Tell me," he urged, trampling my hesitation.

"Jonadab has been seen in this house."

Now Gad took a turn at momentary refuge in silence. Then, he replied, "Of course he was. Do you for a moment think that Absalom has forgotten that your brother violated you? The longer he ignores Amnon, the closer he must be moving toward action."

"What action? And what could it possibly have to do with Jonadab?" But before the last of my words emerged, the answer began to dawn on me, and the sorrow I saw in Gad's eyes told me he knew it too. He plucked a grape from the cluster in the bowl in front of him and rolled it between slender, ink-stained fingers. I felt the walls of my treatment room closing in on me. All healing had fled.

"Jonadab is cousin to all of you and closest advisor to Amnon, your father's heir apparent. But that never stopped him from scheming to do away with Amnon. All Jonadab has ever wanted is to back the man that will bring him the most glory and wealth—far more than that foolish, weak, and reckless man who has nothing but the good fortune to be born first to David.

"I don't have to tell you about concoctions that kill instead of healing. Think of what happened to Chileab, the brother who stood between Amnon and Absalom."

Chileab, the son of another of my father's wives, Abigail. They say that as a baby he was as beautiful as Abigail, but David insisted on giving him a name that would glorify his own famous good looks—Chi-Le-Ab. *Like the father.* I remembered this half-brother as a happy, harmless child, always ready to follow my lead at driving our nursemaids to pretended distraction. And then one day, word came that he had died mysteriously during the night.

Although a child myself, had I somehow known what had really happened? Death came frequently to our family, just like it did to everyone else's. Sometimes it crept, sometimes it pounced. Poison was not the first culprit considered when death visited, even in David's palace, rife as it was with the intrigue of feuding wives and angry children. In Chileab's case, perhaps it should have been the prime suspect.

Now, if Jonadab and Absalom had their way, it might next be Amnon's turn.

"This time, though, it's different," Gad said. "Poison might work once without raising suspicion, but not twice." He stopped there. It was enough. As always, he had read my mind.

A chill shuddered through me, starting at the back of my neck, then creeping down until it reached my bare feet and curled my toes. Bile rose in my throat. I turned away and gasped for air. When I unclenched my fists, my palms were sticky with blood from my piercing nails. Now I knew. I had been nothing but the victim in a plot to bring my brother Absalom closer to our father's throne. If Absalom could convince our cousin to persuade the wretched heir apparent to violate the princess, the king would have no choice but to eliminate him.

But the plan had gone awry. Amnon continued to wait in the wings for his crown while my own dear brother kept me prisoner within walls pretending to protect me. So now the plotters had formulated another plan. If David could not—would not—exact justice, then they would. They would kill Amnon for a reason so convincing that no one would ever suspect . . .

Me.

There was yet another piece of this deadly puzzle to consider. "And the king? Is he part of it?"

"Absalom and Jonadab have conspired to ensure that he suspects nothing. They have played your father for a fool."

The image of my father with the huge crown of Malcam the Moabite balancing precariously, ridiculously, on his head invaded my mind.

"Those two have been waiting now for two years for the perfect moment. And now it has come. Yesterday, in the royal council, when the king announced his arrangements for greeting a vassal delegation from the east, Absalom showed up, unbidden. Right then and there he asked your father to come to the sheepshearing celebrations at his Ba'al Hazor estate. The king turned him down—affairs of state, attending to Moabite delegations, he said, came first. Then, a strange thing—the more David declined, the more Absalom insisted. But Absalom knows your father all too well. . . ."

I stopped him with a raised hand. "Strange? To ask my father to leave the comfort of his palace, his capital, and his doting vassals and travel to some ranch in the north, to sit on a rickety dais as the air fills with frenzied bleating and thickens with dust and flying wool? Are you sure Absalom knows him so well?" The very mention of sheepshearing would be enough for my father to stay away, I reminded Gad. "My father, who almost lost everything because of a wretched attempt to enrich himself from the great prince of Maon, Nabal, during a sheepshearing when he was still a bandit in the desert? As for drunken festivities, my father's greatest sins were committed at such times, with Bathsheba. Everyone knows though no one dares talk about it. So why would it be strange that he avoid such festivities this time?"

The sarcasm was not lost on Gad, but he remained silent; he seemed to know I had guessed the rest.

"Not strange at all," I went on. "Next you're going to tell me that Absalom then asked my father to let Amnon go with him."

Gad put his hands on his knees and leaned toward me. "Not only Amnon, but all your father's other sons. Even if you're right and David has suspected something, Absalom knew that your father would want to distance himself from the death even of adversaries, just as he did when King Saul died on Mount Gilboa, not to mention from the death of his own heir. And Absalom also knew that once your father had refused an invitation from his beloved son, he would think of some way of compensating him, and would allow all of his sons to go with him."

I stood and paced the small room like the prisoner I was.

"When will they depart?" The inevitability of the unfolding events had quenched the fire from my voice.

Now Gad stood as well and reached out. He placed a hand on my arm to stop my incessant to-and-fro. "They're already on their way. But there is another odd thing: Jonadab is still in the city. Dare we wonder why?"

No, we need not. Wondering was not for seers, nor for anyone who knew their enemy.

The time had come to act.

I tore my arm from Gad's grasp and dashed through my doorway and across the tiny courtyard that fronted my room. I didn't care who saw me; I took the fastest way to the outside world, down the wide smooth stairs to the massive cedar-wood doors that led to the street. I could escape easily now, even by the mansion's front door. Because I knew . . .

Absalom would have taken all his best men with him to the sheepshearing and left the door unguarded. If anyone tried to stop me, I could—I *would*—once again talk myself past them. Then, somehow, I would blend into the crowd. Then, somehow, I'd . . .

I didn't see them until it was too late to turn back. Two spears came clashing down, crossing a hair's breadth in front of my face just as I reached the door, wielded by two huge, strapping guards who flanked the locked exit. I looked up at one, then the other. They stared into the distance like the grand, sculpted statues of other nations.

How foolish of me! How could I have imagined that Absalom would have left anything to chance? No, there would be no talking my way past these monumental sentinels.

Their gaze was still fixed at some far point above my head; in fact, they never directly acknowledged my presence. Still, I backed slowly away from them as if they were wolves about to pounce. I turned my back only after they uncrossed their spears precisely at the same time. I crossed my hands across my heaving breast and willed my heart to slow down. Freedom was not an option.

Not for now.

And so, once again I sought out the one place in my world where tiny windows high beyond my reach or rows of colonnaded walkways did not circumscribe the sky.

"Any day now," I told Mara grimly when I felt her presence beside me on the rooftop. I curled my sweating hands around on the cool stone curve of the railing and followed her gaze down to the bustling streets.

"It hasn't even been two Sabbaths since Absalom left. Just look at that throng," Mara said, with something of admiration in her voice.

I obeyed. But the stream of humanity below did nothing but remind me that the people felt nothing but the excitement of welcoming back their most beautiful prince. How could they know his true, nefarious nature? All they did was long for their occasional glimpses of him, with his beautiful garments, finely chiseled features, and legendary, perfectly coifed mane of auburn hair.

A thought plagued me; I tried in vain to drive it away. I, on the other hand, longed for him *never* to return. Because the man I had looked up to, in whose presence I had delighted, was gone in any case. In his place—my jailer.

Through a veil of my angriest tears, I looked behind us, up to the palace roof, half-expecting to see the king with his gaze transfixed to the road northward. But the palace rooftop was empty save a pair of guards at each corner.

Mara's tone was sharp. "He won't be up there today, my child. He already knows."

He already knows. . .

Those three words were enough to tell me that Gad had somehow already shared his suspicions with Mara. Absalom would not be back. Not even his standing as the beloved son would help wipe away the stain of fratricide, including the heir apparent's murder. What he had done was so terrible, so unforgivable, that he could only flee for his life.

"My freedom . . ."

". . . is at hand." Mara, who rarely missed knowing what I was thinking, finished my sentence for me, and her tone rankled more than usual because she was about to disabuse me of the notion.

I plowed on.

"Yes, of course. I can leave now. I can go back to Gibeon and Nitzevet will take me in. I will resume my role as healer. It will be time for the Feast of Weeks sacrifices soon, and it will seem natural. I simply won't come back," I finished. Although I wanted to sound triumphant, I sounded like a petulant child, even to myself.

If I harbored any doubts that Mara and Gad had spoken of events to come, my servant-guardian's next words ravaged them. The words were Mara's, but I recognized the message as being from Gad the Seer. She turned away from me, and her voice seemed to float to me on the wings of the morning breeze down the Kidron Valley below the palace. Even the timbre of her voice had changed, deepened.

"Your brother's failure to return will indeed mean your departure, but your destination won't be Gibeon."

"I don't . . .

A slow, rhythmic shuffling interrupted me. Mara and I whirled to face the source of the sound and saw Gad and Nathan appear at the top of the stairs. Red-faced, the old men wheezed and swayed with the effort of the climb as they stepped onto the roof. Instinctively, I strode to them and offered one hand to each in what I imagined was a regal welcome. But one look at their eyes and I pulled my hands away. They stepped aside as shuffling behind them continued. A third man appeared, planting his crutch ahead of him to lift his withered leg up the last stair. Mephibosheth. Jonathan's son.

Now my father's three most trusted advisers were together and had come to me. *To me.*

"Tell me," I demanded.

The three men looked at each other and then down to seemingly inspect cracks in the plaster floor. There was throat clearing and more swaying.

"Speak," Mara said. "One of you. Any of you." Mara was, as usual, fearless when it came to protecting me, even in the face of the prophet, the seer, and David's young teacher and adviser Mephibosheth. The older men had both seen a lifetime of intrigue, danger, and death. Mephibosheth lived with constant pain, not only from his shattered, poorly healed bones, but from losing his father, his grandfather, and his childhood home all within a hairsbreadth of each other.

The prophet and the seer—it was their divine calling to hold the king in check. But Mephibosheth? Back in the king's good graces with permanent place at his table, this young man would never reprimand the king or speak against him. So why was he here?

"Is it Father? Has something happened to my father?" I paused. "Is it Absalom?" I raised my hands to my eyes, pressing my palms so hard against them that colors swirled in the darkness behind my lids, as if not seeing would mean not hearing. I had not realized I had spoken aloud.

"Your father is in no danger," Nathan answered, but his voice weakened on the last syllable and belied his words.

"What . . . are you trying . . . to say?" I seethed through gritted teeth. I stamped my foot repeatedly in time with each word, and the men were so startled they stepped back. *Ah, Tamar, they must have thought. She has been pushed too far, this poor young woman. Daughter of the king. Assaulted and kept prisoner, she has become too angry, and it will be her undoing. . . .* The wisest men in the kingdom, and they thought I was too weak to know the truth. Let them.

The breeze had picked up whirling leaves and twigs into mad dances around us. "Why won't you tell me what you know?"

Gad extended his hands, palms gently pressing downward against the air to placate me. Turning to Nathan he said, "Enough. I'll tell her."

He stepped closer to me and looked down over the parapet at the crowd still filling the street. "They're on their way to the city gate. But it's not to welcome back their princes. Listen closely," he commanded me.

An unfamiliar murmur rose from below. A dirge.

"The people think they know everything now. They have heard that their beloved Absalom has killed every last one of your adult brothers. They fear for the king and for Absalom himself. By the time we were called to the throne room, it was filled with courtiers. We found David curled on the floor, tearing at his hair and robes, wracked with sobbing as never before. His lyre lay next to him, the strings in a pile of wild coils; he had torn out every single one; his hands were bloodied with the effort."

As never before? That was hard to picture. Gad, stately and strong even in old age, with my father from his outlaw days. Gad, who had not shied from giving David a choice of punishments for his disobedience to God's word—between famine, war, and pestilence? Nathan, of the kind eyes, who delivered a horrific, divine message to the king, and then watched him starve himself to save the dying child who would pay for his sins. And Mephibosheth, whose nurse had fled with him when he was a child and had then seen David take him back years later in an effort to right the wrongs he had done to his grandfather, King Saul. None of these men had heard David weep as much as now?

Even Gad faltered and fell silent. Nathan picked up the story—as befitting the man who recorded the history of David's court—and he uttered the name of one of the men I hated most in this world.

"Then Jonadab rushed to the king. Before the guards could stop him, he knelt at David's side and lifted him up as if he were a child. David clung to him." Nathan paused, perhaps waiting for me to say something. But when he saw I had chosen silence he added, "He wailed."

Despite everything, my own eyes welled up over my father's humiliation and loss. Mara stepped up behind me and gripped my hand. That could only mean the worst was yet to come.

"Jonadab whispered into your father's ear, but loud enough to make sure we could all hear it. Only Amnon had been killed, he said."

"Good," I said, leaving them to wonder—was I glad that Amnon had been killed or that *only* Amnon had been killed.

Gad suddenly lurched and mumbled. His eyes clouded, he stared beyond us. He picked up the thread of Nathan's story, recited the unfolding of events as they were happening right then, before us, though he had not himself been there. As long as I had known him, I had never actually witnessed him in the throes of such a trance.

"The princes are dead drunk after the festivities. Strewn across the floor of the banquet chamber in Absalom's country house, covered with straw and dirt from the shearing shed. The servants are exhausted and steal out, one by one. Almost all the fine nobles are asleep, snoring away, Amnon among them. Absalom had made sure his brother sheared more sheep than any of the others and had been rowdily crowned champion of the event, plying him with even more drink than the others. Then Absalom gives the signal and his most trusted men spring to life. They bundle Amnon off. He struggles only a little before they strangle the life out of him."

Gad squeezed his eyelids at the scene that played out behind them and shook his head wildly for a moment. Then, in a whisper . . . "There is no blood."

Silence. The seer came back to us, startled.

Nathan placed a reassuring hand on Gad's arm. "Absalom had killed only Amnon, Jonadab told the king. The other princes are safe and will soon be arriving back in the city. Jonadab told David he should be comforted in the knowledge that justice had been obtained. . . . " He looked directly at me. "For you . . . in Amnon's death."

Then *I* am to be blamed? For *my* assault and *my* imprisonment at the hands of others? Will I never be free of this web that has been spun around my life? I took one long, frustrated breath, but I could not stem the tide of my rage.

"And that comforted my father, did it? That justice had been done in my name?" Mara gave my hand a squeeze in a failed attempt to keep my next words at bay. These were, after all not only the wisest men at court, but also, after my father, the most powerful. "So once again the king will be able to enjoy the sight of his sons parading through in the street in their golden chariots. Great comfort, I'm sure."

Now Mara stepped in front of me to trap my eyes in her gaze. "Think, Tamar. And not of golden carriages or of your father's relief. That is not what they are here to tell you."

"Enough of these riddles." I freed my hand from Mara's and crossed my arms. "Out with it!"

"We have final proof of Jonadab's complicity in the shame and devastation that has been your lot," Nathan began. "I was at the city gate when Absalom and the princes left. Jonadab was not among them." Even though Nathan had risen to my challenge with a terrible message, he delivered it in the same soft tone as before. "Jonadab never left Jerusalem. So how could he have known that only Amnon had been killed, unless right from the beginning he—together with your brother—had devised the horror that befell you?"

Another gust sighed over the rooftop, billowing Nathan's robe like wings. "Burying you in shame is nothing to them, precious *bat hamelech*. Your virtue—indeed, your life—is of little consequence when it's the kingdom they want."

"Jonadab tried to persuade your father that Absalom had executed Amnon for *your* sake," Gad added. "He thinks this means the end of one chapter and the beginning of another. David will see Absalom as a just executioner; your brother will succeed Amnon as crown prince. Jonadab thinks he has lied his way back into the king's good graces and that the king will never know that he was the architect of your humiliation.

"But Jonadab and Absalom did not count on your father's unbridled rage over Amnon's death," Nathan interjected. "He won't leave it alone."

Gad, whose strength seemed sapped by his vision, silently nodded in agreement.

"His anger will boil over at everyone around him," Nathan continued. "I know this better than any of you. I tried, and failed, to counsel him before every outrage he ever committed." Nathan raised a fist to his chest and beat it there. "If only David had punished Amnon when he committed his crime, we would not be here now. Whatever happens now, the king has only himself to blame."

All at once Mephibosheth seemed to rise taller, to stand straighter than I had ever seen him. His face twisted into a sneer that I never thought I'd see on the face of Jonathan's gentle son, nor did I imagine ever hearing the mocking sing-song of his next words: "*Mephibosheth, my teacher, did I decide properly? Did I convict properly? Did I acquit properly? Did I rule the ritually pure properly? Did I rule the ritually impure properly?*" Mephibosheth looked then to Gad and to Nathan. "What does the past matter now? He never failed to call us in for counsel, but he never listened."

I studied Mephibosheth as the full force of his words lashed at me. So, I was not the only one to nourish a grudge. The other two men were as wide-eyed as I to hear Mephibosheth reveal his true thoughts. Only Mara seemed to know the younger man's sorrow. "Hear him out, all of you," she whispered, fearing he would lose the courage to speak his mind.

"He will hunt Absalom down. And you," he said, his eyes narrowing as he looked at me, "whom Absalom has sheltered in his home for these two years. His full sister. Your father will hunt you down as well."

"No!" I said, the word catching in my throat. Confusion and fear wrestled within me with such force that I could barely keep my balance. I had had nothing to do with this. I had *not* allowed Amnon to defile me. I had not *beckoned* him; he had *forced* me. I could not—would not—become their scapegoat. "My father will know the truth. I have been a prisoner in my brother's home, not a co-conspirator. Of course I had no designs on the throne."

I broke free of Mara's grasp and threw myself at the feet of the seer and the prophet. "Tell him, tell him," I moaned, and smashed my fists into onto the roof's rough plastered flooring with every word.

Mephibosheth shuffled to where I crouched, and when he touched my shoulder, I looked up to see that his attention was toward Gad and Nathan. "Absalom is fleeing, even as we speak." Then he looked directly at me. "And so must you."

Darkness had shrouded the rooftop and the city below as the last glow of the sun disappeared behind the mountains. The mourning chant of the crowd was unmistakable in the quiet of the night. The moon was a gleaming scythe in the western sky. I had counted every new moon that rose during the two years I had spent at Absalom's house. I counted the times in between as well. Times when its fullness waxed, and holy days came bringing only more sorrow at my confinement because it reminded me of the joy of the ceremonies I had once led for the women in the palace courtyard near the altar where my father sacrificed. Now the moon mocked me with its cold, miserly light, shining on the men nodding in agreement with Mephibosheth. I flailed against the ache that gripped me, but it was too strong. I gave in to it, then welcomed its message: Absalom was gone now, perhaps never to return. This would be my last new moon in my brother's house.

"Where . . ." I began, then choked. But the sudden clamor that echoed throughout the mansion drowned out my voice. A muffled pounding on the heavy cedarwood was accompanied by deep-throated shouts of men used to being obeyed. "Open in the name of King David!" The guards who just hours ago had blocked my path to freedom through these same massive doors now flung them open to the emissaries of my doom.

My tongue became like a wad of wool. I felt a heaviness so great it seemed a great black vulture had landed between my ribs and beat its wings wildly. And that strange sound . . . was it me? A whimper about to morph into a scream as it rose—escaping the vulture's clutches.

Mara clamped her hand over my mouth—something she had never done before.

"Quickly, quickly," she urged, spinning me away from the three men and pinning a hand around my arms. "This way," she ordered. She thrust me to the edge of the roof. I whirled at the last moment, slamming my back against the cold stones of the parapet. Mara waved wildly at the three men in the near-total darkness, gesturing toward the steps leading back down into the house. Gad took charge. He shepherded the other two, Nathan first and then Mephibosheth, dragging behind.

"Mara . . . where . . . did . . . you send . . . them?" My words forced themselves out between shallow, heaving gasps.

In an answer not an answer, she said, "This will give us time." Her tone was as calm if she were discussing the day's wardrobe. "Even the king's guards will think twice before they bully the seer, the prophet, and the king's trusted counselor. I will get you to safety," she added.

"But if we're leaving the city . . . we have nothing . . . we need food . . . a mule. We need *help*." The vulture fluttered within me.

"Tamar, look at me." Mara cupped my cheeks firmly between her hands, forcing the black bird of prey to quieten.

"Now, look down there," she said, a hand between my shoulders, gently now, guiding my upper body to where I could see, barely, around the edge of the parapet to the outer wall of the mansion. There was our means of escape. A wooden ladder that had seen better days leaned against the wall, leading down to the kitchen garden. But with the flickering light of the oil-soaked, smoking torch burning in the garden wall, I could see the splintered rungs and the fraying ropes that bound them.

With the lithe movements of a much younger woman, Mara kicked off her sandals and disappeared over the side. She raised her eyes and beckoned to me with her chin to follow her down.

The vulture stirred. If a rung broke, she and I would both plunge to certain death.

I took one deep breath and the vulture took wing, taking fear with it. I pried off my own shoes, wondering only briefly how we would flee the city in bare feet. One foot touched the first rung, then the other. I held on with both hands as the ladder jerked with Mara's movements below me. Then another, and another. The ladder of Jacob's dream that we were told of as children could not have been stronger or more beautiful in those moments.

The final three rungs had frayed into nothingness. I hesitated. But Mara had already jumped the gap and motioned me to do the same. She looked down at her hands and, businesslike, brushed them against each other as if she had just finished kneading dough rather than having risked her life and mine. About to flee . . . to only she knew where.

I let go and pushed off the rung, meeting the stony ground an instant later with a jolt that jarred me from my toes to my teeth. After regaining my balance, I rushed to embrace her.

"Careful, you'll knock the wind out of me," she said roughly, but her voice caught at the end.

The pebbled alleyway behind the house was cold and hard beneath my bare feet. I tried to skip along lightly, avoiding the cracks between the stones that threatened my ankles, but Mara's hand clasped around my wrist and pulling me made this nearly impossible.

Beyond the dark valley to the east, jackals howled. I turned toward them, pausing momentarily. "How are we going to get out of the city with no supplies and no shoes?"

"We're not," Mara answered. "Not yet." She then tugged again to lead me upward into the shadows.

To my father's house?

The walled outer courtyard of the massive royal residence appeared. I continued, passing Mara, up the wide road toward the palace like a sleepwalker until Mara wrenched me back by a handful of my robe. "Do you think that walking straight into the storm of your father's anger will help you? I told you I would keep you *safe*," she whispered, then rushed me away just before the guards would have caught a glimpse of our two shadows in the torchlight near the palace entrance.

Then came the two words that seem to have guided me my whole life long, or at least since my mother was sent back to Geshur and I was alone at court. "This way."

Of course. I knew this house well from my younger years. My arms rose to the dark heavens in thanks, as if of their own accord. Like all the others in that quarter, the intricately carved door announced the seer's status and wealth. It was open a crack. Gad stood within, peering out, alone, and motioned us inward. His own guards were nowhere to be seen.

"The others are waiting," he said, addressing me. "We have a plan."

"I already know. I'm to be sent to Gibeon. Thank you so much."

"Now who's the seer," Gad asked. Through the darkness that small, indulgent smile in his voice warned me gently, as it had so often before, that I was many things to him, but a seer was not among them.

We followed Gad to a small reception room off his main courtyard where Nathan and Mephibosheth stood on the opposite side of a wooden table. They didn't raise their heads to acknowledge us. Instead, they pored over an open scroll as we entered. Others, rolled and unrolled, piled up around it, the unrolled held open with oil lamps. The air crackled around them.

"Here they are," Gad nearly shouted. The men looked up, startled out of their frantic consultations.

"We're going to get you out of here," they said in unison.

"Yes, to Gibeon. Grandmother Nitzevet will take me in and I will serve in the Tabernacle there. I do not mind if I spend the rest of my life doing that. I will be doing good."

Nathan's head snapped to where Gad stood and looked accusingly at the seer.

"You haven't told her?"

"And when would I have?" Gad's answer was petulant, in a tone reserved for the special camaraderie these men shared—which spanned joys and sorrows, triumphs and defeats, and had survived greater barbs than the one Nathan had just cast. It was a bond that left me on the outside looking in.

"Tell me? Tell me what?" I demanded, desperately trying to take control of my own fate, perhaps just this once, finally. "What's next? That you're going to tell Zadok and Evyatar of our plans? Of course, the priests must know, they'll need to . . ."

"The priests? *No!*" Nathan raised his hands to cover his ears, wild wisps of the remaining gray hair dancing through gnarled fingers.

I shifted my eyes from Gad to Nathan to Mephibosheth and back again. Was Nathan right to be aghast at the idea of involving Evyatar? Over the years, Evyatar, who ministered at the altar in Jerusalem, had made it abundantly clear he disapproved of my New Moon rites. But my father allowed them, and Evyatar was fiercely loyal to my father. So what could Nathan mean? Was I to remain here? A prisoner still?

Gad's eyes were on the scrolls scattered on the table in front of him. He picked up one, put it down, picked up another. His voice was even, smooth, quiet, seeking a soft counterpoint to the prophet's panic. "Nathan is right. The priests must not know. Evyatar has declared his loyalty to Absalom and is already trying to persuade your father that Absalom did what was best for the kingdom. Evyatar would gladly paint you as co-conspirator if he believes it serves the king and the kingdom."

"—and himself," Mephibosheth added.

"Then what about Zadok? He'll help me get to the Tabernacle in Gibeon. That's *his* realm, and Grandmother Nitzevet will take me in. I know he will. I know *she* will."

I must have sounded as desperate as I felt. I looked toward Mara for confirmation of my plan, but she shook her head, then nodded in the direction of the men across the room who held my future in their hands.

It was Mephibosheth who broke it to me. "You'll be going as far from here as possible . . . to your mother's lands."

Not my grandmother's lands . . . my *mother's* lands. Geshur.

The young counselor read my mind. "No, not to Geshur. That's the last place we would send you. Absalom is probably on his way there at this very moment."

Mephibosheth seemed to have taken charge of delivering my fate, and in his next words I understood why. "We're going to send you north to your mother's *ancestral* lands. Abel Beit Maacah. In Gilead, where I grew up, people often spoke of Maacah. It was said that your mother was named after the wife of Makir, the ancestor of the man in whose house I lived after I was rescued from King David's wrath."

His voice faded and his eyes grew distant as he gave himself over to childhood memories. Light flickered from one of the lamps, illuminating the handsome contours of his face, and the traces of copper in his thick beard. Leaving his crutch leaning against the scroll-laden table, he stepped out from behind it and walked toward me unaided, strengthened by purpose, his telltale limp suddenly barely detectable.

"Makir often hosted traders from Abel, and it was one of them who brought me my first bow and arrow and taught me to shoot straight and true, even when I could not walk at all. More importantly, I still have contacts there. It is a place known for the counsel of wise women. It's the perfect place for you to continue to practice your art of healing, to hone the wisdom you have already gained, and to keep you safe."

Mephibosheth's honeyed depiction of my future—one I could never have imagined until that moment—enthralled me. I was flooded with the warm-cold tingling I had only known when I heard my father play the harp and sing praises to God at the altar.

Then the voice of reason intruded, and my euphoria vanished. Mara had had enough. She stepped in front of me, standing as she so often did between me and a threat. She faced Mephibosheth, her back straight and hard. "How will Tamar be a healer to a foreign people in a foreign place? Do they even know the Lord, the God of Israel?"

"Tamar . . ." Nathan said, and dutifully, immediately, I turned to him—to the authority in his voice, which was enough to cause both Mara and Mephibosheth to step aside, placing me squarely in the prophet's field of vision. "True, the Maachathites don't know our faith and practices. But they have accepted their status as King David's vassals and now live peacefully among the Israelites. So they are not a foreign people. At least not to you, *bat hamelech*. Abel even bears your mother's name. You'll be able to begin a new life there—and you must choose a new name to go with it—and someday, perhaps, you'll be able to be Tamar again, and see Geshur, and perhaps even your mother."

He half-turned to Gad and raised one hand to the seer and one to me.

"They won't know yet who you are. And they must not know. But Gad will see to it that you're prepared to join their ranks as a wise woman."

"And someday," Gad offered, "one act of yours will change everything for your people . . . and for you."

Mara's hand came to rest on my arm, which trembled as the wellsprings of memory overflowed. The assault. Our visit to Grandmother Nitzevet at Gibeon, my hope to flee to her unconditional love, to reweave the threads of my torn life with her, serving the penitents and thankful who sacrificed at the Tabernacle. The pain of my ruination two years ago flooded back. But so did

Nitzevet's words. It was if she now stood next to me, as if when she spoke them, she had envisioned this moment:

"Do not forgive and do not forget. But do not hide yourself away forever as I have, nor vent your anger on others as your father does. Cloister yourself if you must, but only as long as it takes for you to discover who your true enemies are. Do no harm to those who do not seek to harm you. But be watchful. When the time comes, you will know what to do."

I stepped forward, gently removing Mara's hand from my arm. I was ready for my journey.

A servant showed Mara and me to a bare chamber in Gad's house. Two straw-leaking woolen sleeping pallets were revealed by a single oil lamp flickering in a wall niche, more inviting than a heap of fine linen bedclothes. Still, Mara's pallet remained unused that night; she placed a low, three-legged wooden stool by the door, and watched over me until dawn. My eyes burned behind heavy lids, but I couldn't sleep either. Only a few hours remained before dawn when travel preparations would begin; the sooner we would be on our way, the better.

The black sky pearled through the row of small windows at the top of one wall, and finally a ray of sunlight pierced the room and the house began to stir. A soft knock and then the door opened, admitting another servant with a jug of water and a bowl. Plain woolen gowns were slung over her arm to replace our garments, torn and soiled from the indignities of the previous night.

We had barely finished washing and dressing when another knock came, louder this time. Mara's red-rimmed eyes went wide, met mine and spoke for both of us. Had Absalom's men entered the house? Were they waiting outside the door?

"Come," I called out, infusing that single syllable with a coolness far from what I felt.

Gad stepped into the room, faced us for a moment, then turned away slowly and deliberately to close the door behind him. He turned to us again, one hand cupped in the other against his gaunt belly, his chiseled face inscrutable.

In the presence of the seer, chills of excitement and apprehension entwined within me. My questions tumbled out. "How long is the journey to Abel? What will we need to take? How will we get my potions and instruments from Absalom's house?"

Gad raised a thin, veined hand to silence me. Then, with a courtly flourish, he motioned us out. "After you."

Mara gasped when we entered the room to which Gad led us. She had never been there, but the resinous air, redolent with the smell of old scrolls which I had first come to know in my lessons here as a child with Gad and Nathan, was like a greeting from an old friend. The room was lined with wooden shelves, partitioned to securely hold the hundreds of rolled scrolls that held generations of wisdom, ritual concoctions, and court chronicles, from which the scrolls last night had no doubt been taken for consultation. A broad wooden table atop a sparingly carved but elegant stone pedestal stood in the center of the room. It was piled with scrolls, much higher than the ones I had seen the men poring over last night. Some were yellowed with age, while the smooth vellum of others was only partially inscribed. An inkpot, quill, and unlit oil lamp, its pinched spout blackened with soot, rested next to it. Dust motes danced in the morning light that filtered through the high windows behind the writing table.

"Do you know why I have brought you here?" Gad asked me, his voice the gentle coo of a mourning dove.

Ah, now I understood. My counselors did not intend for me to leave right away after all. I folded my arms protectively in front, grasping an elbow with each hand, as if to postpone acknowledgment that, once again, others controlled my fate.

"No, *hahozeh*," I answered. In this setting of sacred tomes, it seemed natural to use his official court title—seer.

"Precisely," he said, in a strange, almost jovial tone, unwrapping my arms and taking my hands between his.

Mara stepped away unobtrusively into the shadows that still darkened the doorway.

"Well, I believe you do know, or at least sense, why you are in this particular room. But you aren't sure now, are you?"

"Yes . . . no . . . I don't know."

"It's all right. Those words are the beginning of your wisdom. You'll come to this room every day from now on," he said, tilting his head slightly toward where we both knew Mara was standing, listening. "By yourself. You are already a healer with more wisdom and experience than some of the highest-ranking counselors at the royal court. Nathan and I have decided that by the time you leave my house, you will have gained all the knowledge you need to make you a woman of standing in your new home. In Abel. That knowledge will be both shield and weapon for you."

My palms sweated in Gad's hard, boney grasp. "But no one will know who I am . . . where I have come from . . . what my skills as a healer are."

"Again, precisely," Gad responded, his tone a calm counterpoint to the quick, shallow breaths that punctured my own words.

"When you dispense a potion to break a fever, you've been taught that your patient would rather hear that the potion is the magic of the ancients than the simple workings of the plant from which it comes, no? This will apply to your new role as a wise woman. People love an air of mystery in their seers. You're right, no one will know you at first. Tongues will wag. But your arrival with a servant, and with the proper baggage and clothing, will present you as a woman of means and status. As you begin to meet the people—and heal them—admiration for you will grow, and the sense of a secret past will only help you. At the right time, you will enthrall them with your powers. You'll be far from your old home, but safe in your new one."

I closed my eyes to summon a vision of myself in this role. But there was only darkness. It felt too much like my father's plan . . . to send me—no, abandon me—to Amnon and to my devastation, and then Absalom's plan to imprison me at his house on the pretext of protecting me. I staggered backward with the unfairness of it all. I turned to look for Mara. She was there to steady me, as always, but her face was impassive.

Gad could not have missed the effect *his* vision of *my* future had on me. On that balmy late spring morning, cold air suddenly wrapped me like a shroud. And yet, his next words came with the same strange exuberance. "You must be ready for a meal after last night's travails. Come, let's eat. Work will begin after the morning meal."

The grapes had already ripened on the vines as summer blended into fall outside Gad's study, where I spent nearly every waking hour learning the secrets of my new role, when the day came that had been decreed for our departure. The streets thronged with Feast of Tabernacles pilgrims, as Gad and Nathan had intended. Two women traveling alone would ordinarily merit suspicious glances, but on that festive morning we were invisible.

Day after day, I had plunged into the sacred texts, expanding my mind. But the deeper I went, the more my soul begged to expand as well. I wished I could worship at the Ark of the Covenant in the palace courtyard. But the city was rife with spies, and with rumors about my father's weakening hold on power. A journey to Gibeon, the Tabernacle, and Grandmother Nitzevet was out of the question for the same reason. As long as I was a suspect in the plot to kill Amnon, I had to remain in hiding.

Hiding also meant concealing my true name—my mentors had made that clear to me from the onset. And so, before surrendering to exhausted, dreamless sleep each night after long hours of studying, I went in my thoughts to each of the women of our sacred stories to seek permission to make her name my own.

Since childhood, I loved and admired them all. But it was the one I had begged Gad to tell me more about who stretched out her hand with a smile and welcomed me as her namesake: *Serah*, the daughter of Asher.

There I was once again, an insistent little learner at the knee of the seer. "Was Serah Jacob's only granddaughter?" I inquired of him. "If not, why was only she mentioned?"

"No one knows," he answered me simply. "But we can imagine. What do you think?"

This was what I had loved about my learning with Gad; he still brought forth from me thoughts I didn't know I had.

On the cusp of wakefulness and sleep, I smiled at my long-ago reply.

"She was beautiful and wise, and she lived so long that she went down to Egypt with her family and was the only one to live for all the years of wandering in the desert. Could that be?"

Gad had nodded tenderly, and that was that. I never forgot the long-lived Serah, and over the years I aspired to the wisdom I had accorded her.

I whispered the name over and over, and it floated down around me like the finest linen coverlet. Serah I would be.

On the day we left, the men agreed to my idea to pause on the sacred mountain I remember my father calling "God's footstool" in an exuberant moment of song: the Mount of Olives.

And so on that first of our ten-day journey to Abel, there I stood with Jerusalem spread before me across the Kidron Valley. I felt my heart stir, but prayer escaped me. Instead, my thoughts wandered to what I had been taught. Do not practice augury using sticks or any other objects . . . do not look at the shape of the clouds or the stars to find messages about the future . . . do not ask people to close their eyes as did the magicians of other peoples before performing some sleight of hand that they then credited to their gods. . . .

I pushed errant curls under my veil, damp with the effort of the climb to the top of the Mount of Olives. My eyes swept the city, perched on its narrow ridge, from the grand fortifications around the Gihon Spring, to the formidable walls that my father had infiltrated to conquer in his youth, past his palace with the grand courtyard I missed so much, where he worshiped before the Ark, and up to the very pinnacle, where a vast open space beckoned south of the city wall. The space reminded me of the only time in the three months of my studies that Nathan grew truly angry. It was after he had admonished me, once again, never to reveal my knowledge of the future. His face had darkened at my question: What if he had not told David his future—that he would not be allowed to build a temple to the Lord, as he longed to do, on that land I looked at now, land he had purchased for that purpose at the very top of the city?

"That prophecy was a true prediction, as will be known by the eventual outcome. Your father will indeed *not* build the temple," Nathan had railed at me. "Furthermore, it is not your role to predict the future," the prophet had admonished, and not for the first time. I already had the skills, he said, to know by the whites of eyes, the color of fingernails or a gentle pinch of parchment-like skin, who was mortally ill. "But you must not reveal this—such a revelation will only take them more quickly. Instead, in addition to drinking the herbal infusion or powder you have made for them, give them an exercise to perform, such as cupping the plant in both hands each morning and evening as they recite the healing verses you give them."

This, Nathan explained, would give people comfort and a sense of power over their illness. "It will strengthen their belief in you as a leader with many options for their future wellness."

Nathan had been more patient, warmer, when it came to teaching me how a well-worded parable could induce people to the actions I sensed were right for them. That, he said, was more important than predictions of the future, which could mean a death sentence for me, for witchcraft, idolatry, or both, even in outlying Abel, where people of many faiths dwelled together.

I was also never to reveal my dreams, he warned, for as prescient as I believed a dream to be, if it fails to come true, people will doubt my wisdom. Dreams, he explained, may correctly predict the future, but God takes note of good intentions and actions, and allows one's fate to change.

Better, Gad and Nathan taught me, to comfort those in need by sharing the songs Grandmother Nitzevet had taught my father and which I had heard him sing countless times at the Tabernacle, songs that beg healing from the Creator of the World. "These words have unimaginable power," Nathan concluded.

If so . . . this moment, after all, was the time to call on that power myself.

"*Esa einai el heharim* . . ." I chanted. "*I lift my eyes to the mountains.*" I looked around, making sure to avoid eye contact, not wanting anyone to recognize me simply by these differing irises of mine. I was immersed in a sea of pilgrims, and my words were echoed by hundreds. The sacred words ebbed and flowed with the rhythm of each syllable. So much more than a song. This was the prayer I sought. I breathed in the melodious blessing and called on its protective mantle for the road ahead.

The sun shall not smite thee by day, nor the moon by night.

The Lord shall keep thee from all evil; He shall keep thy soul. The Lord shall guard thy going out and thy coming in, from this time forth and forever.

Journey

As the road seemed to lengthen interminably Mara and I drew closer than ever. She wouldn't let me ride more than she did, and I would not let her walk more than I. When the food we had brought from Jerusalem ran out, we purchased supplies in villages and towns on the way. When the crowds on the road thickened as we approached a bigger village or a town, Mara ordered me onto the donkey in such a way as to remind me that—although she was a servant and I the daughter of the king—I had not quite seen eighteen summers. I had studied to be a wise woman, but she was wiser still by simple virtue of her age and experience.

"You must be seen as a lady of means," she insisted.

Bethel was only half a day's walk from Jerusalem, but I had never seen it before now. If I had pictured that place where Jacob dreamed of angels would be a huge and vibrant hub, I was wrong. It was just another little village belonging to the tribe of Ephraim. Still, when we showed what we had to trade, the merchants there served us more willingly than those of the Benjamites through whose territory we had just passed, where strife with our own Judah was always just below the surface. We stocked up on dried goat's milk cheese that when doused with water to moisten and fatten it again, and sprinkled with cumin, would last many meals. We refilled our sacks with the barley kernels that we ground into the bread that we baked every dawn, sometimes over ashes buried in the ground and sometimes in the courtyard oven of an inn where we spent the night.

Shechem, another name that had been no more than a backdrop in the sacred stories of my childhood, was not as I had imagined either. Its main gate lay unguarded and in ruin. The foundations of many of its dwellings had been turned into terraces on which olive groves and grapevines now thrived. Still, most of the other travelers who had joined us on the road by then bore goods to trade in its meager market.

Meager, but a market it was, and that meant encounters with strangers. And so, when we were still a good way off and both walking to ease the fully laden donkey's burden, Mara suddenly stopped.

"We want to be ready any time, any place, to tell the story Mephibosheth invented for us," she said. She gestured me toward the donkey and bent down, cupping her hands around my foot to help me onto the animal's back.

Dinah, Dinah, Dinah. As we walked through the market, while Mara bought food, in exchange for silver tokens so rare we feared they might give our origins away, I realized it was not only my inner voice that cried out for Dinah, my sister in sorrow. Girls and women called Dinah were everywhere in a city itself named for the man that had cruelly violated her here. At the inn where we spent the night, a storyteller was on hand who, in exchange for a meal, was all too willing to regale travelers with that woeful tale. We put in our share of flour and a small flask of wine and joined the circle around the hearth in the courtyard, hoping to blend in.

This was one of the most tragic, shocking, and yes, salacious, stories of our ancestors, and every Israelite knew some version of it; I knew it so well I could have told it myself. But in our small circle at this mountain crossroads were people of many tribes and nations. For some the story was new. I could see it in their eyes, riveted on the storyteller, bulging at the prurient parts.

"Dinah, ah yes, poor Dinah," the storyteller began. "What does she have to do with this city, you ask?" He paused and looked around the circle expectantly.

No one had actually asked, but this was the accepted formula, and so the circle listened patiently.

"Well, once there was a wealthy man. He was the patriarch of the twelve tribes of Israel who inhabit this region, and his name was Jacob. Now this chieftain had traveled far from northern lands with his wives and his many sons and daughters. Of all his daughters, we only know the name of one. Who is it?"

"Dinah," some in the circle murmured on cue.

"Indeed! Dinah!" the storyteller confirmed jovially. "Now, Jacob bought some land here from a local chieftain of the Hivites named Hamor, whose son's name was given to this very city, called . . ." The storyteller pointed a finger around the circle, seeking a response. A few obliged, calling out the name of the town—"Shechem." Now the man picked up his narrative pace. He must have sensed the same restlessness as I in his little audience, at least among those who knew what was to come. "Now, this Dinah was so very beautiful . . ."

We then had to sit through a litany of praise for Dinah's allure, taken from a thousand tales of beautiful women that everyone had heard before. Nonetheless, everyone else drank it all in.

". . . and an adventurous, curious type, as well. And so one day she went to visit the women of the land. Unfortunately, oh yes, so unfortunately, before she could go far, Shechem, a huge, wild-haired tribesman, caught a glimpse of her. And then he *grabbed* hold of her as she walked along, *dragged* her into a thicket of oak trees, and *lay* with her by force."

Tense, silent anticipation filled the air and told the man he had his audience well in hand. Then, suddenly, everyone looked at me.

Only then did I realize that I had broken the mood with a gasp. Dinah's story was my story. Mara unobtrusively put her hand over mine and squeezed. But the storyteller seemed pleased, as if his dramatic presentation had properly titillated me.

His eyes caught mine but I refused to look away. "For some of delicate spirit, this story may be too harsh. I will take no offense if some among you need to leave," he said. Some in the circle glared at me. Those who knew the story were intrigued to hear how the teller would frame the gory end, some of those who did not were licking their lips.

I forced myself to reply calmly. "No, no, my apologies. Please continue," I said. Mara patted my hand approvingly but did not let go.

"Well, wouldn't you know it, after he did what he did, he confessed to her that he loved her so deeply he could not live without her." Now came a huge, suspenseful sigh and another look around at his audience. "My friends, these things happen, don't they? And so wouldn't Shechem's offer be her salvation?" He paused a moment. "Yes!" he shouted while heads bobbed in agreement in the reflected firelight. "Jacob would receive whatever he wanted as a bride price. Dinah would not be shamed; she would not have to hide or be banished by her family. On the contrary, she was about to become the prince's wife, the powerful Hivite chieftain's daughter-in-law, sealing the ties between Jacob's tribe and these locals forever.

"But is that what happened? You ask? *Lo valo* . . . certainly not! Instead . . ."

I could almost see people's ears perk up. Those who knew the story could hardly wait, and those who did not leaned forward in expectation.

"Dinah's brothers made an offer to the men of Shechem. To seal the deal, to have access to all of Jacob's women and all of the clan's riches, their men would all have to be circumcised."

"Circum-*what?*"

I looked around the circle to see who had spoken. It was a young woman I had not noticed before. Now, in the flickering shadows, I saw the mask of tattooed spirals and circles around her mouth and over her brows. Then I noticed more intricate designs on her hands and her forearms, which protruded from her robe and rested on her knees. So, not a Judahite, and hence, her question. The storyteller waited patiently as the man next to her leaned over and whispered something in her ear. A titter rippled around the circle when her eyes widened in confusion, then disbelief.

With an irritated sigh, the storyteller took up his tale again. "Would you believe it? All the men of the town did as Dinah's brothers had proposed. And what do you think happened *then?*" The man raised his arms, palms up, as if asking the night sky for an answer. "As the men's wounds were healing, Dinah's brothers, their names were Simon and Levi, fell upon the house of Hamor and slaughtered all the men. They found their sister Dinah in the women's quarters and took her back. What do you say to *that?*"

I felt Mara's eyes on me, and I stole a look at her. No one noticed our exchange; they were utterly drawn into the turn the story had taken. In her eyes I saw my own thoughts. Violation and violence— the stuff of a good story to pass the time for our fellow travelers— were my story. Brothers who planned horrific, immediate revenge. Brothers who stood up for their sister. Absalom had certainly learned it, just as I had, at the feet of Gad in our childhood lessons on our sacred texts. Absalom had not learned its lesson, for he never truly stood up for me. Thoughts tossed and churned in the rough seas of my mind as I struggled to keep my features calm.

Or had he, eventually?

After all, he had murdered my attacker.

But, no. He did this for reasons of his own, to clear his way to the throne, a plot I had been maliciously, ludicrously, accused of abetting.

Simon and Levi, too, had used their supposed revenge for their sister's dishonoring to their own ends.

"What became of Dinah?"

I looked up. Had I spoken? No, it was the same tattooed woman. The storyteller seemed pleased that his recitation had sparked the question, for he had much more to tell, it turned out, and more livelihood to be earned.

"Ahhh, well asked, madam. Some say she married one of the Hebrew heroes, a man named Job. Still others say she lived as a widow, went down with the Hebrew tribes to Egypt, and her bones were brought back together with those of the Hebrew patriarch Joseph. By the way, our heroine is buried right here in this town, and I can take you all there tomorrow." He raised a finger. "Now, do not believe anyone who says her body was dug up and reburied in the north overlooking the Sea of Chinneroth." The finger rested as he continued, "Others say Dinah never left this spot, that she lived in seclusion on the edge of the Hivite tent camp, abandoned by her brothers and her father." And, with a nod, he gave his assessment. "This is probably what happened."

Had the man finished this installment authoritatively, conscious of the need to earn tomorrow's livelihood and everything he would show people for the mere price of a straw pallet at the inn for tomorrow night? No, he couldn't help himself. He went on and on, spinning endless versions of Dinah's future, although his voice had faded to an unintelligible hum as I plunged into a sea of my own memories, sparked by the tale of Dinah, my long-dead sister in sorrow. Would anyone lean close around a fire somewhere to listen to my story someday? Would it, too, rise heavenward like the sparks from the courtyard fire now swirling and dancing before my eyes?

The tribe of the men who had violated Dinah was long gone. But the town, though in ruin, bore the name of Dinah's violator, and I couldn't wait to leave it. It had been no great temptation to refuse the storyteller's offer to go with him in the next morning to the house where it was said Dinah had lived as a recluse after her assault by Shechem, also passing the graves of his men, slain by the Israelites, her brothers, Simon and Levi.

The breathtaking view on the day we left Shechem brought some healing. For the first time I beheld the mysterious, white-mantled Mount Hermon of which my father liked to sing. How magnificently it sparkled on the distant horizon in those last clear days of autumn, as if God himself had suspended it from the sky.

We spent the next few days making our way down to the fertile valley of Jezreel by way of Tirza and Ein Ganim. When we arrived at bustling Beth She'an, we rested, basking in anonymity. I had seen them before, those painted-eyed Egyptians who dominated the streets, even in Jerusalem. But my mouth had dropped open at the sight of the merchants and their entourages, people of every color boasting lavishly embroidered costumes and elaborate headdresses.

I was taking in everything hungrily when I suddenly felt Mara's familiar squeeze of my elbow to rein me in. "What now?" I snapped. "Just look! Have you ever seen anything like these people?"

"Stop staring," Mara commanded.

"I'll stare if I want to. No one will notice us. Look at them, they have eyes only for the goods they haggle over. And what fruits! Have you ever seen anything like this?" I said, not knowing where to point first.

Mara followed my gaze as we made our way down the street and as we restocked for the rest of our journey. She seemed willing to let me lead now, forgetting for a day the past and the future. We were just two people, like all the others.

But at dawn of our third day at Beth She'an we returned to the road. Soon we were making our way along the coast of the glistening Sea of Chinneroth. In Jerusalem at this time of year, autumn breezes promised relief from the long, hot summer. But here even the rippling beauty of the water and the fresh fish we cooked and ate with a fisherman's family at our lakeside camp were small comfort in the clammy, torrid air. And so before dawn broke, we were on our way up into the mountains again, moving ever northward toward Abel.

Each day at sunset, as we made camp near a spring or took a pallet at a village inn, Mara sought safety in numbers—finding a family we could travel with and blend into, to mask the oddity of two women on the road by themselves. But I could feel the eyes of strangers, even if only gently curious, on us from dawn to dark.

"Perhaps it's time to tell my story," I said quietly to Mara on the evening of the second day, taking advantage of the whirl of activity after our arrival at a roadside campsite.

"No, it is *not*," the older woman said. She had busied herself unpacking provisions for the night and unfastening the donkey's bridle, and she motioned me to do the same. To catch her words, which she delivered in an intense whisper, I had to lean close as we worked in tandem, following her from one side of the donkey to the other.

"Remember what Mephibosheth told you when you left Jerusalem. '*Trust* is your most precious commodity. Don't squander it.' I believe we are beyond the reach of your father's agents." Her eyes narrowed. "But not your brother's. He's safe in Geshur, where the king, your father's ally, would not dare harm him—your father saw to that when he married your mother. Now Absalom has both your mother—if she is still alive—and your grandfather to protect him. Killing Amnon was not the end of your brother Absalom's purge. In his pursuit of your father's throne . . ." She nodded once, ". . . he has agents everywhere."

Mara was right, of course. If we were caught and revealed as imposters, we could never return to Jerusalem; our flight would be more supposed proof of the ludicrous idea that I had thrown my lot in with Absalom against our father. Even Absalom would probably have deluded himself into believing that I had sided with my father, and that I had come north to punish Absalom with my own hands.

And so I kept silent when circles of travelers gathered under the stars to spin and listen to stories of the road and their small lives. I kept silent, but I wondered—when would the chance come for me to spread the tapestry of my own artfully spun tale, the one Mephibosheth had deemed essential for me to make my mark in Abel?

The valley of the High Waters was speared by a road straight into the heart of the unknown. The sun had surrendered for the day; the last of its rays sank behind the mountains, and a cool, welcome breeze ruffled my veil. Flocks of birds flew low overhead, skidding skillfully to a halt for the night on the lakeshore to the east. I envied them.

As more travelers joined us, Mara had insisted I ride, and I shifted in the saddle to catch my balance when the donkey's hooves slipped on the rock-studded path. And slip it did, frequently now as Mara tugged impatiently at the bridle to hasten its progress. And then . . . from nowhere, heaps of mudbricks and ashlars appeared—the once-powerful walls of Hazor.

We arrived with the last of the day's travelers—seafaring Phoenicians, Aramean and Damascene traders, Israelites from the north, and even some from Judah, farther from home than anyone else.

Passing through the unguarded, once-proud gateway, Mara handed me the donkey's reins and loped awkwardly ahead to catch up to a knot of people on the cobbled street. An exchange of gestures, and a brief question that had elicited as brief a reply. She doubled back to me and reached for the reins again.

"We have a place to stay tonight."

A slap on the animal's rump brought us into the group of travelers, road-weary and wordless like us. And, like us, blessed with the means to exchange goods or tokens for a night's shelter and a meal.

An alley, so narrow that our shoulders nearly scraped the walls of the houses that lined it, led to a large courtyard. At the back was a stout stone doorway, its jambs scored by the saddle frames of countless pack animals over countless years. Chaos reigned—braying donkeys and grunting camels kicked up clouds of dust as goods were offloaded for the night. Like Shechem, even in a ruined city there were people who lived, ate, drank, bought, sold. The animals, once relieved of their burdens, slurped greedily from a well in the center while a stable slave darted here and there to pick up their steamy droppings.

I was about to help Mara unload our bedrolls and other supplies for the night when she stopped me with an almost imperceptible shake of her head. "Go with the others," she said—her way of instructing me to assume my traveling persona as a pampered noblewoman while she slipped into the role of servant. But then, a moment later: "No . . . wait." She restrained me with a hand on my hip. As if she were merely helping me straighten my garments, she reached around under her robe, and brought forth a large, oval bone bead, crosshatched intricately on top and bottom. Once it had adorned a necklace I wore on court occasions. Part of the now-depleted cache of jewelry I had tucked securely in the folds of the sash at my waist and carried from my father's house to Absalom's, it would buy us shelter for the night.

"Go, go on and pay," Mara said, with a little nudge. "I'll join you after I've watered the donkey and bedded him down."

I followed the caravan masters and other travelers who had formed a ragged line leading to a table. There stood the innkeeper, a giant of a man, his pale, red-rimmed eyes peering over an unkempt beard that barely hid the stains on the robe covering his considerable paunch. The eyes darted back and forth, skillfully sizing up one traveler after another as they waited in front of him, making sure that each had been parted with as much as they could afford in merchandise, personal possessions, or tokens to pay for night's lodgings. Servants then directed us all to vacant rooms that we would share with strangers for the night.

I went where I was shown and stood in the doorway for a moment until my eyes adjusted to the dim interior. My bone bead had purchased two of the six sleeping pallets in the small chamber. A row of small, high windows in one of the roughly plastered walls emerged from the gloom but emitted scant light at this late hour and did little to draw off the smell of stale hay and previous occupants.

The room was undisturbed; I was the first to enter, and so I made for the pallets next to the one wall with the windows. I sank down to unlace my road-encrusted sandals and lifted the veil from my dusty, matted curls. I bent forward, ran my fingers through my hair to shake it out as best I could, allowing the veil to flutter down to my shoulders. Then I slid the pallet next to mine a little closer, to lay claim to it as well.

Let me just close my eyes for a moment. Now I was astride the donkey again, descending a stony path, leaning back to keep balance, trembling with fatigue. The tremor became so strong, I opened my eyes.

"Tamar ... *Tamar.*" Mara gently shook me back to the present. She grasped a small pottery tray bearing an oil lamp, which illuminated the lines in her face, deepened by the dust and stress of our journey. But her eyes were bright with hope.

"We've been noticed."

I scrambled to my feet and lifted my veil hastily over my head again. "What do you mean? Should we leave? I'll be right out. Is the donkey saddled?" There it was again, the fearful flap of the great vulture's wings.

"Nooooo, this is a good thing," Mara said, placing a hand on my shoulders. "The manservant of a wealthy man, from Abel of all places, met me at the well. While we poured the water into the troughs and the animals drank, he whispered that his master was curious about you. He wondered what a high-born lady was doing so far from . . . wherever home was."

"You didn't . . ."

Mara put her finger to my lips. "Of course not. I told him nothing, neither the truth, nor even the story Mephibosheth prepared for us. I leave that to you. His master has private quarters upstairs." Her chin raised a fraction. "He has invited you to dine with him."

With one smooth, practiced movement, Mara tucked a few sleep-tossed locks behind my ears and under my veil. With another, she licked her thumbs, and cupping my cheeks in her other fingers, wiped away what may have been some real or imagined grime from the road. Then she hastily adjusted her own robe and veil and motioned me out of our door into the courtyard. We walked across it to the door to which Mara had been directed.

"Welcome, welcome!" Smiles were not something I was used to, but the man who greeted us at the doorway had the widest grin I had ever seen, revealing a full set of teeth—unusual, even for a nobleman. And for such a small person, his bray of a voice was so startling I couldn't help jumping back.

The man cringed almost comically at my response and then, in what he must have imagined as a softer tone: "I'm happy to have such auspicious company, and I'm sure we're all in need of a good meal, no?" Grandly, he stood aside and waved us in, giving us a glimpse of a finely woven robe of soft linen, whose ample sleeves were embroidered handsomely with bronze threads.

My mouth watered at the aromas that wafted from the array of dishes set out temptingly on the colorful woven mat at the back of the room. I couldn't remember when I last saw such sumptuous fare, including whole fish, a delicacy almost never served in Jerusalem even at the wealthiest tables, and roasted quail that I suspected had been cooking for hours in the courtyard below. Mara must have been as hungry as I, but she took up a position near the door to remain true to her role in the story we would tell this stranger. My response to the food was not lost on the man.

Hands clasped over his ample belly, he bowed as deeply as his girth would allow. "I am Eved-Atar'ate. I have come from Damascus and am on my way home to Abel Beit Maacah, the city of my birth," he offered. Settling down with surprising grace at one edge of the mat, he motioned me to join him.

As I sank down opposite him, the man looked at me fleetingly, then focused intently on fashioning a scoop out of a floppy piece of bread and dipping it into a bowl brimming with red lentils. The better to politely wait for me to respond by revealing my own name, I imagined.

"Please, join me. My kitchen is famed in the town, and with good reason, as you'll soon find out." His tone was pleasant enough, and I tried to muster a grateful smile in return.

But I could not speak. One more time, I trained my thoughts on going over the story I had practiced with Mephibosheth. Most of all, I remembered his admonishment: "The falsehood most difficult to uncover is one based on truth. The story you tell should not contain too much truth to give away your identity, but not too little as to be unbelievable."

Eved-Atar'ate appeared happy enough to keep on talking and eating without my response. "Ah, yes, Abel Beit Maacah." He seemed to relish even uttering the name and for good measure rubbed his hands together in delight. "Do you know what the name means?"

I barely had time to shake my head when he pushed on. "'Watered fields of the House of Maacah,' that's what!'" He circled the air with a raised index finger for emphasis. "Yes, indeed, you should see it. Springs so numerous you cannot count them, walls so high when you stand at the bottom you cannot see the top, fields of grain stretching in every direction. Why, we're as famous as the Valley of the Great River of Egypt, not to mention Damascus and Tyre. And do you know why?"

I had recovered my poise by now and could have answered, but my host never gave me the chance.

"We're so wealthy, so well situated, so satisfied with our lot, that we need not fear our neighbors nor do our neighbors need to fear us. Now that's something one doesn't hear every day, eh? True, in recent years our kingdom of Maacah has seen times of unrest and deprivation that no one wants to relive—wars raged around us as the greater powers sought control of our riches. Then came the battle of Helam, in which hundreds of Aramean charioteers and thousands of foot soldiers were slain by David, King of Israel. Now . . . those of us who truly love our city are loyal to King David and his emissaries, and there is peace.

"Our wise men sit daily in the city gatehouse and receive people who come from far and wide to have us mediate their disputes. By the time most of them get there, after days together on the road, more often than not they've found a way to resolve their differences on their own," he continued with a hearty laugh. "But if not, there we are, to help them go the last part of the journey and smooth things over. And we even have—*had*—an oracle, can you imagine?" But here, suddenly, his voice went flat, and then he fell strangely silent.

Finally, when he had stopped eating, he eyed me expectantly. "And you, my dear? What brings a young noblewoman to ply these harsh roads?"

Mara coughed quietly from the shadows. Her message was clear. Now or never. This was the chance we had been waiting for.

But I was not so sure. I had attended many celebrations in honor of my father's distant conquests; slaves from distant lands were a common sight in the city. But the names of these far-off places, were just that—names. I never had faces to put to them until this journey.

But all the more so, if I began with truth, one so uncomfortable, given Eved-Atar'ate's tale, that it might put him off guard, to my benefit.

"My name is Serah." It was the first time I had uttered that sentence aloud, and I was surprised at how natural it felt. A well-traveled merchant like Eved-Atar'ate, used to strange names, responded with only a polite nod, leaning toward me just slightly, head cocked, an invitation to continue my story.

"I am from Jerusalem," I said, placing a knuckle over my upper lip almost hoping to disguise the name of my city in a mumble.

I sensed, more than saw, Eved-Atar'ate stiffen. It was such a brief moment that only my training and practice at reading people told me he had even heard the name of the city that had so aggrieved his people. Still, hadn't he just told me that he had made his peace with Jerusalem's control of Abel? Indeed, the shadow passed and the man's warm smile re-emerged. Here was a man who had come to terms with what was and what is. But then of course, he was a merchant, and for them, war is good if one waits long enough. The next part of my story, the invented part, would be even more believable. And so I continued. "My father and brothers run a lucrative family business." Here, I could be vague; only a poor or unpracticed storyteller would reveal all the details at once—even I knew that. His ears perked at that. Yes, I had him, and so I plunged ahead.

"Since childhood, I have had the power to heal body and soul and have learned the health-giving mysteries of herbs and concoctions from the best teachers. In just a few years, more and more people came to me with all sorts of questions and problems. Somehow, I seemed always to have the answers they sought. People said I must have already lived a full life in another world to have such a wise old soul."

Eved-Atar'ate leaned so close toward me then over the food-laden mat that his embroidered sleeves brushed the bowl of lentils, coming away with orange stains. "So why did you leave?"

"My father and brothers were seeking a suitable match for me and had already presented several candidates. I refused them all, and that came at a great price." I lowered my eyes to dramatize my next practiced words. "My father and brothers stopped speaking to me and my mother was powerless to intervene. I begged them to allow me to go to worship at our shrine at Gibeon, to hear God's plan for me, and they finally agreed."

"Indeed, I have heard of this shrine," Eved-Atar'ate mused, and I looked hard at him, wondering what else he may have heard. "Unbeautiful, no statuary, but still thronging with pilgrims and penitents."

I lowered my eyes again and picked an imaginary crumb from my lap to focus on what I had practiced—patience, silence. But the loquacious Aramean saved me the trouble. Before I could draw a breath to respond, he raised his index finger, as if a new thought had occurred to him.

"In fact, you'd be the one to answer a question I've had for a long time. I heard that on one occasion, soldiers returned to your Jerusalem from a battle in Ammon with half their beards shaved off and half their tunics cut away. Is that true? That wasn't long before our king joined the Ammonites to fight him. We lost that one to your king, right enough; it was after that that we became his vassals—not that I'm complaining, mind you, it all worked out for us in the end—but people like to say that divided faces and divided tunics presaged the divided House of David."

Out of the corner of my eye, I saw Mara nod slowly, and I did the same. To confirm the story would be to encourage the man to our side. And indeed, I did remember all too well the sight of our humiliated soldiers entering the city, battle weary even after they had rest in Jericho, bizarrely colorful with the hodgepodge of scraps, blankets and even women's veils covering their ragged half-tunics, one sunburnt cheek stubbled, the other a bearded tangle.

"Ahh, such divisions in those royal households. Ours have our quarrels, but nothing like that one in my memory. Wasn't the crown prince murdered by another of the king's sons over some trouble in the palace?" he asked between bites and nibbles as my breath caught in my chest. "Didn't I hear that murdering prince then fled, as did the princess who had caused the whole upset, leaving the king bereft over the loss of his son and the palace seething with intrigue?" Eved-Atar'ate went on, his tone suddenly lighthearted, seeming to relish this downturn in the family fortunes of his overlord. "They say the son who fled is not only a murderer, he's both audacious and cunning as well. Travelers from Geshur, which also belongs to the House of Maacah, say he has fled there, where he has close relations, some say even the king himself." A frown pursed his lips. "No one knows where the princess went."

Bereft over the loss of his son. Not over the loss of his daughter? It was all I could do to keep myself from asking this stranger that question out loud. But that was not my purpose.

His narrowed eyes seemed to reach right into my thoughts. "Ah, but be that as it may, how did *you* end up here, so far from your Jerusalem? When you returned home from your shrine, did they not choose a husband for you?"

Eved-Atar'ate had wandered dangerously close to the truth. I had to draw him away from affairs in Jerusalem's palace and my father's conquests. I had to paint the aura of the rest of my story. I took a deep breath and continued. "The road to our shrine was so well traveled that my father acceded when I begged him to allow me and my serving woman to take it alone." Eved-Atar'ate's eyes followed my hand as I gestured at Mara, watched it come to rest again in my lap, and moved up again to my face.

"How odd. How *very* odd. I would never allow a daughter of my household to take such a risk. I don't know anyone who would."

Would he believe me? Or was this the moment he would unmask me? But his next words were merely an invitation to continue. "Is that how things are done in Jerusalem?"

"Sometimes, yes, as in my family, who believe that my great learning has rendered me capable of warding off any evil. No one was prepared for what happened to me. . . . " I allowed my voice to trail off. I looked for the pulsing under the skin in the man's neck as I had been taught, to measure response to my medicine, counsel, or vision. There it was, throbbing imperceptibly. He was waiting and seemed open to believing anything I would say next.

"We were attacked by bandits. Before I knew what had happened, they dragged us into the brush. They held their filthy hands over our mouths so I couldn't even scream . . . not that anyone would have heard."

Mara played her part perfectly. She drew a sharp breath as if terrified at the very memory of it all. The story I told was Mephibosheth's invention, of course, but my own terror? That was real. All I had to do was conjure up Amnon's hands and his fetid breath.

"But surely your family ransomed you?" He knit his brows. "And still, that doesn't explain what you are doing *here* . . . why you are so far from home where even Israelites from the south are few."

"My family?" I placed a hand over my chest and swallowed the bile that rose at the thought of my treacherous father and brothers. On went the mask. Anything to win the trust of this man who, from moment to moment, seemed the key to my future. When I spoke, my voice was calm, cloaking the scream behind it. "No, there was no ransom. I don't know whether my family even knew I had been taken. Our captors may have planned to ransom me, for they fed us well and kept their distance from us. They forced us to collect wood for their campfires and bring water from the nearest spring, as well as to collect herbs to season their food. And that was our way out." I fell silent, then looked away for a moment as if weighing whether to confide the secret of my escape from the man. Then I locked my eyes onto his. "Once, by chance, we camped near a huge *kanei bosem* tree. This is a tree whose bark I had learned long ago to boil to relieve joint pains, earaches, and to heal sores."

Eved-Atar'ate's eye brightened. "I know of it! We call it honey-berry and we are told to keep chips of the bark in the folds of our girdle to guard against evil spirits."

"Indeed?" I said, feigning interest. "Well, in large doses, when imbibed, an infusion of this honeyberry leaf induces sweet repose one wishes never to end. One night when the moon was dark, I prepared a brew so powerful that they fell into a sleep as deep as death." I looked at Mara and she nodded in assent. "And this is how we were able to flee. We've been on the road ever since." I opened my arms at the elbow, palms up, offering my story as all that I had. "I seek a place far from my home and my past, where I can start a new life and practice my skills in the wisdom of healing for the benefit of all."

It was done. The story had been told, at the right time and with the desired effect.

The next day, Mara and I joined Eved-Atar'ate for the last day of our journey. Every day had been exhausting, but by the end of this one my strength was utterly consumed. The moment the sun rose, Eved-Atar'ate questioned me again, but perfunctorily, as if to confirm a decision he had already made. By the time we stood at the foot of the massive fortifications of my new home, he had fallen silent. But the telltale clues I had learned to recognize as relief—mouth soft, brow smooth and dark centers of the eyes large and quiet—told me he was satisfied. I had found a new home, and he had found a wise woman for his city.

Abel

Another city gate. Another entryway to the unknown. But, unlike Hazor, this one massive and well-protected. Girdled by courses of huge black boulders the height of three men, topped by two more stories of smooth mudbrick.

"Ah, Abel! Amazing, isn't it?" Eved-Atar'ate said, his gaze following mine.

On the roof, the purple dusk sky over a ruby fringe lining the mountains framed spear-clutching guards who paced tensely as they eyed the crowds pouring into the city.

Eved-Atar'ate's little figure disappeared in the crowd as he plowed confidently ahead toward his home. I, however, had stopped in my tracks. I barely heard the annoyed shouts of the travelers who collided with us as Mara, walking behind me, maneuvered our donkey to a sudden standstill as well. I rolled the name off my tongue again in a whisper: *Abel Beit Maacah . . .*

House of the Watered Fields of Maacah. The fields of my mother's ancestral house. Her name tasted like honey. But though her name was in this town, I had only imagined her living in Geshur after she left Jerusalem.

"Mara, do you think my mother is still alive?" I sieved the words through my teeth without looking at her.

"How can I know? You are the one . . . who has been taught . . . to see what ordinary folks cannot," Mara replied, her words interrupted as we were jostled and pushed. "Tamar, I beg you," Mara continued. "Stay with the present. We'll go to Geshur when the time comes, as you were told, and perhaps she will be there to embrace you. But your task right now is to keep sight of Eved-Atar'ate—your future is in his hands."

In his hands . . . for now. I drew in a deep, calming breath. With it came the sour scent of way-weary travelers along with the stench of their thirsty animals and the dregs of their food supply. The home of a wealthy local citizen suddenly seemed attractive. Mara had all she could do to keep up with me until I caught sight of our host's high brown turban.

Wood scraped on stone and doors banged as the last of the shopkeepers lugged their tables and goods back into their shops for the night along the pebbled main thoroughfare. Despite the dimming of the day, we tracked Eved-Atar'ate more easily now; the crowd around us had thinned out as people peeled off this way and that toward home or host. At the far end of the street, we followed our own host, who had turned down a side street and stopped at a tall wooden door in a smooth plaster wall. The guard lowered his head deferentially at Eved-Atar'ate, opened the door, and stepped aside.

The doorway framed a slice of broad, busy courtyard, bathed in the flickering light of resin torches. "Welcome!" Eved-Atar'ate boomed, turning to us.

"We thank . . ." I started.

But he had already turned away, besieged by a cluster of laughing, shouting children who greeted their father with joyous adoration.

Mara's hand blocked my view for a moment as she lifted the edge of her sleeve to dab my cheek of a tear I didn't know had fallen. Children greeting their father was something I had never seen, and that it moved me to tears astounded me. I smiled and brushed her hand away lightly.

The children poked their hands into their father's voluminous robes, emerging with dried dates and even sticky honeycomb. They giggled as he raised his arms in mock surrender, as if they had found all the sweets, but then, eyes twinkling, he raised his hands higher and produced a few more dates from within his turban and handed them over.

"All right, children, all right," the father soothed, patting a curly head here and there. "Shhhh," he said repeatedly until calm reigned.

We waited patiently while he parried their pelter of questions about his journey until he finally shooed them off to their mothers' quarters before curling his index finger at a manservant standing in the shadows. "Now you will be shown to my guest quarters," he said to us. "Tonight, I will have a meal brought to you there so you can retire early."

His next words stirred me with hope and excitement.

"Tomorrow, you'll see where our wise woman will live."

The voices outside our room that filled the gray, pre-dawn air were Aramean. I had heard it more often as we made our way north, and before long, every tenth word I recognized from its similarity to our native Hebrew fell to every five.

But this time I strained to fill in the gaps. This was no casual travelers' talk or Mara's halting attempts to purchase food and lodgings in a language not our own. Eved-Atar'ate and a group of men were arguing about something. His tone had rapidly become more strident, theirs more adamant. His parting promise of the night before seemed to recede with every word.

"She . . . the woman . . . a healer for our city . . ."

"A stranger who could . . ."

"Better that we find . . ."

Eventually the voices fell to murmurs. Silence. Then a command summoned a servant. The murmuring grew distant. The flip-flop of sandals struck the pavement outside my room, followed by a knock at the door.

Mara and I both stood hurriedly, smoothed out our robes and veiled ourselves. Mara motioned me to stand behind her as she opened the door.

Eved-Atar'ate stood on tiptoe to look at me over Mara's protective shoulder. Once again, the affable, enthusiastic host, all traces gone of the unmistakable rancor of moments before had disappeared. He spoke only four words, but they flooded me with relief. Gratitude coursed through me for the counsel of Mephibosheth, Nathan, and

Gad, whose strange plan had brought us here, to this place, this moment.

"I've done it," he said. "Come." Eved-Atar'ate reached around Mara and took my hand to lead me out of the room. He tugged, but I remained rooted to the spot—Mara held me fast by my other hand.

"Wait, please . . . if you will," Mara said in her servant's voice. "My lady has not washed, eaten, or dressed properly for the day." Her polite words were encased in a tone as cold as brass.

Stretched between the two of them—my odd new ally and my oldest protectress, between my past and my future, my weakness and my strength—I knew what I should do. But Mara would not let go, and I surrendered to old habits.

"I will be quick, sir," I said, gently unpeeling his hand while keeping hold of Mara's. Eved-Atar'ate conceded the moment and bowed out of the room. Mara closed the door behind him, a little harder than necessary. I cringed at the sound, then turned to glare at her. How could she not know how important these next hours would be to the future we were planning?

Mara turned and looked sharp at me. Had I spoken aloud? No, it was just Mara, as usual, reading my thoughts as if I had. "Yes, I *do* know how important these moments are to you. Never mind food, but do you think I would allow you to take up your new post dressed in the garments in which you slept? If you are to be paraded through the streets, you will do so as the healer that you are. As the new wise woman of Abel."

As she spoke, she busily went through our meager bundles, which had been piled in a corner. Out came my magnificent robe of office, the one I had worn *that* day, when I went unknowingly to my desecration, the one I was sure Mara had burned. But, no . . .

Mara had secretly mended the tear and cleaned away the ashes of mourning that had fallen from my head and clung to it. She rested it on her upturned forearms and offered it to me. I thought I would never want to see it again, let alone wear it. And yet, I was drawn toward it. I took it from her.

She placed the robe lovingly over my head and arranged the pleats neatly around my feet. After kneeling to lace my sandals, she reached into the folds of her belt. *What could she still have there that we had not sold on the way?*

My pendant of office, the huge white bead bathed in an early ray that streamed through the high window of our room, hung from her fingers, the coils of sea-blue glass amazingly still intact despite the rigors of our journey. She placed it around my neck and straightened it on the embroidered breast of the robe. Then she put my veil over my hair. It was my simple, dust-caked travel veil, but the robe and my pendant made me feel royal again.

Mara looked me up and down. "*Now* you're ready," she pronounced, and opened the door.

Eved-Atar'ate's open-mouthed gaze told me better than the finest burnished mirror that I looked every bit the part he had chosen for me. "Yes, well . . . very good . . . here you are. Come along," he said gruffly.

Heads turned as we emerged from the alley to the main street. After days of forcing myself to blend in with the crowd, I had to fight my urge to duck into the nearest doorway. But this was where I had to be, and so I did my best to summon the sense of pride in my status and powers. To my surprise, there it was, standing shoulder to shoulder with the courage Grandmother Nitzevet had planted in me. Pride and courage—the twin guardians she had instilled at the familiar, beloved shrine of Gibeon—flanked me as I headed to an unknown shrine where I was to rule. I fell more easily than I could ever have imagined back into the role of healer and held my head high—for the first time in a long time. Mara, tall and imposing, and Eved-Atar'ate, one of Abel's leading citizens, walked half a pace behind me, heightening the sense that this young woman they followed, clothed in a multicolored garment, shot through with royal purple, was as unique as she was mysterious. The crowd parted as I passed, people shielded their eyes with their hand against the morning sun as it glinted on the golden threads Mara had skillfully woven back together.

These were to be my people; I was in Abel Beth Maacah to show I could help them with their troubles large and small. To step over the threshold of a new life, for them and for me. I remembered to incline my head from time to time, and smile softly as if I recognized them, not regally, but in gratitude.

The thoroughfare, paved with huge, smooth blocks of stone, led up and up, straining my calf muscles like the mountain roads. But here, finally, knowing I was moving toward my destiny, the pain thrilled me. This must be the kind of pain I encouraged pregnant women to expect—good pain that boded future joy. Not even the acrid smoke that rose from among the alleyways, which I would learn came from bronze workshops in the city, could distract me from this moment of triumph.

I raised my veil to block out the smell. Eved-Atar'ate caught the gesture, and said, "Never seen bronze works before, eh? Once, our bronze weapons and tools products were famous from Damascus to Tyre. Once it was the source of our wealth. That was before your king defeated our alliance with the Arameans and took over our city. Now our furnace serves the king of Jerusalem." Then, as before, the shadow of anger that fell over him vanished as quickly as it had appeared. "But we've learned to live with it, and we enjoy peace and prosperity even without all the bronze we once had. What we have left we still make—we always have, in the quarter over there," he said gesturing toward the source of the smoke. "Come, now, let's get where we're going."

He quickened his pace, and soon we left dwellings, workshops, and the marketplace behind, and another wall loomed up before us. The structure was unlike anything I had ever seen before, its dark stones interlocking and flowing into smooth curves to my right and left. And its gateway had its own pair of armed guards. Eved-Atar'ate had moved in front of me, his eyes fixed straight ahead, intent on our destination. But I allowed myself to look around freely now that the door had closed on the knot of people.

Behind the wall. A new home, a new ally, a new means of practicing my art. If only the wall within me, built high by the men who had torn me down—Amnon, my father David, and yes, more than anyone, Absalom, my supposed protector—were stone and mortar like the one I stood before now. At least then it could be breached by a warring army or felled by an earthquake.

Eved-Atar'ate encircled the air behind me with one arm and gestured ahead with the other, guiding me past the smelting works and the well-built royal storehouses and toward my new quarters. More curious stares, less open-mouthed this time, from a small cadre of slaves that moved in two orderly lines—empty-handed in one direction, burdened down in the other, like busy denizens of an anthill.

Eved-Atar'ate stopped before a nondescript wooden door and rattled the handle. "Locked, of course," he mumbled. Then, half-turning to me he said, "No one has been here since our wise woman disappeared during the campaign your king launched against our allies and the raid that brought our city to its knees. No one knows whether she fled or was taken captive, or perhaps lies dead somewhere."

The faint flap of wings within: My fear vulture was about to sink its talons into my heart. Despite the man's warm words for his city's overlord in Jerusalem, had he somehow realized that I was that master's daughter? Would the city risk everything and kill me if he did realize it? Hold me for ransom? My eyes darted around the courtyard, calculating the distance between this all-but-stranger and the door from the courtyard to the street.

"Let me just get you inside, and you'll find your bearings," Eved-Atar'ate said, although I couldn't tell if he had noticed my near-panic. But his tone was comforting, and the vulture let go of my heart. He motioned me to step back. He set his shoulder against the door, but as usual, he kept on talking, punctuating his words by launching his solid little body against the planks. At first it did not budge. "She . . . was gone . . . in an instant . . . leaving behind , . . all her *possessions.*" With the last word, accompanied by a loud *ooomph,* the door gave way and Eved-Atar'ate was thrown, stumbling over the threshold, into a little courtyard.

He made straight for another doorway across the courtyard and pulled aside a ragged curtain. "Come through, come through," he gushed after catching his breath. At first, the scant morning light that filtered in from the courtyard seemed to reveal all that I would need to practice my art. But as my eyes adjusted to the dusty gloom, I realized that the only bundles of plants still hanging from the rafters and walls were shriveled and gray, which meant I could expect whatever valuable tinctures had filled the rows of vials in wall niches below to have also curled up and dried. A low stone bench lined the wall opposite the door, next to which a wooden table on stout legs occupied the corner. In another corner was a large amphora filled with dark lumps. Niches in the wall were covered by the ragged remains of cloth. A small table stood on a low podium in one corner. Another room lay beyond this one, through a doorway partially blocked by a moth-eaten curtain.

Never mind more exploring right now. There would be time for that and for examining what was left of my predecessor's work. I had one task now: to make this my home. I calculated quickly. "Please send for Mara," I said. "Have her bring my everyday robe. And can you provide two servants for us? They would help Mara and me restore this room for the work of healing and counseling. Then we can scour the fields for the herbs I need for my new healing cornucopia."

"Yes, yes," Eved-Atar'ate said in compliance. His eyes had followed mine around my new refuge, but now rested on mine. The corners of his lips curled in a smile. "Ah, you *are* pleased, I see."

"Yes," I answered swiftly, because, in spite of myself and my new uncertain circumstances, I had finally begun to feel hope breaking down that cursed inner wall.

Somewhere in the ensuing years, every healing, every counsel dismantled that inner wall, stone by crumbling stone. Even the times when life flickered and went out added to the change, the strengthening, within me. The horrific memory of Amnon's assault, which at one time invaded my thoughts day and night, finally seemed to be receding.

Early on, I ran out of the small store of dried healing herbs Mara and I had brought with us on our journey, but I planted a garden in the courtyard of my quarters, and in setting down its roots, I fostered my own. The hills around Abel produced more anise and aloe than I would ever need, and in early winter purslane crowded the banks of the stream near the city. With its bruise-healing flowers and roots, when crushed, the thick green leaves strengthened a baby's hold in the womb. Other plants, like the all-powerful *la'ana*, so vile I had to beg people to take it until it conquered their ailment, were desert lovers and rare here, so I had to send for the seeds from far-off market cities on the edge of the eastern desert markets via Eved-Atar'ate's contacts. Those seeds, too, had taken root, and now, if unattended and allowed, the billowing bush would take over everything else.

I learned to use the knucklebones of sheep, goats, and deer that I had seen when I first came into the wise woman's quarters—the dark lumps I saw on my first day in the healing chamber piled high in a vessel in a corner. Though I had pledged to Gad and Mephibosheth never to do so, they were not here, and I had a great deal to prove. When I cast them on the floor in front of me with all the ritual dignity people anticipated, then rightly divined the troubles of the people who sought my counsel, or rightly predicted their future, it had nothing to do with the shape of the knucklebones or what side they landed on . . . I had only done what I always do: reach deep inside myself to the wisdom the Lord God had placed in my heart. And so, I was able to help them in a way they found familiar.

But plants were the mainstay of my healing art. There was one so rare that, before coming here, I had never seen it in the wild—the ground-hugging *duda'im*. Few knew how to use it; some died after eating its bulbous fruit or consuming a leaf or a blossom. But in Jerusalem, I had used its powerful secret to give many women in my care what it had given tender-eyed Mother Leah—a child.

Years into my sojourn at Abel, news finally came of my brother Absalom, thanks, of all things, to the *duda'im* and a strange woman who swept into my healing chamber unannounced. "If you seek wisdom, go to Abel," she said as a scowling Mara moved up behind her with the swiftness of a gazelle but too late to stop her.

The woman needed no invitation to sit. She continued talking as she sank to the bench against the wall near the table that bore my vials of brews, extracts, and tinctures. "I want a child and that's what I was told. . . ."

I waited for her to finish her statement, but I must not have been able to hide my surprise and confusion, because she repeated impatiently that "'if you seek wisdom, go to Abel.' That's what they say in Geshur. So here I am. You will provide it."

Eved-Atar'ate's gamble on me had long ago paid off. By the time a single summer and winter herb harvest had passed, sheaves of redolent, curative greens and blossoms crowded each other for space on my rafters. Soon, I had a long list of healings to my credit and word had spread of my powers. I had grown used to a certain deference on the part of those who came to this room seeking my help, even if they were greater than I in age and stature. Treatment began when, with a gasp, they first looked into my mismatched eyes—one green one blue—and saw them shimmer. My apparent youth no longer concerned them. And so it was with this woman. I calmed myself and waited, wordless, which threw the woman off balance.

Now, finally, after so many years of waiting, this woman had brought me one step closer to Geshur where I was truly meant to be. Mara hovered close, hoping to ward off a misstep that would reveal my true identity. Absalom was surely still in Geshur; perhaps through this woman Mara feared he would get to me.

Lost in thought, I didn't respond to her arrogant speech. "If you please," she added begrudgingly, scowling at Mara.

With a nod, I signaled to Mara that she could leave us. The woman's eyes followed Mara until she closed the door, and then turned back to me.

"What is your name?" I asked.

As always, I began by probing the woman at length about her life. Shamuni, it turned out, was not much older than I. Her clothing and manner, as well as her girth, which well exceeded the width of the stone bench, showed me that lack of food was not the cause of her empty womb. I discovered that she had never been pregnant, despite what she boasted were the unflagging amorous attentions of her devoted husband. But he was growing impatient, she said, and might soon take another wife.

I gathered her hand in mine as if in sympathy. Then I turned it over, to feel whether her skin was dry or moist, warm or cold, and to observe the pulsating blue line in her wrist. Her glistening eyes as she grasped my hand in response told me the barrier had fallen. I could treat this woman.

In a quiet voice, I began the story I had chosen to relax her and make her more amenable to the treatment. "When I need my most valuable herbs, I wander the foothills above our town. I chant the psalms of healing I learned as a child . . . and I pray to find what I seek. One day early in my time here at Abel, my servant and I were assailed by a fragrance so powerful it stopped us. Only one kind of plant that has such a fragrance, and there they were, a whole cluster of bright green leaves cupping purple flowers, right at our feet—*duda'im*. We pulled it carefully from the ground to keep the precious root intact. I still have the same root I pulled up then, years ago. This is the root that will give you a child."

Shamuni was now watching my every move. I rose. I took my mortar and pestle from the table next to me and placed it on the small table on the platform across the room. At a slow, deliberate pace, I made for a niche in the wall, and drew aside the finely woven tapestry that now covered it. I had turned away, but I knew her eyes were locked on me.

"In the sacred stories of my people, our matriarch Leah was given it and soon bore a son."

My back still to her, I broke off a tiny piece of the precious root. "I am going to grind the root now and I am going to chant. You may hum with me if you wish, to empower the potion," I said as I began. "*Adonai Elohai shavati elekha vatirpani*."

Clearly this woman was not used to chanting . . . or to remaining silent. She interrupted me right away. "What does it mean?"

"*My Lord, my God, I cried out to you and you healed me*," I answered, then resumed the chant.

After briefly trying to follow along, she stopped and spoke again. "Your people? Where are you from? Isn't it strange that a city's wise woman would not be of that city?"

"I'm from Jerusalem, in Judah." There it was, before I could help myself. Not everyone was as understanding as Eved-Atar'ate when it came to my past. But this woman was from Geshur, and I was almost certain, a sense honed by years of training and practice, that my risky admission would bring me news of my brother's fate, and perhaps even my mother's.

The woman continued, and I was not disappointed. "Jerusalem, eh? Our king, Talmai, married off his daughter, Maacah, to the one who calls himself King of Israel. Much good that did us. The sons of the desert allied themselves with the Arameans and the Maacathites, and anybody else who would have them to protect themselves after they had insulted your king somehow. They fought your king and lost. That was how we lost Abel—Geshur too—to his rule. I lost my own good brother in one of those battles."

I had finished grinding the root and had already added the requisite honey and cinnamon to the mixture. I continued my rhythmic chant under my breath as she spoke. Of course, I knew this part of the story all too well. Many households in Abel had lost sons in that needless war. Then, just as I was about to turn to her with the potion in hand, she said, "But with all the trouble between our peoples, King Talmai remained true to the king of Israel, his son-in-law. When your king rejected Maacah after years of marriage, King Talmai took back his daughter without a word of protest. But when the time came and the king's son—Maacah's, too, mind you—rebelled against him, King Talmai took the prince in and protected him. They say that was Talmai's revenge, although the king insisted it was nothing of the sort."

If I faced her now, my mask would surely crack and all would be lost, even after all these years. Keeping my back to the woman, I moved my hands and arms enough for her to think I was still busy with the potion. But, in reality, I only tried to still my shivering shoulders.

"Yes, and they say Princess Maacah is still there in Talmai's palace, although we never see her, not even on feast days and ceremonies. But word is, the son has been sent for. Your king is apparently willing to forgive him. What do you think of that, then! He's gone back to Jerusalem. They say your king has also allowed the prince to roam the city free and . . ."

She finally paused.

I didn't trust myself to respond as a stranger would to the parade of people . . . my people . . . she had brought forth as mere marketplace gossip. Not to mention the unintended news that my brother was no longer in Geshur. That, finally, there was nothing keeping me from going there.

I peered over my shoulder at her. "And what?" I asked as quietly as I could. What did this woman hold back?

"No, nothing . . ."

Her sidling eyes told me different. The potent aroma and smoothness of the potion informed me it was well mixed. But I stirred some more and pressed on. "You were saying . . . ?"

"The king is calling up our troops and they say the same is true in other cities. They say Abel is already under siege. Well . . ." Shamuni lengthened that single syllable into a suspicious sing-song. No wonder. Why, she must be thinking, does she have to tell me, the wise woman, the woman of second sight, the healer, what happened right outside the gates of our city.

"Is something wrong?" she asked.

I had been holding my breath and had let it out in a one huge sigh, knowing I should move quickly now. I aligned my features into a relaxed, reassuring smile and turned to face my patient. "No, of course not." I pushed aside the unwanted images. "I always take a great cleansing breath before handing over a potion. It helps maintain the power of the mixture on your journey home."

I held out the vial as she stood and almost ran across the small chamber to take it from me. The vial was my lifeline to this world I had made my own, so I held onto it for another moment before I lost it again. With my free hand, I brought hers to rest around mine, grasping the vial. I looked into her eyes and summoned my healing authority. "Take a tiny drop of this mixture on a spoon no bigger than the one you use to apply color to your eyes. Place it under your tongue every day for two weeks after your bleeding stops, and make sure your husband's attentions persist during this time. You will be with child soon enough."

I clapped my hands twice and Mara stepped over the threshold and back into the room. The woman understood she had been dismissed and turned to follow Mara out. In the doorway, she stopped and turned again. "What do they call you? Besides 'Wise Woman'?"

"Serah," I replied. After so many years, the name rolled off my tongue without a second thought. How ironic, just as I was about to lose it.

Mara and I were alone in the room, but the shiver I had tried to hide now turned to an uncontrollable tremble. I longed for Mara's embrace, but she remained where she stood. Something was amiss.

"So, you know," Mara said, her voice calm.

The trembling stopped and my fuming anger filled the room. "I *know? I* know? Are you saying *you* knew about Absalom and you kept it from me? You let me sit in this room, day in and day out, dispensing potions and powders for ailments real and imagined, while my pain waited only for the words I had to hear today from a stranger?"

"I did what I have always done. What was right for you to keep you out of danger."

The corner of Mara's mouth slanted upward in the wry smile I knew so well, which only infuriated me more. Our servants had heard plenty from this room; weeping from pain or painful counsel and even screams of anguish. But my own pain remained silent, always. Until now. A cluster of worried faces appeared in the doorway. Mara shooed them back, then closed the door in their alarmed faces lest they hear our truth.

"Mara . . ." I had to stop, swallow, and begin again, bruised with the effort of choking back my screams. "You knew Absalom had left Geshur and you didn't tell me?" Arms akimbo, I waited.

"Yes . . . and yes." Her calm enraged me all the more.

"And you lived this lie because . . . ?"

"Because it is my task, above all else, to save you from yourself. Now that you know your brother has left Geshur, you would head there this very day if you could. You've never gone on a gazelle hunt, never seen a doomed creature trapped at the end of the stone-wall funnel built by the hunters. She runs and runs, and the walls become narrower and narrower, and in the end, she has nowhere to turn. The arrows and spears take aim, and the end comes quickly. All her running, fleet as she was, for nothing."

I clenched my fists and stamped the floor with such force that a puff of dust rose from the packed earth. I pushed another scream deep into my throat and ignored her long-winded description of me as a hunted animal. "That is *not* true. You've kept this from me because you're comfortable here and you're too old to leave."

I was indeed trapped, but not by my brother, his agents, or my father's long arm. Mara, who had been like a mother, kept me from my future. At that moment I was anything but the wise woman of this city. I was once again a helpless, angry, sputtering child. But I could not get Mara to rise to the bait. Instead, she persisted calmly.

"It was not for nothing that Mephibosheth and Gad instructed you to shun prophecy and keep to healing and counsel. You're a poor seer, especially when it comes to yourself, *Serah*. You never mention the worsening of noise and smoke from the bellows in the artisans' quarter. Do you think it means nothing? There are weapons of war being made there. You never learned to understand the outside world, even after all these years. You do not see what is happening right outside our compound, even on the rare occasions when you leave these walls and walk the city's streets." Her brow rose. "Now . . . it is time for me to show you." Mara ducked behind the curtain into my private quarters and returned with my cloak, but I remained rooted to the spot. "Right now. Come with me," she commanded.

Mara was right. When I ventured out, accompanied by Mara and the two servants Eved-Atar'ate had given me, it was to the meadows, streams, and rocky hillsides where I found my treasures of healing. I had never been able to shake the feeling that I was being watched when I was in the street; my work was my retreat.

We went through the door in the wall that separated the inner compound from the city's main street, Mara pulling me by the hand like a child. But once we reached the street, she let go and fell into place behind me, assuming her servant persona.

Passersby stopped when they recognized their wise woman walking among them. Many bowed and poured out greetings and blessings, impeding the progress of the walkers behind them, who jostled each other and my admirers to get by. Soon, a little knot of people accompanied us.

I bowed and smiled in response to the greetings, but my thoughts were elsewhere. *She's taking me to the marketplace. Why?* I looked back at Mara, but her look was inscrutable.

"Here. No need to go any farther." She gently pulled me out of the eddying crowd.

So, not the marketplace.

"Look down," Mara said, with her chin lifted toward the lower city. My first glance revealed nothing out of the ordinary. But then I saw what Mara had brought me here to see. Interspersed among the men and women in the crowd moving through the street below, their shawls like colorful blossoms nodding in a passing breeze when they greeted acquaintances, or negotiated over a purchase, toddlers riding on their fathers' shoulders, babies strapped tight in voluminous shawls on their mothers' backs, servants weighed down with baskets of food and other goods, the conical metal helmets and armored vests of foot soldiers glinted in the sunlight. The more I stared at the scene below, the more there seemed to be.

I turned to Mara.

"Don't," was all she said, touching the bottom of her chin unobtrusively to signal to me that my mouth had dropped open.

"Since the prince left Geshur, Abel and all the surrounding cities have summoned their soldiers," she said. "Anything might happen now. Who knows what stories Prince Absalom told about his time at Geshur to get the king to take him back. The king might launch a campaign against Geshur to take revenge for deeds Absalom invented to explain his long absence from Jerusalem. And if Absalom has betrayed King David, he might march against Geshur out of fear Absalom has allied himself with the Maacathites. In any case, our people are preparing for war."

Tears blurred not only the scene below. My destination, Geshur, and a reunion with my mother, grew distant in the shimmer. But then the strongest parts of Serah/Tamar surged through me. "We'll go to Eved-Atar'ate. I must hear this from him."

"As I suspected," Mara responded. "You don't even believe your own eyes." With a sigh of resignation, she followed me toward the town council chamber.

Back up the main street. Even though I held my veil over the lower part of my face, some recognized me and tried to stop me. I gently pulled away with a murmured blessing, and our pace quickened as we retraced our steps to the upper city and Eved-Atar'ate's compound.

The household of Abel's leading citizen was always a busy one, but now it was a simmering cauldron. The standing order to admit me at any time brought us immediately into the spacious chamber where the council met. Ten men occupied the row of woven cushions on the stone bench that lined the back and side walls of the chamber. I had treated most of them at one time or another over the years, which explained why some first seemed surprised, then confused, to see me on their territory. There was only one man I had never seen before. A soldier—an officer, I presumed by the round metal medallion covering his chest—and an archer, his bow slung across his back.

Eved-Atar'ate rose when we were shown in, and the rest of the council followed his lead, before settling down again against the cushions. "You've seen?" His eyes moved from me to Mara, and Mara's slight nod made me realize he had asked her to bring me to that vantage point and then to the council. "Well, so you know. Absalom son of David is more cunning than we could have ever imagined."

If only they knew.

"Absalom has left Geshur for Jerusalem. King David finally called him to court and gave him permission to travel the country at will. It has been some time now since we've heard anything, but the last we know of from our agents, the king even gave his son a letter that gives him the power to appoint two elders from every town and village of note. He chose them and insinuated that they were the favorites of the king himself. By the time he was finished, he had two hundred leaders from throughout the land, including our very own region. Then, Absalom put on a fine banquet. The wine flowed, magnificent food never stopped coming, and the women danced before them from dark to dawn.

"I have heard the prince knows how to put on a banquet," I interjected, working hard to keep my tone even, wondering why I was being subjected to this litany.

"You've always been impatient, from the day I brought you here," Eved-Atar'ate said. "Please don't interrupt." The other men's squirming told me they were glad it was not they who were the target of Eved-Atar'ate's exasperation. None of them would dare speak to the wise woman as he had. But none of them could know the debt I owed this man. So I fell silent with more obedience than I felt. I had to remember that the information was key.

Eved-Atar'ate waited a beat before continuing. "At the banquet, Absalom had seen to seating arrangements himself—he placed one of his own trusted followers between each two of his guests. Our agent said Absalom's men by turns flattered, cajoled, and threatened the man on his right and the man on his left, until it seemed they had been won over to his plan. But our agent tells me that even before the festivities were over, and certainly in the days that followed, the prince's guests, while they saw no choice but to stand by him, hoped for King David's victory over this upstart prince."

I could have guessed Eved-Atar'ate's next words.

"We already have the troops assembled. We will have to decide where we stand—with Absalom or with the king."

"But why have you sent for me?" I looked from my patron to Mara, and back again.

"You wield as much influence in this town as any of us here. Influence well earned over your years of service. But you are from Judah, and so . . ."

He's going to ask me where my own loyalties lie. Before I could compose my answer, the door to the chamber blew open admitting a runner.

Pushing aside the jug of water a servant offered him, the young man approached the councilmen, who stood, alarmed and silent. The man gulped at air like a beached fish, and shouted over the din, his voice bouncing off the walls of the small chamber. "Absalom," he gasped, "the crown prince of Israel has been killed!"

The men's mouths moved, their eyes bulged, but I heard nothing beyond the roar of rushing water that pulsed through my ears. Why could I hear no more than this? Perhaps this was another of my vengeful dreams?

But it was the pounding of my heart that had drowned out their voices. I began to feel the faintness that always followed the pounding when a vision overtook me. But this was no vision.

Come back to yourself! Show them nothing! Mara had not spoken aloud, but it was her voice I heard within.

The messenger looked helpless as the councilmen peppered him with questions, each man no doubt distilling what the news would mean for him, his family, his business. I barely heard him; my thoughts, so different from theirs, were distilling as well.

My revenge was complete.

I could go home to Jerusalem. My father would finally love me, as the only surviving child of Maacah, if not for myself than for his alliance with Geshur. But . . .

Who had killed Absalom? If the Geshurites took his life, I would be putting myself in even more danger by going there.

"How did the young man die?" I feared it was I who had spoken aloud, but it was Eved-Atar'ate speaking to the messenger. The council fell silent as his voice overrode their confusion.

"Do you know?" he pressed the messenger, who nodded woodenly in response. I almost felt sorry for the man. "Tell us," Eved-Atar'ate commanded.

The messenger saw that he had a rapt audience, which seemed to please him. It certainly calmed him. He reached for the jug of water from the servant and took a swig. Then he focused on some unseen point as if the scene were playing out there, in the air, and sighed into his answer. "The word has already spread. I heard many versions of it on my way here. As well as I can make of it, the army of the king's general, his nephew Joab, faced off against the forces of the rebel prince Absalom in a great plain bordering on a forest. Tens of thousands were killed on both sides. But Joab's men wanted only one thing, to find Absalom, of course, and to rid the army of its leader and the nation of its chief rebel, as their king wanted."

I wondered, bitterly, at that. David's love of Absalom outstripped anything else. I knew that, even if no one else did. No, this much I knew to be untrue; my father would not want Absalom dead, no matter what.

"Joab's men spotted the prince—the general's own cousin—easily on the battlefield. His height gave him away, not to mention that magnificent mane of auburn hair—it was said he was too vain to cover it with a helmet like a normal soldier. Joab's men had the day, and in the prince's haste to flee the battlefield on his mule, his hair became entangled in the low-reaching branches of a stubby oak. There he was, hanging, swinging back and forth. No one has ever seen anything like it, they say.

"One of Joab's men reported this to him and the general said he wished he could see Absalom dead, although his men said they had all heard the king, when he dispatched the troops and stayed behind at Mahanaim, urge them to spare his son."

Of course. No level of infidelity would make the king denounce his beloved son.

"Joab made his man show him the place where the prince hung. As soon as he saw it, he plunged his spear straight into the prince's heart. Joab's armor-bearer pulled down the body, threw it into a gorge and had his men cover the place with boulders."

"As if to hide the act from the king, though it was witnessed by dozens of soldiers, hence you know the entire story." I had spoken aloud.

The men all looked at me, including the messenger, as if they had forgotten I was there. Now they remembered. A Judahite in their midst. And their wise woman, whom they could not do without. "What now, then?" I asked in an attempt to place their attention back on the messenger.

"Now," the man continued, his eyes glowing with pleasure that I had handed the stage back to him, "Sheba son of Bichri—a Benjamite—has gathered the people of Israel to revolt against King David."

"Has he returned to Jerusalem, then?" Eved-Atar'ate asked.

"He has. And, it is said . . ." He glanced toward me, then lowered his eyes. "It is said that he has made provisions for the ten concubines he left to care for the palace in his absence. The ones who Absalom forced into his tent as a show of power. They will be cared for, I have heard, until they die."

Blood rushed from my head and pooled in my toes. I closed my eyes, knowing that any man in the room looking at me would imagine that I, as a woman, would feel the grief of those ten. But they could not imagine and could never know the truth behind my sudden show of camaraderie: *the king would care for those raped by his son . . . unless the one raped by his son was the king's own daughter.*

I righted myself and opened my eyes to find Eved-Atar'ate looking directly at me. "So then, if the prince is dead," I said with a strength I hardly knew I had, "why are the king's soldiers building a siege ramp against Abel?"

"Because," Eved-Atar'ate answered, "Sheba has somehow managed to make his way into our city. Sliding in like a snake between the stones of the wall."

Now they all turned to look at me, each with one question in their eyes. Did I stand with Judah who, even now, attempted to besiege the city, or did I stand with my adopted home of Abel?

My goal to reach Geshur and find my mother would have to wait. I would put my burning anger against my father and my dead brother to good use.

"I stand with Abel. Even if General Joab casts blame on us to save himself with his king, this is my city and I will protect it."

Eved-Atar'ate looked from one man's face to another, scrutinizing each to assure they would not give me, a Judahite, up. He then turned to me and bowed. I had been dismissed. The other men were caught up in the crisis and everyone spoke at once. The air filled with panic and snippets of fear-drenched words swirled around us as we turned to leave.

"The Judahites are already . . ."

"We are under siege . . . Who has seen to our emergency stores?"

"Some of their men have infiltrated the city . . ."

How long had we been in the council chamber? The street in front of Eved-Atar'ate's house had changed, grown more crowded, and everyone who could carried bundles of food, stocking their homes against the dreaded siege. Fathers scooped up toddlers who dawdled, mothers covered babies in their shawls against their breast.

"There will be no leaving now," Mara said under her breath. "The Judahite army is already here, building their ramp to take this city captive. And now that Absalom is dead, do you think the king will mourn for his daughter the way he did for his beloved son? No, he'll blame it on her, and his mourning will turn into blind rage. David's agents are everywhere. You must try *not* to draw attention to yourself. Well . . . " Mara looked me up and down. "Try to be inconspicuous . . . try . . ."

I rolled my eyes at that, and Mara gave up. My fiery tresses had taken only a few years in Abel to turn a silvery white. That would have been enough of a disguise for many women and men. But no one in Abel had eyes like mine—"Serah's brilliance shines through rainbow eyes," I'd heard the people say. This alone could stir my fear of being recognized, but I consoled myself knowing that as long as they never knew the eyes of the king's daughter were the same eyes of their wise woman, I remained safe.

"I will try. I promise you," I said. We both knew I would do what I had to do, yet I—for the first time in the many years since I came to Abel—had no idea what that would be.

The door to my courtyard cracked open as we approached. A servant peered out, her face a mask of apprehension and confusion. "A stranger is here. He says he will speak only to you." The servant gestured to a shade-dappled corner of the courtyard where a cloaked figure crouched, a bowl of water before him. Without standing, he jerked the cloak from his head, revealing a filthy beard right up to a pair of beady black eyes, oily hair covering his low forehead.

I folded my arms, waiting. Surely the stranger would rise respectfully before the wise woman of Abel, especially if he needed healing or counsel.

"It's not what you think," Mara said through barely parted lips. "I know this man."

I shook my head at her; I wanted to hear for myself—see for myself—to what lengths his insolence would go.

I pulled myself up a little taller. "You obviously know who I am. But I do not believe I've met you before. How can I help? Are you ill? Would you like to come with me to my treatment chamber?"

"No!" Mara shouted.

The servants—who should have been used to Mara freely telling me what to do—jumped as her voice sliced the air. An almost imperceptible shadow of confusion crossed the stranger's face as well, that a servant would speak thus to her mistress.

"It's Sheba son of Bichri," Mara spat out, her eyes never leaving him. "You Benjamites are troublemakers from the moment you emerge from your mother's womb. Looking at Jerusalem as though it were yours," Mara said, her voice as thick with rancor as if she had been a high-born noble with lands to lose to Jerusalem's northern neighbors. "And here you are, pursued now by Judah, turning yourself over to Abel, throwing yourself on the mercy of this city. How dare you?"

"Silence!" I demanded. The servants jumped again, and no wonder. They had never heard me speak to Mara as mistresses usually did. I didn't want this man to know more about us than he already did. But I took her cue. "You speak out of turn, as usual, Mara. But that makes what you say no less true. Indeed, the Benjamites have long been jealous of King David, who has extended his gracious sovereignty over the rulers of the north, from Jerusalem to the realms beyond Abel."

Finally, Sheba stood, and stepped forward. His cloak fell to the ground revealing mud-caked armor covering a thick torso, and greaves that protected stocky, bowed legs. Even when I spotted the glint of a dagger in his belt, I forced myself to stand my ground.

How had he escaped the standoff of his army against King David's outside the gate of Abel, not only getting into the city but to my very courtyard? How had he gained entrance, looking as he did? "What is it that you want from me, man of Benjamin?"

Sheba stared into my eyes, as so many did. But he did not do so out of astonishment or intrigue. Instead, a knowledge seemed to grow within the dark pools of his eyes. He stood silent. Then . . . "Nesicha." *Princess.*

For once, it was I who stood speechless, and he took advantage of it. "Of course I recognize you," he continued in the language I had not heard for years. "Those eyes of yours are a legend that refuses to die. I remember you as a child in your father's court, and when you became a healer your fame only spread further afield." He looked around fleetingly. "So, you are the wise woman here in Abel now. Rumors were rife about where you had fled after you were accused of conspiring with Absalom against the king to kill your brother Amnon. It seemed you had disappeared into thin air. But when I heard of the wise woman with the mismatched eyes . . ." He snickered. "Ah, but this is perfect. You understand what it is like to be an outcast and an enemy of the throne, as I am now," the man called Sheba went on. "So, hear me out: I believe I can beat the army of King David. I've known it for years. I have no part in David. The tribe of Benjamin and the House of Saul were destined to reign, *not* David's line. And you, *you* Nesicha, can help me make this happen."

"How is that?" I dared ask, which brought Mara one step closer to me.

"We will reign together. Perhaps even a wedding . . . depicting everlasting unity between Judah and Benjamin. Take me to the leaders of your city, allow me to present myself to them. We will work together toward greatness."

My stomach turned, my mouth filled with bile and my thoughts churned with the desire for revenge for that ravaged young girl of so long ago. I clenched my hands in front of me beneath the broad sleeves of my robe. I gripped the hilt of an imaginary dagger in my interlaced fingers. I pictured myself raising my hands high and plunging the blade into the black eye of this panting, sweating, lustful little man.

But I hid my rage completely behind a forced smile so that all he saw in my gesture was a thoughtful pause. "Your victories on the battlefield have turned your head, Sheba of Benjamin," I said lightly, continuing to speak to him in our tongue. "I will not turn against my adopted city. But I will take you to the council, as you have requested. But you must trust me fully that I will work to free you to safety from Joab and his men, and that I will succeed." I paused to allow my words to penetrate his minuscule mind. "And . . . in exchange for your life, you will keep my secret and leave this place, never to return."

It was the only thing I could do, I told myself again and again all the way to Eved-Atar'ate's house, where the council met. I waited with Sheba in the deserted council chamber while my patron sent runners to fetch the council members. The room slowly filled and hummed with curious murmurs and glances at the stranger. Finally, they were all present. "I'll leave you to your deliberations," I said, with more deference than I felt, "to determine how best to get this man safely out of Abel and, in doing so, to send the king's general away from here. But please wait with your decision until I return from consulting..." —I thought quickly, knowing I could not divulge my real plan—"the augers." I would do no such thing, of course, and I silently prayed for forgiveness from Nathan, Gad, Mephibosheth, and especially faithful Grandmother Nitzevet in our beloved shrine in Gibeon, who would be aghast at the very idea of my true intent.

I turned and left the chamber.

Sunset had nearly blanketed the city with its smoky but brilliant colors. On a normal day, people walk companionably home from the marketplace, while visitors and merchants made their way to the inn. But the waning light revealed scurrying, panicked crowds, who knew more than I. With Mara in tow, I turned against the human tide and made for the walls.

I didn't stop until I reached the main gate, facing south, deserted and shuttered. The sentries stood on the wall above, their backs to the city, facing whatever lay below, which I was determined to see. Mara was still breathlessly trying to catch up as I mounted the narrow staircase, hugging the wall as I climbed and reached the roof of one of the two massive towers that flanked the gate. The older woman could not make the steps. I knew it; it was what I had planned. After a failed attempt, she stood at the foot of the stairs and looked up helplessly. I gave her only the briefest of nods.

The sentries didn't see me until I was standing between the crenellations. "It's the wise woman!" the one nearest me alerted the others. They all swung their heads in the direction of their shouting comrade, then back to me.

"Get down, my lady! You're in full view of the enemy's arrows!" The soldier next to me clumsily swung his shield aside and tried to pull me behind the higher part of the wall, but my powerful pull in the opposite direction caught him by surprise. My travails may have turned my hair white, but I was never stronger than at that moment. He stumbled and released me.

I placed myself back into full view of the field below. The tense quiet of a siege prevailed. I saw two high earthen berms, one in front of Abel's walls and one in front of King David's army, with a deserted meadow in between. A line of watchers lay prone just behind each army's fortification. On the far side, a lone figure stood. A man I knew well from my father's court—his nephew and general, Joab. No job had ever been too bloody for this man in the service of his king. Nothing and no one would stand in his way. And here he was again. He had not shrunk from finishing off the king's own son, and he would not shrink from attacking what he believed to be a rebel city.

Joab, doer of David's dirty deeds for my entire life, not only my fellow Judahite, but my own cousin, right there at the base of the walls. And back in the council chamber, the rebel Sheba the Benjamite, expecting me to act for him. How would I make this right? For myself? For others?

Standing as a lone woman, erect on the wall of a city, I set my trap. "Send to me your general," I shouted, hoping my pretense of not recognizing the man would help keep me safe. "Send to me Joab so that I may speak to him!"

My cousin stepped forward, the metal of his armor casting golden prisms from the brilliant orb inching toward the desert's horizon. He placed one booted foot up on a boulder to demonstrate his authority but said nothing.

"Are you Joab?" I shouted.

The soldiers on the wall with me crouched lower. They placed their shields over their heads, all pretense of protecting me gone now. I seemed even more foreign to them than ever, I suppose, speaking to the enemy general with such boldness, my accent in their native tongue more prominent than ever.

"I am!" he called back. "But how do you know my name?"

Ah. "*How do you know my name.*" The wrong question. Weakness. This was my entry. And he had answered me in the language I had used to address him, the language of my adopted city. He did not know who I was. More weakness.

Out of the corner of my eye, I saw the shields protecting the soldiers on the wall moved slightly. I looked aside; they stared at me open-mouthed. They thought my question ridiculous. All the better.

"Listen to what your servant has to say. I know your name in the same way I know everything else. . . ." I paused for effect, knowing that two warring armies had fallen silent at the sight of the shouting woman on the wall. "Because I am the wise woman of this city. When people need answers, they come to me from all lands and tribes." I had never been above exaggerating my own power to help people believe in me to lead to their healing. Now I did it to save an entire city. "And so, I know not only your name, but your tribe."

"What is that to me, *O great one?*"

Ignoring Joab's question and its contemptuous tone, I plunged on. "Some say you are called a *takhkemoni* of the Tachkemonites, a tribe that takes its very name from wisdom. But you are foolish and have broken the laws of your own faith."

His laugh was chilling. "They should call you fool woman, not wise. I can order you pierced through where you stand, if you don't fall off first," he replied. He gestured to the pair of archers that now flanked him to draw their bows.

"But you won't," I countered, "because you're too curious. You want to know what I mean." I swallowed. My throat was dry from shouting, and I wondered if I could continue. But the general took my pause as a threat . . . that I might *not* continue.

"Speak then, woman, if you know."

"Listen to what I say. We are the peaceful and faithful in Israel. Why would you want to destroy a city that is a mother in Israel? The laws your God handed down require you to ask a city for terms of peace before you besiege it. And the penalty for breaking such a law is well known among your people. Why would you want to swallow up Yahweh's inheritance?"

In truth, I didn't know the penalty for breaking the law, but I knew that the mention of our great God would cause Joab to pause. From the distance that stretched between us, I could see Joab shift his weight uncomfortably. "Who are you, really?"

Another question, another sign of weakness. Or had he recognized me, the way Sheba had? No, from this distance all he could see was my white hair, which was flaming red when last he saw me, if, in fact, he had even noticed me as a child. No, I was safe.

"I am Serah, the wise woman of Abel, and I am faithful to the welfare of my city. I only want to save it."

The general's response came before I had even uttered the last word.

"If this is true, then let us discuss terms," he said. "I do not need to destroy your city; far be it from me! I require only the head of the man hiding within its walls, somewhere among you. He is a rebel against my king, and he must die."

One man. I had accomplished the first stage of my plan. "Then stand down and wait. I will return with his head."

I climbed down from my perch. "Tell your men to return to their posts," I commanded the officer in charge of the gatehouse roof, then turned to find Mara.

There she was, at the bottom of the precarious staircase, muttering under her breath and shaking her head. When I reached her, she grabbed me as only a mother would, and fumed, "What is this you have done, Tamar?"

"Shhhh," I hissed, and put a finger to her lips. Every shadow seemed to undulate at the unfamiliar sound of my real name.

"How could you risk your life in this way?" she persisted, now in a ragged whisper. "What did you accomplish?"

"Oh, a great deal, I hope," I replied, much more lightly than I felt.

We made our way through now deserted streets, their shadows vanishing with the sun's slipping behind the wall, back to Eved-Atar'ate and the council. An eerie silence greeted us when we entered the chamber. Had the councilmen debated themselves into exhaustion? I looked for Sheba, afraid that they had come to some conclusion without me. But no, there was the rebel, in the corner on the floor, where I had left him. He eyed me warily as the men began again to babble. No, they were far from argued out.

"We're deadlocked," Eved-Atar'ate said. "We decided to wait until you returned with the word of the augers."

The air pulsated with the men's attempts to outshout each other.

". . . Give him up now! He is not one of us . . ."

". . . surrounded . . ."

". . . when we're slaughtered, they'll kill this man anyhow . . ."

"No!" one of the men exclaimed. "After all, what crime did he commit . . . how many of us wish we could be free of King David's tribute . . . perhaps the rebel has brought us the opportunity we have been waiting for."

"Speak for yourself . . . I've made my peace with the tribute," one of the city's wealthiest men argued. "I pay it, and have plenty left over, thanks to my new trading routes with the south. . . ."

I folded my lips into a tight line against my teeth. I could not stay silent much longer. And, after all these years, Mara's hand on my arm would not stop me. I was a wise woman—*the* wise woman—on the verge of saying something worse than un-wise. Just as I was about to speak, Eved-Atar'ate shouted over the din, "All right! Silence! We have been over and over the same issues. Some of us have grown rich sucking on Jerusalem's teat, I among them. Others would risk our wealth to stand up as a free kingdom the way we once were.

Has this Sheba, son of Bichri, committed a crime, you ask. One that deserves death? I say—yes! It's a crime to rebel against the ruler whom our gods, or their God, or military might, or all of these, has decreed for us. He deserves to die for his crime, and we and our families deserve to live." My eyes shot to Sheba, who now stood, his fear threatening to expose us both. I raised my hand but slightly to shush him as Eved-Atar'ate continued. "Now, let us listen to our wise woman's word as we said we would."

They turned to me in one swift movement as Sheba slid against the wall toward a door.

"I consulted the augers and they told me to go to the walls and speak to the Judahite general myself."

A murmur of disbelief engulfed the room.

"But . . ."

"But . . ." I repeated the word more softly after Eved-Atar'ate's raised palm brought back order.

"He said he will kill a thousand people of Abel to teach us how his king treats a city that harbors a rebel fugitive," I lied. "Each one of you will have to choose from among your family and clan. There is no other way."

I waited. Narrowed eyes told me the men were trying to take in what I had said until they widened in horror as understanding dawned on them. Faces went ashen. I let the full force of it engulf them. Then I spoke again. "But perhaps, just perhaps, he'll agree to a smaller number of sacrifices if I go back to him with a counteroffer."

"Let some of the council members go with you . . . it will give your proposal more weight," Eved-Atar'ate said.

"I think not," I said, in the same determined tone familiar to many in that room of the one who had held in her hands the fate of their health or their wife's or child's life. "There is more safety for you if I handle this alone. He knows I am the wise woman and he trusts me. No. I will go alone and I will return with the general's reply."

I turned and left with an imperious whip of my robe, followed by Mara, leaving them open-mouthed behind me.

Night fully engulfed the street now. Shadows danced in the lamplights flickering from a few high windows, but people were already rationing their oil, and most had probably rolled out their sleeping pallets. They were hoping, I suppose, for the night to pass swiftly and retreat when the sun rose and brought a new, better day.

I pulled Mara with me into a dark corner.

"What are you doing now?" she said testily, moving much more slowly than I would have wanted.

"Precisely nothing. We'll wait here until enough time has passed that they believe I am returning with a message."

We sank against a wall outside a shuttered market stall, squatting in the shadows. A soft snore soon came from Mara, but I waited tensely until the brightest star I could see had moved beyond the line of the buildings across the street.

"Mara . . ."—I shook the older woman gently to rouse her. "Mara . . ." Her lids trembled and finally she opened her eyes. As she had done for me countless times over my life, I tucked away tangled hair, and the thin wayward gray strands obeyed me immediately and disappeared beneath her veil. When I started to help her up, she pulled back, and waved me off.

"You go on," she said. "Don't worry, I'll be fine here. I'm tired."

This time, silence fell as soon as the servant opened the door and the men saw me standing in the doorway.

"The general has reduced his demands. Now he wants only five hundred instead of a thousand people of the city."

"Is it then time for us to accede?" A man of Eved-Atar'ate's faction—only much wealthier—asked.

But to my surprise, it was my patron who responded, his eyes not leaving mine. "No . . . no, it is not, is it, wise woman?" Without waiting for my answer, Eved-Atar'ate pressed on and as my heart trembled. "Go back and see if you can persuade him to lower the number further. I believe in you. We all do."

When he looked from one man to the other, daring anyone to defy him, the room grew suddenly cold. What was this? Had they hatched a plan of their own? Had Sheba done his own bargaining in my absence? Had he revealed my identity in exchange for his own life? I could do nothing now without endangering my secret except persist in my ruse. I returned to Mara and reported what had happened.

"Good, very good," was all she said, leaving me unsure if she had understood.

By the time I calculated that I could end my imaginary negotiation with Joab, a bright band pushed back the curtain of night and the stars had begun to fade. I returned to the council with the news that Joab had lowered his demands from five hundred, to one hundred, to ten, and then, finally, to one. Most breathed a collective sigh of relief. But something about the room had changed. One man stared at the wall, another nudged his neighbor and imperceptively raised his chin toward me. Most damning of all, Sheba, curled up in a corner, slept peacefully.

"He only wants one man." I looked toward the sleeping rebel. "If he receives the head of the rebel, Sheba son of Bichri, he will depart in peace."

The debate grew heated, their whispers crackling like a freshly made fire.

"We must put the good of the city before the fate of one man!"

"And he's a rebel—we owe him nothing! Remember who our overlords have been for these past years—the Judahites . . . I mean, the Israelites! Our loyalty is to the king of Israel."

"Loyalty, eh? The same kind of loyalty you showed in your rebel days against the Israelites before you found out how convenient life could be under them?"

The argument seemed interminable. Clenched fists were raised, and fingers stabbed the air and then poked ample bellies as red-faced adversaries refused to budge.

And the rebel himself . . . his soft snoring had stopped when whispers turned to shouts and he bolted to a sitting position. His future now hung over an abyss, swinging between life and death. I looked away from him on purpose, but I could feel his eyes boring into me. Would he keep my secret if my own plan were accepted? Had he already divulged it?

"Enough," I said calmly. A startled silence fell over the room as if I had drawn a weapon. Before they could recover, I plunged ahead with the idea I had mulled over in my last walk back from the walls. "We'll give them what they want."

The rebel merely looked puzzled, but men began to nod as if they realized what I meant.

Eved-Atar'ate spoke up first. "Then it is your counsel, as our wise woman and healer, who alone negotiated with the enemy and knows his strengths and weaknesses? To deliver the head of this man, a man who committed no more of a crime than many of us here in this room did in our youth, and perhaps even to this day? This man who sought refuge among us by slipping into our city?"

My sponsor spoke gently but his opinion was obvious.

I could feel Mara's restraining hand on my forearm as if she were in the room. It reminded me to swallow scorn and utter words commensurate with my station.

"Yes . . . and no."

A dozen pairs of eyes narrowed. They were all in my hands now, waiting, hoping for a cure to their woes, as people always did. For a change, it would be for my own as well. I would cement my unspoken bargain with the rebel, he would keep my secret, and I would keep his, and no more lives would be taken.

"As your wise woman, I counsel you to deliver the head of *a* dead man. You will wrap *a* head and bring it back, and you will fling it over the wall to Joab. The face will be so mangled when it lands at their feet that they will never be able to recognize the man it once belonged to."

The men nodded as if they understood. But it was Eved-Atar'ate who was the first to realize the ruse I had planned. Then Sheba.

His scowling, fearful features realigned themselves and he smiled wickedly, satisfied.

Their wagging heads now turned side-to-side as disbelief took over. But Eved-Atar'ate was the only one who spoke.

"Yes, we understand, don't we," he said, his voice like forged iron, locking each man's eyes in turn with his own. They came to rest on Tukulti, the youngest member of the council, and the only one in the room who had recently lost a relative, his uncle.

I forced myself to stand still, to remain silent. Tukulti had grown up under the Israelite occupation and his family has prospered. He would consider it an honor to bring Sheba's head to Joab, to save and further his family's fortunes. And, like my own people, these Maacathites were meticulous about their funerary rites. It was one thing to sweep aside dry bones in a burial cave to make room for the newly dead. But Tukulti would not easily agree to desecrate the grave of his uncle by slicing off the head before the flesh had desiccated. Before I could think of a way to disagree with my ally and advocate these many years, Sheba cleared his throat and stood. All eyes, including my own, turned to him, incredulous.

"And what of me?" It was hard to imagine that the sheepish voice belonged to a man who had led an almost successful uprising against the great king of Israel.

I turned to stare him down. He obviously needed to be reminded of the pact I had made with him earlier that same day. "You? You will remain here, under the protection of Eved-Atar'ate, until the besieging army decamps. When they do, that very night, you will leave Abel. You will tell no one your destination or what transpired here."

As I spoke, I realized my life in Abel was about to end. Or perhaps life itself, and that would be because I had spared the life of this oily little man with a ludicrous pact. "Fool woman" would indeed be a better title for me; Joab had been right.

Sheba knew my identity. Even if he had kept it a secret from the council, would he not deliver me up to my father in exchange for a pardon? Would my father not pursue me, as he had pursued Absalom in his blind, misplaced rage at my supposed treachery? I was back where I started before arriving in Abel.

I turned to the rebel. The fear I sensed told me he had seen fire in my eyes. "You will leave this place forever. You will be dead to all who knew you." I summoned up the practiced, dire tone I reserved for people who sought a spell against their inner demons. "And all whom you knew." I turned away abruptly so he would not see that the fire he had seen previously had been doused with my own fear.

Eved-Atar'ate followed my lead. "We are adjourned," he said coolly, opening the door of his council chamber. The men filed out, stunned but satisfied. Their city had been saved, and no one else had died. Their masks were on, the secret plan safe. Eved-Atar'ate murmured to a few as they made their way out, setting out details of the plan, I assumed. Then I joined the line, motioning to Sheba to follow me, leaving Tukulti to follow last out of the room.

"I must get to Mara," I called from the back to Eved-Atar'ate. "I left her on a doorstep down the street. Do you see her?"

"Wait for me. I'll look for her, I . . ." he began to call from the street.

The rest of his instructions were swallowed up in the sounds of grunts and scuffling behind me. I turned. Sheba stood, his eyes bulging as Tukulti held him in a strange embrace, a dagger gripped in his hand. He shouted gurgled obscenities, then cried out for mercy until blood pulsed and arched, shooting from a gaping wound as Tukulti continued to saw at the rebel's neck.

I gasped as Tukulti's blade finished its work. He lifted the dripping knife with a flourish and let go of the body, which thudded to the ground. The head, held by the hair in Tukulti's grip, stared with eyes wide open, mouth frozen in horror. Blood covered the assailant's hands and soaked his sleeves.

The commotion drew the other men back from the courtyard and the street. They crowded into the corridor leading to the council chamber, then pressed in close around the body, their faces frozen in horrified awe.

"There. It's done. No need to disturb my uncle's eternal rest for a ruse that might endanger our city." Tukulti looked from one man to another, daring any to oppose him. My own first instinct was to run, but the men hemmed in so tightly I couldn't even lift my hands to my nostrils to shut out the smells and the pumping spatter, now slowing to a trickle.

Tukulti's next words were meant for me. "And no need for anyone to keep secrets now, is there, Lady Serah?"

Animosity dripped from each word like the blood from his knife. His words stood out in the blurred swirl and rush of my thoughts. I looked at Tukulti, then back at the mangled form at my feet. So . . . I hadn't been mistaken about the change in the room when I returned from the walls. Sheba was a betrayer to his soul. He had broken our agreement and told Tukulti my identity, out of earshot of the others, hoping it would save his life. He had no idea that the man he confided in would sign his death warrant.

"Move aside there, move aside," came the agitated voice of Eved-Atar'ate. He pushed the others out of the way to stand next to me, just in time to hear Tukulti's ominous tone.

"What . . ." he began, looking at me. Then he took in the full horror of the bloody scene.

"How . . . how dare you," he sputtered at the killer. Tukulti tore his eyes from mine briefly when Eved-Atar'ate spoke. But his words meant nothing now. The knife that had butchered the condemned man had also sliced through and bled away every last drop of Eved-Atar'ate's power. And with it went my protection in my adopted city. The fog was lifting. Without hesitation, holding the head by its matted hair, Tukulti had sawed sickeningly through sinew and bone and pulled it from the body.

The other men shoved each other aside, craning to see for themselves. Some turned away retching. Others seemed rooted to the spot, shocked at the carnage and at their leader, drained of power, somehow even smaller than before. As for me, I could not help thinking that, although I had gone to great lengths to avoid this very moment, this was for the best.

Covered in blood, Tukulti breathed heavily in battlefield euphoria. Eved-Atar'ate looked from him to me, his features a mask of bereft puzzlement, begging that the next move had to be mine.

It would be.

"Bring me a sack," I ordered, to no one in particular. "And stand away," I added unnecessarily as the men had already backed away in an awkward, macabre dance, their eyes still glued to Tukulti, already giving him their allegiance.

"You will take the head to Joab," Tukulti said, as haughtily as if he had been born to rule and had not just ferociously ripped the mantle from another. His sudden bloodletting had cowered the council, but his high-handed tone had no effect on me. My eyes bore into him until he wrenched his gaze away.

"Here, my lady," the man closest to me said, and handed me a large, rough swatch of woven black goat hair.

"Do the honors," I said flatly, passing the piece of fabric to Tukulti.

He looked around for a moment as if considering whether to delegate the task to one of his allies. Then he seemed to think better of it and did as I had bid him.

He shook out the fabric and laid it on the floor with a mock ceremonial flourish. Then he placed the sole of his foot on the glistening head, shoved it onto the cloth, bent to bring up the four corners of the cloth and tied them with two firm twists.

"My lady," he said derisively, handing me the grisly burden.

It was heavy. And it would not be easy to carry it to the walls. The blood was invisible against the dark cloth, and women bearing heavy loads drew no special attention. But would I? When had anyone ever seen me in the streets without my servants? Still, they might no recognize me without them, and the streets would be mostly empty, given the early hour and the enemy still at the gate.

I made straight for the doorstep where I had left Mara. She lifted her head when she saw me and extended her hands in a relieved welcome. I avoided touching her with my own crimsoned hands but sank down next to her. She leaned exhausted against the rough wooden door, and I leaned against her. The house behind us slept deeply so our presence went undetected.

Haltingly, I began to tell her what had transpired outside the council room. "Shhh, never mind that now," she said. She gave the sack no more than a cursory glance. "What's important is that our time in Abel has come to an end."

"Who is the wise woman now?" I asked wryly. The lucidity of vision that had taken me years to master seemed to come easily to her at times like this.

"Finally. This is how it ends. We'll go to Geshur," I said.

"Yes," she replied. That one tiny word. It embodied my hopes and dreams for so many years, to be in my grandfather's court and in my mother's house, at her side, safe.

"I have one more mission, and then we can leave. Do you think you'll be able to go home ahead of me and prepare for our journey?"

Only when Mara's lips disappeared into a stern, indignant line did I realize that she had caught uncertainty in my tone. My doubts seemed to fill her with renewed strength because she rose more briskly than I thought she ever would again, and headed for our dwelling.

"You'll come to me when you're ready," she said over her shoulder as she walked away.

One thousand. One hundred. Then One. One Thousand. One Hundred. Then One. Events distilled into a cadence of clarity by whose rhythm I strode toward the city wall.

I shifted my bloody burden from one hand to the other. Both were now slick with blood, and my robe was splotched with crimson. Anyone encountering me would think the deprivations and stress of the siege had driven even the wise woman mad. Who would not make way? Without breaking my stride, I slipped off my veil and ran my free hand through my hair, my fingers catching my white curls, streaking them with gore, the effect now complete.

The six sentries on the gatehouse roof shrank back gasping, three on each side, and unwittingly created a trembling honor guard through which I passed as I approached the wall. I stepped to the space between the crenellations that I had occupied before.

The risen sun glanced fiercely from lances and swords in the camp below. If Joab kept his word, the city need no longer fear them. But as I stood tall among the stones, bloodied and strange, I was still the enemy, too perfect a target for some marksman to ignore. I willed an invisible shield to surround me. A stir among the men gesturing, shouting, and running to and fro told me their commander would soon appear.

Sure enough, Joab stepped out from among them. Sunlight shimmered along his breastplate and even from this distance, I could see the oil glistening on his hair and beard. His sword arm bulged with strength below the short sleeves of a crimson tunic. His legs were slightly apart, the better to effectively stand his ground, and his thighs were like two sculpted tree trunks sprouting from his greaves. The consummate general, tall, handsome, and composed, battle-ready, his appearance belying fatigue at the unexpected siege, and inspiring his lieutenants unconsciously to assume exactly the same stance as they flanked him. Such beauty, such strength, brought a flash of memory. As a child I thought I'd grow up to marry him. No wonder my father loved him so.

His eyes went straight to the gore-caked sack.

No more words now.

I lifted the bag over my head.

The general sheathed his weapon. Then he raised both hands and with rapid flicks of his wrist, summoned me to keep my part of the bargain. Silently, I repeated my chant. *One thousand. One hundred. Then one.* With all my strength I heaved Joab's reward into the air. It arched upward, spun through the air for what seemed forever, and hit the ground with a sickening crunch, almost precisely at the general's feet.

Joab signaled to a lieutenant to untie the sack. The head, or what was left of it, was dumped unceremoniously onto the ground, revealing a gory mass of flesh, viscous hair and beard covering most of it. Joab stepped forward and picked up his prize with both hands holding it flush with his own face. He looked into the dead eyes, turning it this way and that, as the men nearby bent over to retch. The corners of the general's mouth turned down and his lower lip slid forward in a satisfied grimace. He nodded, and kicked the severed head aside, his lieutenants scrambling out of the way.

Then, he looked up at me again, drew himself erect, placed a clenched fist over his heart and bowed his head in a mocking salute. He murmured a few words to his underlings, who shouted them back through the ranks, their echo filling the air. "Break camp! Break camp!"

I turned to go home.

Mara's back was to me when I stepped over my threshold. She was more energetic than I had seen her in years, and I paused just to watch her barking orders to the two servants, inspecting the snugness of this or that bundle, setting aside to leave here what the donkey could not bear and would not be necessary for our three-day journey south to Geshur. As soon as she spotted me, she rushed forward with a bowl of water. "For your hands," she said quietly, and then, as I cleaned the blood away, she raised her chin to indicate that we were not alone.

On a stone bench in the corner of the courtyard, where the servants usually fed our chickens, sat Eved-Atar'ate. There was so much commotion, I almost missed his presence. Hens pecked the hard-packed ground and clucked at his feet. The bench was shaded from the morning sun, but sweat glistened on his ample cheeks.

"I can explain," I said, but not knowing how I would. My plan to save the rebel had unintentionally taken everything from the man who had taken me in, supported me, and given me a new life. I only knew I would not tell him the truth. I was Serah, and as Serah he would say goodbye to me forever.

But he saved me more lies.

"I know who you are. I knew it before Tukulti did, before the siege, before the rebel came. You were described to me as one with fiery curls like your father's. Your hair soon turned white after I met you, but yours are not eyes one can hide behind," he said, his arms raised almost in adoration. "Don't you think I would have inquired about you on my travels after I brought you here? Every day since I learned the truth, I decided anew to be your father. Every day through these long years I have loved your skills and your courage."

"So much more than a father," I murmured.

"And so I know why you must leave. Tukulti has taken over and I will live with that. But my time is over, and I can no longer protect you. Mara has told me you are going to Geshur where you can finally live as yourself again."

He stood and walked to me, pulling his defeated shoulders back and infusing his rotund body with all the dignity he could muster.

Mara stood respectfully still at a distance and motioned the bustling servants to do the same.

A shiver passed through me when he took his hands in mine, and I knew it was more than the sheer exhaustion from the past twenty-four hours. I would miss this man more than I had missed my own father, for he had given me love and acceptance in a way my father never had. Or, perhaps, never could.

"Your secret is safe with me," he whispered, and I knew it was. "If you are hiding, you must have your reasons."

I nodded. It was all I could do.

"Blessed be your going out and your coming in. May your God guide your steps," he said.

I tightened my grasp on his hands, but he unpeeled my fingers and turned to leave without a backward glance.

As always, with one word Mara brought me back to the present and the task at hand. "So."

"We'll need to wait for nightfall. The city is in chaos, but still someone might see you leave otherwise," she said.

I wiped away tears and cleared my throat. The scent of death lingered in my nostrils, but washing away the source would have to wait. "Agreed. Now, where have you put my herbs? I want to make sure they're safe."

"Of course they're safe. Or do you think I would let them fall out on the way?"

I smiled. Mara was back, and I set about my tasks.

The postern gate was unguarded as I knew it would be; once the besieging troops received the order to decamp, home would be the only thing on their minds. The people could not have known the threat had been lifted; they would not leave the shelter of their houses until given the word.

We set out southward, walking half the dark night, putting enough distance between us and Abel to make sure no one followed. I knew this place. It was the farthest afield I had ever gone in search of my rarest herbs, a small natural, overgrown terrace on the hillside. The cave where my servants and I had sought respite and shade after our gathering was awash in moonlight, and, with Mara, I made straight for it.

"Come on in," I said as I ducked inside. But when I turned, my faithful companion stood frozen and as wide-eyed as a fearful fawn. "What's the matter? Come on," I said, exhaustion morphing into irritation.

She shuddered and headed in.

In the back, a spring bubbled into a small pool hewn by long-ago travelers. It was known far and wide as magical because it would burst forth and fill the pool to the brim, but never, except in the rainiest winters, overflowed. I filled a leather water skin and brought it to the donkey and lifted the loads from his tired back. Then I returned to the pool to wash away the evening's horrors. By the time I had filled our water jug, Mara had unrolled two goat-hair blankets and covers and set them side by side. She never lay down before I did, and tonight was no different. She had waited for me.

I gave her the jug. "You should drink." Her hands shook as she raised it to her lips. I held it unobtrusively from the bottom to keep it from slipping from her grasp. I lay down and allowed her to cover me, as she did every night.

"Only three days separate us from our new home in Geshur," I said, hoping it would assure her, and me. Yes, she would be herself by then.

What was left of the night was punctured by a strange cough that Mara tried unsuccessfully to choke back. As soon as the sky grew light, she stirred. I threw aside my scratchy cover and peered in the dimness to her direction. Something was wrong. I had never seen Mara strain to stand. This was, after all, Mara, for whom nothing seemed a struggle, who lifted me up, in every sense. First as a toddler into her warm, welcoming arms, and years later as a woman wronged, into a comforting embrace, over endless roads.

But rise she did. Even though turning the fire stick back and forth seemed an effort to her, soon the sparks burst into the flames. While she tamped them down and kneaded a little flour into dough, I unpacked my pharmacopoeia to find something that would help her. Sitting cross-legged, I set the little packets of dried herbs and flowers on the ground before me and passed my hand over them, hoping for inspiration. Was this malady of hers exhaustion? Shock? An illness of the elderly? I could not be certain. Certainly not here. Not now. But we would be in Geshur in two days, and then I'd be able to assess her condition better. Meanwhile, a milk-thistle infusion, even if the water was cold, would strengthen Mara for the road ahead.

Geshur

Once on the road, our garments were soon soaked through with sweat under the yoke of humid air that bore down upon us in the valley. We cautiously navigated the main road southward within reach of a murky swamp that stretched in every direction. Mara rode the donkey—I had to nearly order it so—while I walked beside the animal, one hand on Mara's thigh to hold her steady, especially when fits of coughing overtook her. In the afternoon, I kept focus on the western hillside, seeking another cave for shelter. Finally, I spotted one. I left Mara at the roadside and climbed to explore it. It had no water source, but it would do. We would water the donkey at the spring that flowed into the swamp and fill our jars from it before bedding down.

On a normal journey, a rider would dismount in a place like this, to allow the donkey to navigate the pathless hillside. But, taking stock of Mara's hooded eyes and weak hold on the reins, I knew she could not. And so I guided the animal's steps as best I could. With Mara still precariously perched on its back, I pushed and pulled him upward. This night, I prepared the sleeping mats as Mara leaned against the cave wall, barely aware of her surroundings, the coughing now only intermittent. She closed her eyes when she lay down and seemed to fall asleep peacefully. After a short while, I realized the coughing had ceased and, for that, I was grateful enough to fall into my own slumber. But, before the sun rose the next morning my eyes fluttered open to understand the stony silence; the only mother I really knew—my companion, my protector—was gone.

I cradled her, embracing her as if my own body could restore warmth to hers. When the cold and clammy issue from her reached my own bones, I stood, then bent down again to gather her to me, to hold her in my arms as she had so often held me.

"Without your great soul, your body weighs next to nothing." I realized I had spoken aloud, assuming the bantering tone that sometimes made Mara smile despite herself. I carried her to the back

of the cave where a low overhang had created a small niche. I knelt
and settled her carefully beneath it and then set her hands together
on her stomach. "There," I said, as I placed her feet in the direction
of our new home. "Rise when you are ready and follow me."

I meant to stand, but my body disobeyed. I doubled over and
rolled onto my side next to Mara's body, tears searing my eyelids. I
would lie here with Mara, I thought, just for a little while. I would
embrace the notion of lying beside her as I had countless nights. Sure
enough, within moments, I began to drift on a cool, quiet, safe sea.

I woke to a hand on my shoulder, violently shaking me. Choking
with shock, I scurried past Mara and crawled as far as I could into
the back of the cave and crouched. But there was no one other than
me . . . and Mara.

I understood. She would not want this. She would tell me to
pack up and get moving so I could reach Geshur this very day. I
mustered up the memory of a song of strength: "Your right hand,
your arm, and the light of your face . . . *Your right hand, your arm,
and the light of your face.*" As I spoke the words, their melody took
over. The mid-morning sun greeted me outside the cave, and I
headed for the road south.

I surely looked just as dusty and disheveled as other travelers,
but I was the only woman walking alone beside her donkey and I
drew curious glances. My demeanor discouraged anything but the
obligatory nod and greeting, and I stopped only when the midday
sun robbed the road of shade. I sought a solitary tree behind a
boulder on the hillside and waited out the heat. I pushed away the
shadowy thoughts—or were they sun-scorched dreams—of past
and future. Of mothers, daughters, fathers . . . sons. Had it been
only a few days ago that I walked the streets of Abel as its wise
woman? Sought after? Revered? Full of tomorrows.

A cool breeze swept down from the west, and I rose and retook the road. The sky was tinged with lavender when I reached the final rise before the road forked eastward and descended to the great city in the valley; nightfall had blocked me from my destination. Unwillingly, I turned, as did others like me, toward a cluster of lean-tos and tattered tents, too makeshift to be called an inn, where I would have to spend the night.

Even this ragtag shelter had its doorkeeper and its price. A dour, skeletal man, he looked over my meager supplies strapped to the donkey and pointed to a cruse of oil whose rim was showing above the saddlebag. "That will do," he croaked, his hand outstretched. Cradling the jar, he gestured vaguely toward a few tattered lean-tos as he directed larger families and wealthier travelers to more spacious accommodations in another part of the camp. What must he think of me, a haggard and sullen woman traveling alone? Would he be surprised to know that I was a daughter—*the* daughter—of a king?

Exhausted and irritable voices, so close to home or market, and yet so far, bickered over trifles. People and pack animals jostled against me as they raced for the few remaining empty shelters. I staked out a spot on a more distant rise and made for it before anyone else could reach it. Fire circles were started here and there among strangers. After giving the donkey less than it deserved, the last drop from the scuffed leather water bag and the last of the fodder and a few crumbs from the bread that Mara had baked on her last morning—his next meal would have to wait until we arrived at our destination—I unrolled my mat, lay down and faced the back of the rickety lean-to. The goat-hair wall, only a hand's breadth from my face, bore the stench of a thousand travelers. How could it be that only the night before I had lain beside Mara. Had I ever laid down to sleep with no one—no one—to answer if I called out? No.

The tears finally came before quiet sobs shook my body with force I'd never known before. I'd not wept like this after my half-brother's assault. I'd not wept like this over my father's lack of love toward me. Of concern over the horror his daughter had endured. I had not wept like this over my mother's absence or Absalom's treachery.

I must have slept, because the holes in the worn lean-to framed a pinking, pre-dawn sky and the cloth waved gently in the breeze as if bidding farewell to the night. My cheeks were taut with the salt of dried tears and my eyes so swollen I could hardly pry them open. My head pounded, my tongue was thick, my stomach sour. I recognized the symptoms that I had cured in so many others by merely giving them water infused with saltwort. Just water would have to do. I knelt to retrieve my jug and upended it, emptying the last drops.

It took me only moments to gather up my meager possessions and duck outside to saddle the donkey.

I walked to the crest of the hill and looked down. There it was, even more magnificent than the night before, basking in the sun as it rose from the plateau of Bashan, sending a strip of gold streaming across the Sea of Chinneroth, feathered with gently rolling whitecaps. My skin tingled at the sight of it. Carried along by the flow of people, slowly and steadily I approached my goal, and I entered the massive city gates, pulled open from within just as we arrived.

Everyone seemed to know where they were going. I dreaded the moment someone would ask me my own destination. And strangely, when no one did, my heart fell. Still, what would I say? I pictured the exchange.

"The palace," I would reply, and they would look me up and down, dust-streaked and sun-scorched, as if I had lost my mind. Perhaps I had. What would my grandfather say when he saw me? Would he harbor me as he had my brother? He probably rued the day he gave my mother to that red-headed upstart from Judah, a marriage that had produced such progeny as my brother and me. *Mother*. A clouded image bloomed behind my eyes. A warm smile, open arms.

No, there was no answer I could give a stranger. Better to find my way alone. I knew cities and palaces all too well. I needed no landmarks. I tugged the rope around the donkey's neck, then followed the main road until I reached the royal compound, surrounded with its own wall, guards at the ready.

As I stood near the gateway, wondering what I story I could invent for the guards—a tale that would persuade them to open the doors—they suddenly opened and a pair of men emerged, well dressed and well fed, hands clasped behind their backs, heads low, deep in conversation. Each man followed by an older man clutching clay tablets. I knew the scene. Courtiers and their scribes going about the first royal business of the day. I was weighing my chances of slipping in unseen before the gate closed—how could I with my animal beside me—when, of all people, one of the scribes stopped. His colleague proceeded a few steps more. Then they too stopped and turned, brows raised. But the first man waved him on. "I'll join you," was all he said.

The man intentionally placed himself between me and the guards, blocking their view. He stared at me with a mixture of warmth and wonder that went beyond the usual amazement at my multicolored eyes, his fingertips coming to play along his lower lip.

"I know you," he said, and those three small words rewove my raveled world. They did not threaten as when Sheba had recognized me, nor were they the parting words of a beloved guardian as Eved-Aatar'ate had meant them. This time they held promise.

I quickly took stock of the stranger. A spotless woolen robe covered an equally pristine linen tunic from which a portly, well-fed belly protruded over a beautifully embroidered sash. His well-kept beard and long, perfumed hair were white. This man was old enough . . . old enough to . . .

He had read my thoughts and gave a careful nod. Now he eyed me more carefully, pausing at the white strands that peeked out from beneath my veil. "I thought you had your father's red hair, like your brother. It's been years, of course," he mused. "But there's no mistaking those eyes. There's only one other person in the city with those eyes."

She was alive! My hand gripped the rope tighter.

"Don't speak," the man admonished, mistaking my opened mouth as a prelude to a response.

I took a step toward this stranger. What I really wanted to do was embrace him. Have him embrace me.

"That would not do at all." I looked around to see who had spoken, and once again, no one had. But it had been Mara's voice; I knew it well. Her spirit had taken me up on my offer to follow after all.

I stepped back.

He laid one large, meaty hand gently on my shoulder. "I am Ittai of the tribe of Benjamin. I was in your father's honor guard, but I could not stand idly by and see your mother, wife of his youth, cast out by the king. So I came with her from Jerusalem and have been by her side all these years in Geshur. I am vizier to your grandfather, King Talmai." His eyes widened briefly. "You are home now."

The words sounded like a magic incantation. I half expected each one to turn into a dove right there in front of me and fly heavenward. But if the soldier thought this at all odd, his face betrayed nothing.

Without waiting for me to respond, he turned to the guards. "Let her pass and bring a maidservant to show her to Princess Maacah." Then, to me, he whispered, "Keep those eyes of yours downcast."

He motioned me to a bench inside the gateway and called a comrade to lead the donkey away to shelter, feed, and water it.

Within only a few minutes, a maidservant appeared by my side, bowed, and gestured respectfully for me to follow her through massive cedar-wood doors, sunken into intricately carved recesses. I almost pushed her aside in a rush to reach my mother, then paced myself, my eyes downcast as I'd been warned.

The palace was strikingly like the palace in which I had grown up in Jerusalem. I felt I knew the way to the women's quarters. To where my mother had lived all these long years. The servant had to quicken her pace to keep up with mine as I crossed a long colonnaded portico that fronted the palace complex. The next hall, guarded by four stone-faced sentries, I took to be the throne room. I would have demanded that the guards open the doors and move aside if the serving woman had not respectfully but firmly directed me to a corridor that bypassed it, which led to my destination, the women's apartments.

We continued down another long hallway, this one coated with sea-green plaster and gilt flourishes. I glanced up only fleetingly, staying aware of the possibility of being seen . . . of being recognized, even if only by my eyes.

The servant stopped at the last door. She cleared her throat to announce her presence.

"Come," a voice beyond the door called out. The voice I had never forgotten, the voice I yearned to hear for as long as I could remember. There was Mother, standing at her loom, her regal back to us, passing her shuttle skillfully and quickly under and over the warp of a brilliantly colored fabric.

"What is it?" she said. She turned as she spoke, and I raised my eyes to meet hers, which widened, then froze. She took one step forward, still holding the shuttle attached to the tapestry. The entire loom crashed down behind her. But she seemed not to hear. She dropped the shuttle when I flew to her outstretched arms and we clung to each other. Toe to toe, breast to breast. Her hands patted my back softly and rhythmically. My cheek on her shoulder, hers on mine.

I could have stayed there forever. I could have allowed her to hold me until, like Mara, I took my final breath. Never eating. Never drinking. Never sleeping again.

My mother pulled away first and held my face, desert-caked and tear-stained—between tender palms. One hand rose to finger a lock of my hair. Our eyes locked, miraculous colors mirroring each other. Then, in unison, we said, "You look like me." And with that, her bright, warm laugher poured out and filled the room. The memory of it washed over me and I joined in until tears flowed with relief.

Mother led me to a soft couch strewn with colorful tapestries of the type that now lay in a tangle with her collapsed loom where the maidservant attempted to right the damage. Hands still clasped, we sank down and faced each other.

"Why did you leave me?" My hand flew to my mouth, but the words had already escaped.

"Not by choice." She replied. Those dreadful words, the same that had come to dictate every aspect of my own existence, drove away the first heady delight of our reunion. The time now passed as the image of King David—her husband, my father—barged into the room in my mother's rendition of his part in everything that had happened.

"The king insisted I return to Geshur. He said it was for my own safety, given the dangers of war from abroad and intrigues at court. My father accepted it, because trade with Israel and the Israelite mercenaries who served him were more important to him than anything else, more than . . . anything." Before I could ask a bereft child's question, Maacah answered, "No!" And then more gently, "No," she said. "I could not take you with me. You and your brother, fruit of such a propitious, strategic union as ours were too valuable to part with. Your father told me before he sent me away that courtiers were instructed never to speak of me to you, and I was not to know your fate. And so even those who pledged to care for you—Nathan, Gad, Mephibosheth, and Mara—would not have been able to tell you I was alive." Her hands squeezed mine. "You could never know how much I longed for you, and I could never know how much you suffered until your brother came here seeking safe haven and told me what had happened." The odd coloring of her eyes—my eyes—turned to flame. "And he *dared* to speak of you as a burden." Maacah spit her last words like a bitter herb.

"I dreamed of you," I told her, purposefully ignoring her last line. "I dreamed that you had come for me. I dreamed you knew the heights to which I rose at court, that you were proud of my healing skills, and the depths to which my brother brought me." And then I told her about Mara, about Nitzevet, about my learning, my herbs and healing, about Gad, Mephibosheth, and Nathan. My escape to the north from Jerusalem. My years in Abel and the denouement with Joab.

The entire day passed as we shared our lives. Servants came and went, meals were served. A bath was drawn and, as though I were a child, my mother cleansed me, washing away the grime of the road and years of loneliness. As dust motes danced in the golden afternoon rays that pierced the room's high windows, Mother rose and went to a curtained wall niche. She brought out an object carefully wrapped in a soft cloth and then returned to the couch and placed it in her lap. I guessed what it was before she had finished unfolding the wrapping.

"This is the lyre I took with me from Jerusalem. Do you remember I played it for you? Well, when you would let me. You would push my hand aside with your pudgy little fingers to pluck out your own melody, such as it was."

I didn't remember, but my mother laughed as she told me, and it pierced my sadness. My father, who loved the lyre, had seen to my lessons on the instrument every noblewoman knew how to play. I even used it to calm people whose anxiety threatened to overtake them, when no other concoction worked. But I took no joy in it, and I never understood why. I had not touched a lyre since leaving Jerusalem.

She took my hand in hers and brought it to the strings, brushing them gently with my fingers. "Do you remember?" When I shook my head, she plucked one of the strings. Its tune rang out, reverberating in the sweet air around us. Her eyes met mine again—a mother's eyes this time, demanding, insisting. "*Remember*, Tamar. *Remember*."

And remember I did. In the months that followed I was by my mother's side almost constantly, my hand seeking hers, or hers mine, like the toddler I had been when last we were mother and child. Her very presence was enough to lift the weariness of the years. Mara's voice that whispered into my heart had now gone suddenly and strangely silent. I had been cocking my head for its sound, seeking its comfort as I had in the three days after she died, rejoicing upon hearing it as if it were the first turtledove in spring. But I had stopped pining for it. The glowering admonitions that had kept me safe had also saddled me with a heavy burden. That chapter was now over. I had no life-changing decisions to make, for myself or for anyone else. Perhaps, I began to imagine, I never would again.

When my mother was not with me, I floated on an exhilarating cloud from room to room through the women's quarters, out to the main courtyard, up to the roof to take in the grandeur of the city and the glimmering lake beyond, to inhale the fragrance of the river and hear the song of the nightingale nesting on its tangled banks.

I finally looked through the neatly folded tower of fine wool and linen tunics my mother had brought to my room the day after my arrival at Geshur. As the servant laid them carefully on wooden shelves in a wall niche, my mother added a few gentle words about what I, as the king's granddaughter, should wear. For a while, they seemed just too strange. For years, every day I had donned the same plain, dark garments, and I had grown used to them. Perhaps because they were the opposite of the magnificent striped robe that Amnon had torn away when he attacked me and that I had ripped further in my sorrow. My mother was correct. That had been a lifetime ago; they served another purpose. They aged me, the better to look the part of a healer and wise woman when I first arrived at Abel. Later, they simply became my hallmark.

But here in Geshur my life had become a procession of languid days, and I was surrounded once again by courtiers in their finery. I realized that when the servant came in with my morning meal, she unobtrusively opened the curtain that hid the colorful garments. One day, I went to the niche and ran my hand from top to bottom and then up again. I pulled out a blue- and green-banded linen tunic. Neither past nor future, simply a reflection of my new surroundings—blue for the lake in the morning, green for its shorelines.

And for life.

And so I donned the new clothing. And when I met my mother in the courtyard that day, this seemed to be the sign she had waited for. "Today," she said with an approving eye, "you will meet the king."

My mother took my arm and motioned her maids to step behind us as we left the courtyard. They fanned out like a wave as we walked to the royal audience hall. The door, which had been closed to me months ago when I first entered the palace, now opened to greet me. Servants and officials alike bowed and made way for us.

The room was dominated by the huge, magnificently carved ivory throne on its stepped platform, touched with gold, heaped with multicolored pillows, and armrests ending in carved roaring lions' heads. My grandfather stood in front of the platform, arms outstretched, a smile brimming over a silvery beard in the midst of a kind, wrinkled visage. I felt every one of the bones in his aged hand as he grasped my forearms, but the whole room glowed with the warmth of the moment, especially my mother, who stood silently by his side, taking it all in.

"Granddaughter," was the only word he uttered, but it flooded me with more relief than I had felt for years. Ittai was right. This was not my birthplace, these were not my people, but I was home.

An imperceptible nod from the king brought servants scurrying forward with three small delicately carved wooden chairs. He took one, and he motioned for us to sit facing him.

At first, silence. I looked to Maacah, hoping she would speak and break the silence. Her face seemed composed, but her tunic was taut from her belt to her lower thighs, each gripped by an uneasy hand. She returned my glance by unobtrusively raising all ten fingers from the fabric, her wrists still resting on her legs. "Wait," they signaled.

"You are nothing like your brother," he said, his tone more of a question than a statement.

So he knew the rumors about me. My brother had challenged the rule of our father, one of King Talmai's greatest allies—his son through marriage, but still, King Talmai had harbored him. Absalom had denied the bizarre story that I had allowed my half-brother to assault me in order to lead to his death and put Absalom on the throne. He had told everyone that, after what happened, he had protected me as any loving brother would. But King Talmai had had his doubts, and I could hear in those first words that seeing me had put those doubts to rest. I was safe. The rumors were dead.

"Blood is the tie that binds us all here. The blood of my beloved Maacah flowed in your brother's veins, and whatever his sins, I sheltered and defended him. You, on the other hand, did nothing to deserve your fate. Moreover, you molded a life from it that would make any grandfather proud. Sheltering and protecting you is more than my obligation, it's my privilege."

Grandmother Nitzevet, can you hear this? Do you see? This is what you wanted for me, isn't it?

These two grandparents of mine—here before me my mother's father, and left behind in Gibeon, my father's mother—could not have been more different. Grandfather Talmai had never known want; the magnificence of his palace was legendary. He had little use for deities; he left those things to his priests, appeared at the temple when he was told to, and donated what he was asked to. He had navigated the great kingdoms successfully for his own and his people's wealth. His many wives and children filled the palace courts with laughter and song. He had confidently taken in my rebellious brother and my rejected mother.

And then, there was Nitzevet, wizened and sick, rejected by husband and sons, living out her circumscribed life alone, her "palace" a single, perpetually dusky room, with a floor of packed earth. And yet, she was a queen, in another realm—a servant at Gibeon whose faith had rewarded her with another kind of riches.

Cloister yourself if you must, but only as long as it takes for you to discover who your true enemies are—and whom you can trust. The first discovery I had made all too successfully and had been victorious. The second, I made then, in that very room. When the time comes, Nitzevet had said, I would know what to do. Indeed, the time had come. I let out a great sigh in the same moment my grandfather stood, signaling that the audience was at an end. The twinkle in his eye and the warmth in his voice made me want to rush to embrace him, but my mother's arm around my waist restrained me. "It's all right," she murmured to dampen my enthusiasm. One did not hug the king in this court, even if he was one's grandfather and even if he had a twinkle in his eye.

But the spring in her step as we left the audience hall was infectious. "Come! I'll show you your new home," she said.

The following months were a blur of new faces and places. As in Jerusalem, my favorite perch was the roof of the palace. But from here, the view was not of rolling terraced hills studded with olive groves and grape arbors. This view was of majestic mountains rising from the east, gray and mysterious in the rising sun and purpled when it set. It was of a verdant valley through which the narrow Jordan snaked. It was the azure swirls of the lake and the fishermen working their nets by the shoreline. I grew to love it. True, this was the king's house, as my father David's had been. But it was also the house of my mother. And as such, I felt it mine in a way I had not felt in all the years since fleeing Jerusalem.

The seasons did not change here with the arrival of driving rain as in Jerusalem, or cold winds and streams rushing down from snowcapped Mount Hermon as at Abel. Still, change they did. The air grew cooler, but the rain was warmer, and the wildflowers blossomed more riotously than anywhere I had ever been before. With winter, the sense of Mara's presence, her endless prodding to constant action, constant caution, even after her death, sank slowly into the well of memory. My new life had quieted her voice, and I was sad to no longer hear it. In the Jerusalem palace where I was raised, princess or not, I had to bake bread every morning. But baking bread had become another horrific reminder of Amnon's assault, and so I never took my hand to flour again after Mara and I fled Jerusalem. Here in Geshur, it was the custom for the women, even princesses, to bake their own bread, as I had before. The first day the ingredients were brought to my mother and me in the courtyard, my whole body trembled when I realized what they expected of me. My mother pulled me away from the hot oven with a jolt that shook me back to the present. She demanded I tell her what was wrong, and when I did, she motioned a servant to take over the task.

"When you are ready," was all she said. I heard those four words at least once a day from my mother, and they became a healing balm.

Weaving was another matter. I had never been able to weave with the skill of the courtiers' daughters with whom I spent my childhood days. The mistress of the loom was constantly unraveling my sorry products and giving them to others to complete. But alongside my mother, weaving became a quiet, joyful time, and the resulting garments and wall hangings drew her warm praise.

Moreover, Maacah had received the king's permission for me to open my pharmacopoeia, and I spent hours laying out my healing herbs in a space provided, a room off the women's courtyard, sunny in the morning, cool when the sun was overhead, and glowing warmly at dusk and through the evening. Eventually, this part of my life began to feel like the best moments in Jerusalem and Abel. The king now let people from the city visit me, people from all walks of life, when he realized the magnitude of my skill.

I rarely saw my grandfather, as his days were filled with diplomatic missions from neighboring lands. I became aware of them when he sent some of the high-ranking officials to me who sought relief from their ailments, and generals who needed dressings for wounds suffered as they fought nomadic incursions that threatened everyone's crops and cattle. I learned from a grateful Maacathite officer as I bathed his wounds with a soothing aloe poultice, that his people, and my own mother, were named after a son of Nahor. To put the man further at ease, I shared with him that Nahor was the brother of our founding father Abraham, who had crossed this very region so long ago. This made us distant relatives. But that, I learned, had not stopped the Maacathites from joining a confederacy to fight against my father. But whereas the Maacathites had thrown their lot in with the great kingdom of Aram, my grandfather Talmai led a policy of appeasement, most obviously represented by giving my mother to the Israelite king in marriage.

After the officer left, it came to me that my own diplomatic skills in Abel harked back to my grandfather, a peace-seeking leader of a nation in the heart of a region where swords and lances most often decided the future.

Sometimes my mother and I, along with my grandfather's wives, attended special banquets for foreign guests and local dignitaries, where I sang and played my lyre. On occasion, when I sang and my fingers flowed over the instrument—as the music coursed through me—despite all that had transpired, I found that I missed my father.

We heard that Israel's king belied his advancing years and continued to scheme, plot, and form alliances. Word of a famine in Judah was followed by another purge of King Saul's family, except for my old ally Mephibosheth. "You wouldn't have survived this if you had stayed," Maacah once said to me.

Messengers told my grandfather that David fought the Philistines again and had been left weakened. This, of course, brought thoughts of my three allies in Jerusalem: Gad, Nathan, and Mephibosheth. What type of advice had they given the king?

Would I ever see them again?

One afternoon, the sky darkened early, and the first rain of the season came with a mighty wind that slashed the pomegranates from the trees and the rest of the summer grapes from their vines, and roiled the lake into an angry froth. The palace women raced indoors to our sitting room and the servants rushed to set the braziers burning for the first time that year. In the midst of the excited chatter, Maacah came in.

"I have news, my daughter," she said, as composed as the rest of us were breathless. She sat next to me and cupped her hand over mine. "Tamar," she said. The sound of my name still shot a chill through me, warm and cold at the same time. I had been called Serah for so long; I had not been called anything at all by my own mother in a time longer than that.

Our eyes met, and as always, it was as if I were looking into my own. Not through the dull, scratched surface of a copper mirror, but with the clarity as if she and I were one person, one soul. I had quickly learned to love these moments of deep comfort. But this time, I saw nothing of myself in those eyes. What I did see ripped the fragile fabric of my new life.

"Your father is dead."

The servants nearest us quieted when they overheard their princess, and at their urgent hand signal, silence rippled through the room. Everyone turned to look at us.

Maacah waited to allow the words sink in.

I opened my mouth, but words were drowned in a flood of images. My father, red curls bobbing as he danced with abandonment before his people on feast days. Playing the lyre in the throne room or in the Great Courtyard before the Ark . . . singing his poems, every pair of eyes fixed on him. Holding forth in his study circle, pacing before Nathan, Gad, and Mephibosheth as they tried to get a word in edgewise.

And then . . . seething at the son who assaulted me and stole my life, yet failing to act against him, and hunting down another son for stealing the throne. Capable of believing that his daughter had played a part in her own defilement for the sake of palace intrigue.

Worst of all, he would never know the truth.

Maacah's glittering eyes never left my face, and her bitter smile told me she could almost see that same parade of images in mine.

"I know, my daughter, I know," she cooed. "When I first heard he had died I saw him as I once knew him—I remembered when he first came to this very palace, brash and full of bluster, to ask for my hand. The days and nights we spent together, when I believed the marriage my father had arranged would produce more than a dynasty through which nations would grow rich and powerful." Her eyes narrowed. "The shame he caused when he sent me away . . ."

She put her hand to her throat, choked and overcome by her litany of pain and humiliation, and her whole body convulsed. But with a sigh more sorrowful than weeping, she exhaled and went on. "He was not the man you remember. How long since you left Jerusalem? In that time, he faced a starving people, enemies new and old, committed new sins and atoned for them, wrote and chanted songs of thanksgiving whose beauty astonished all who heard them."

"How could you know so much?" *And yet so little.* The whereabouts of her daughter had been a mystery to her, one I had perpetrated too successfully.

"I have always had my sources. That is how I know that my father never gave up his alliance with King David. It was more important to him even than his daughter's wellbeing. That should not surprise you. These are the ways of kings."

I looked down so my mother could not see I was seething at all the things I could have known but had not. But what she could not see, her answer told me she sensed.

"Your anger is wasted, Tamar. How would it have helped you to know these things? He was the father you grew up with, no more and no less. I tell you these things only for you to picture him as he was at the end, beaten and weakened. Old and ready to go down to Sheol."

She put her arm around my shoulder, and I placed my own over hers. We sat companionably until time seemed meaningless. Until she spoke again. "My allies in Jerusalem tell me there is a new king now. All the time you were in Abel, your younger brother Solomon has grown stronger, and finally he has beaten his path to the throne with the help of Queen Bathsheba, his mother, the woman who replaced me in your father's heart. King Talmai will leave soon to pay his respects in Jerusalem."

New images crowded my mind at the mention of the little brother who, when I left the palace, had only been a boy. The sight of a mischievous toddler running to and fro in the throne room or courtyard, in and out amid a forest of colorful robes, his nannies trailing after him desperately. This was the new king? Of course, he would be grown now. Twenty, perhaps? Tall. Handsome. Composed and groomed by his mother for this day. And I had missed it all. This is what it meant for those chapters of my life to have fallen away, swallowed up by the years no longer living in the home I once thought I would never leave. This was what it meant—to miss it all.

Over the next few days, the court buzzed with preparations for the king's departure. Excited snippets of conversation flitted through the air as supplies collected for the journey filled the kitchen, spilled over into the pantry, and then into the kitchen courtyard. "Are you going?" was the most common question, and people—whether servants or courtiers—usually said yes, even if they had no idea if they would be part of the entourage. "Anything to serve the king," some said with a sigh, while widening their eyes with self-importance, as if they were taking on a great sacrifice. But I knew better; people who had never left their village or even a great city like Geshur—and never imagined they would—grew hungry for stories of the world beyond. My own journeys had given me the special aura of mystery that helped turn me into Abel's wise woman. As for healing, sometimes all I had to do was tell a patient that I had brought a certain concoction "from the far-off hills of Judah where the great God Yahweh reigns." Fifteen days on unknown, sometimes frightening roads would be a small price to pay for the journey of a lifetime.

At sunrise on the morning of the king's departure, my maid laid out a stately robe of gleaming linen with an intricately woven pattern of costly purple thread, which I had not yet worn, along with its matching linen veil. My mother and I, Talmai's wives, and seekers of the king's favor—court officials, judges, and assorted sycophants—would stand at the gate to see him off.

My mother arrived, wearing the same garment, her purple veil over one arm. "Not yet ready? Not even dressed? *Hurry*," she instructed the maid sharply. "Come now, everyone is already at the gate!" She all but pulled me out of the palace and down the road to the city gate. Joyful, rhythmic chanting and clapping floated over the morning breeze from the mountains, even before the gate came into view, where a crowd had gathered, flanking the gateway. The courtiers remaining behind were an eddying sea of riotous colors, their finery designed to attract attention and advertise wealth and position. Their garb contrasted sharply with the subdued browns and blacks of the traveling party as it flowed between them.

"Typical of your grandfather," my mother said, softly enough that only I could hear. She read my thoughts. The fact that the little group wore the plainest travel garb did little to disguise the wealth of a royal entourage. The king, flanked by an armed guard and followed by his officials, servants, and five heavily laden carriages pulled by oxen, filled with gifts for the new young king of Israel and supplies for the journey. I set the thought aside as I joined the throng in their chanting, cheering, and joyful waving.

Finally, the last of the wagons rolled out, and men and women bade farewell to the festive hiatus in their lives and returned to toil in their fields and fishing boats, workshops, and looms. Courtiers lingered, chatting with pretended nonchalance. Mother smiled wryly at me at the gist of the conversation, as they explained away a variety of invented reasons why they had not been chosen to accompany the king. She put her arm through mine in preparation to head back to the palace as her ladies fell in behind her, ready to move when she did. But before we could turn away from the gate, a man stepped in front of us.

He looked vaguely familiar to me, but my mother knew who he was. "Pirshaz, friend of the king, peace unto you," she said. Her usually melodic voice held a tone of pointed cold politeness. She clearly wanted to put an end to the encounter as soon as possible. At first the only reason I could think of for her reticence was the overpowering smell that clung to him, penetrating the cloying sweetness of the calamus and cinnamon fragrance with which he had all too obviously doused himself. But no matter, the smell of the stables clung to him.

Now, I remembered. I had seen him in the king's vast stables and the yard—within view of my rooftop perch. I knew little about these spirited, glossy-coated creatures; we had hardly any in the royal stables of Jerusalem because my father kept to the ancient commandment and therefore possessed few of these spirited, great-limbed creatures. As a child, I had watched the horses prancing and snorting as the stable slaves struggled to harness them to the king's sleek chariots, and I mused over the strangeness of that commandment and the others given to us long before my people had kings. Thanks to Gad's tutelage I could still recite them word for word.

However, the king is not to acquire many horses for himself or have the people return to Egypt to obtain more horses, inasmuch as ADONAI told you never to go back that way again.

Gad had never failed to answer my incessant questions, but when I asked him why the divine commandment had forbidden the king to have many horses, many wives, and silver and gold, and why my father had plenty of the last two and few of the first, he turned away and kept silent. The highest I had ever been off the ground was on donkey back, although my brothers had loved the impression the horses made on the crowd, and they insisted on maintaining a few for themselves. Fleetingly, I wondered if my brother Solomon preferred a horse to a donkey.

I now realized that the tall, shapeless hulk of a man my mother called Pirshaz, who had stepped back to bow obsequiously to us, was the same Pirshaz I often spotted in the courtyard, almost always with a whip in hand, which he snapped in rhythm with the orders he shouted at the stable boys and as he put the animals through their paces. Urine- and feces-tainted dust swirled around him. He always wore the same fine, filthy robe he had on now.

When the man rose to full height, all I could see was a grape-sized mole in the middle of his cheek that I tried, but failed, to stop staring at. Hairs cascaded from it and disappeared into his unkempt beard. It overshadowed all the other unpleasant aspects of his face—a huge, red-veined nose that the healer in me recognized as the sure sign of an overabundance of wine coupled with rich food moving too slowly through a distended belly.

"And peace unto you, my lady," the man responded, his voice as oily as the long strings of hair hanging to his shoulders.

Holding my hand, Mother turned on her heel and walked off, more suddenly than court etiquette would prescribe. It was clear she detested the man. I could not see his response to the slight; I hurried after her as she strode back to the palace, our maids in our wake.

"That *man*," Mother said with a shudder, wrinkling her nose and pushed exasperated air through clenched teeth. I rarely saw my mother respond so violently to anyone; as the king's daughter she had been taught, as I had, to surround our feelings with a fence of calm, unrevealing diplomatic demeanor.

"I've never seen him up close before," I said, then described the view I had had of him and of the stables from the parapets. "And this oaf is a friend of the king?" *Friend* meant so much more at court. Confidant, comrade, ally, closer than counselor, was more like it. I tried to think of those my father had called friend in his court. And I could not help remembering that the accursed Amnon had had a "friend," Jonadab, with whom he had plotted my downfall. This man fit none of those categories.

"The ways of court are strange," Mother answered. "Pirshaz can whip up a chariot force more formidable than any you could imagine. Not to show off, as Absalom said he did while he was in Hebron building his rebellion, enraging his father to the point of no return. No, his would be a force to be reckoned with by all the surrounding cities. He could use it for or against your grandfather as he saw fit. So the king brought Pirshaz close, at least in coveted title, and that seemed to please the lout." A sudden breeze pushed its way into her veil, causing it to billow and soften her already beautiful face. "He loves to lurk the palace halls as if he belongs here. At least we can smell him before we see him, and usually avoid having anything to do with him." She stopped so suddenly the maids walking behind us almost collided with us, then faced me. The black circles in her eyes, sometimes so large that I could clearly see my reflection in them, had shrunk to the size of a needle's point and the iridescent colors surrounding them glowed. "You must never find yourself alone with him," she finished.

. . . Alone with him. I told you never to be alone with him.

The almost forgotten black bird of prey beat his wings frantically within me, grasping my heart in its talons. . . . Absalom had used almost the same words when he accused me of ignoring his warning about our brother. But both my brothers were dead while I was very, very alive.

I shook my head fiercely, more to banish the memory than to acknowledge my mother's warning. "I won't, Mother, you can be sure of that," I said.

With the king gone, languor settled over the court. Opulently robed and gift-bearing diplomatic delegations ceased to parade through the city gates, depriving the people and the palace of one of their chief diversions. Meals were simpler and briefer. Courtiers took advantage of their lack of official obligations to leave the palace and pitch lavish tents by the Sea of Chinneroth, and it was then that Mother took me there for the first time. On a rise overlooking the shoreline, servants pitched an airy tent fronted by an awning under which we sat as my grandfather's normally staid officials cavorted in the shallows. They left their dignity behind, shouting with glee as they caught a sizable fish or cornered a fearsome, snorting boar along the banks of the swampy tributaries that gurgled their way into the lake.

One morning, when only a sliver of gray, pre-dawn sky announced the new day, mother shook me gently awake. "Come," she whispered with a conspiratorial smile, holding out my robe. Obediently I slipped my hands into the sleeves, my feet into my sandals, tying them hurriedly, as mother waved off the servants who had jumped from their sleeping mats as soon as they heard the rustle of her bedclothes.

Rubbing the sleep from my eyes with the heel of one hand, the other already ensconced in my mother's comforting grip, I allowed a warm, long-forgotten feeling to envelop me. We went around the back of the tent to avoid the guard out front, whose snores told us we could have saved ourselves the trouble. Where she was leading me, I could not imagine, but something good would be waiting, of that I was sure.

Mother led me down a narrow path barely visible in a field of tall, light green fennel plants, whose tart-sweet fragrance welcomed us as our legs brushed against them. Barely had we emerged from the field when the lake water gently eddied and lapped at my feet. Mother slipped off her robe and let it fall to the pebbly beach and, before I knew it, she had stepped behind me and slipped off mine, and we were clad only in our night shifts. She stepped into the water ahead of me, tugging me with a gleeful laugh as I hopped forward while trying to untie my sandals at the same time.

"Never mind that now, *yakirati*. They'll dry. Just be with me now."

Yakirati, my dear one. Echoes of a time before. A time when my hand in hers meant all would be well, and it was. Sandals would dry, scrapes would heal, nightmares would flee, home was here. With her.

I gave myself over to my mother and at her signal we immersed ourselves and came up laughing and sputtering. The first birds of the day chirped and the date palms rustled as I turned onto my back. By the time we emerged, the sun was sparkling on the water and the birds in the reeds had quieted. My teeth chattered a bit as the morning breeze teased us. Mother picked up my robe before I could and wrapped it around me. "There, now," she said, patting it for good measure. As she swung her own robe over her shoulders, I said goodbye to the gentle water.

That faithful breeze from the lake anointed the summer-blooming herbs in my garden and they flourished of themselves, drinking in the moisture and turning it into pungent, promising, healing aromas. Harvest was months away, and all my plants asked of me was to keep the weeds at bay so they could grant me the best of their gifts when the time came. Early mornings saw me work alongside the servants, turning the soil and keeping roots free to stretch and grow.

The rest of my days passed in the women's courtyard, where I divided my time between loom and lyre. As it had been when I was a child, here too, I listened to the stories the women told as they passed their shuttles back and forth from one strong hand to the other, tales no man would ever hear. The warp and weft of their lives found their way into the colorfully designed tapestries that we would drape over couches or over walls. When the weaver spied one of her creations donned by a noble or the king himself, she nudged her companions gently and pointed with a proud raise of her chin.

The hours at the loom were precious, but those with my lyre were incomparable. I turned the tales of the women into the ballads of their lives. Magically, as time passed, I recalled more of the songs my father had sung at court and before the Holy Ark and, in doing so, I made my peace with him.

Shira l'Yahweh shir hadash. *Sing unto the Lord a new song*—a song my father had composed and sung before the Ark in the palace courtyard. Verses of it had somehow made it to Gibeon where I evoked the memory of my time there, and the priests sang of the strength and beauty in the Lord's sanctuary. For me, my life here was truly a new song. I could not recall the melody my father sang and played, but I picked out my own on the lyre. After all, I was surrounded by the very sea and its fullness, the fields and forests of which he sang. My new home. I began to repeat and improve on the melody. When Grandfather returned from Jerusalem and the sealing of his alliance with my brother—the new king and son of the man who wrote these words—I would surprise him with my composition.

These were times when Mother knew to leave me alone in my quarters, and my maids understood that they could venture away, because this was a time of aloneness that I sought and cherished.

Such was the day he came to me.

I had just set aside my lyre and to watch the late-day sun creep though the row of high windows in my room, forming beautiful golden squares of light on the polished stone floor. I must not have heard the door latch click or the iron hinges creak. But when I raised my eyes, Pirshaz stood in front of me. What he must have thought passed for a smile revealed yellowed, gaping teeth above the dirty beard.

I looked behind him for a servant or a guard to enter and remove him, but there was no one. *Where had they gone?* The maids knew they need not return for hours. Mother had made herself scarce until I asked the servants to call her or went in search of her myself. Still, I glanced suddenly over the shoulder at the door, hoping he would do the same. His eyes followed mine, but he did not turn.

"There's no one out there, Lady Tamar. Even the guard for the women's quarters was dozing as I passed by," he said dismissing my feint. He paused only as long as it took him to take a deep breath, and strode brazenly toward the couch where I sat, legs curled beneath me while the old vulture, the one I thought banished forever, clawed at my heart once again.

I backed to the edge of the couch where it met the corner of the room and held the lyre against my chest like a shield as he spoke.

"Lie with me."

His words tore into me. How could this be happening again? Had I gone to the man as I had when I heard those very words before? That was what they had said the last time, although it had been my father and my brother who had sent me . . . sacrificed me.

No, of course I had not gone to him. He had come to *my* room, *my* space, and without warning. At first, I put my hands over my ears, and uttered that same, single, useless syllable as the *last* time. The last time? No, this could *not* be happening again. It just could not. *Wake up!* I screamed inwardly. But this was no dream, I knew because my fingers bled where the strings of my lyre had cut into them.

His leering, clouded eyes never left mine. As if gently, he unpeeled my fingers from around the lyre, and set the instrument aside. He was making his move, and my own will was of no consequence. I watched, unable to turn away, as it prepared to abandon me.

No! I would not allow this to happen. Not here. Not as then. Then, in that long-ago princely room, where a child faced a man, fear and helplessness had been the accomplices to my downfall. But this room belonged to a princess. A blast of rage, full of images of the men who had wronged me—both my brothers and my father— threatened to engulf me, but I rose above it. I stretched to my full height slowly, contemplating my next move. Let it be deceitful. Let it be cunning.

Let it save me.

"My lord . . ." I lowered my eyes, pretending submission, and lightly drummed my hennaed fingers along the embroidered sleeve of his robe to distract him. They left a bloody trail, but he did not seem to notice. In his ridiculous sense of his own attractiveness, with one touch I had made him believe that I welcomed his disgusting overture. But carefully, very carefully. "Let's not." I continued softly. "Such wantonness is not befitting a king's daughter." I glanced up. His eyes followed my finger like a hawk calculated the movements of its prey. I was in dangerous territory, no doubt about it, but a plan had taken shape. Words would not be my only weapons. Not this time.

"Daughter . . . and granddaughter," he mumbled.

I bit my lip to keep from blurting out what I knew about men like Pirshaz. His lust was apparent. Once upon a time, I had tried to dissuade my attacker—my own half-brother—by offering myself up in marriage. But I didn't know then what I knew now: it was not me this man craved; it was power at court, and the riches it would bring him once he persuaded my grandfather that the only way forward was marriage to his granddaughter. But would my grandfather refuse his "friend"?

He lurched and emitted a belch that reeked of beer. The now familiar odor of his body, mixed with horse urine and fermented hay wafted over him, forcing me to inhale through my mouth. The fool seemed to take this as sign of ardor because he moved closer. With one beefy hand he seized me by the back of the neck and pulled me toward him while the other picked at my tunic, fumbling for the hem.

His arms were open, his body vulnerable, and I pictured myself kicking those violent loins. But I was wise enough to realize that my waning strength would be no match for his.

If I said that what happened next was one of the most difficult things I had ever done, who would believe me, with the life I have lived? But it was. I unpeeled the hand from the back of my neck, then lifted the other away from my skirt.

"Listen to me, my lord," I cooed. I gestured languorously toward the lyre that Pirshaz had shoved aside. "Why not lie here, upon my knees, and allow me to sing and play for you? After that, you will have your heart's desire."

As a healer, I had used my hands this way. The sick needed to be helped to find a different path. Getting them to fix their eyes on my hands had always been the first step. It distracted them from their pain, calmed them, and made them mine. Indeed, Pirshaz's hooded eyes followed my every move slavishly. As many times as I had done this before, in another life, faced with disease and horrific wounds, never had revulsion threatened to spill over and break the spell.

I willed my legs to stop shaking and veiled my disgust with a lavish, inviting gesture toward my lap. It was enough. He lay his head on my thighs and placed his arms around my hips, locking his hands at the small of my back. Gingerly, I picked up the lyre and set it in position on the outer edge of my thigh, slightly raising my knee and extending my lower leg. My fingers, aching though they were, caressed the strings and brought a melody I had not known I possessed. The deep voice of the long strings, interspersed with the sweet chirps of the shorter ones, brought comfort. As I played, the words drifted up unbidden from some deep, other place. I chanted, silently, words, the brute would not hear.

Yahweh, King of my father David . . . Send your light and truth to hold me . . . and do not allow the desire of a wicked . . . and impure man . . . for you have known what is in my heart. My father David, my father David, my father David, look at your disgrace and your daughter's disgrace. Go before the Throne of Glory of Shaddai, and ask for mercy, for me . . . to help me by his help. I beseech you . . . I call on you the day I am frightened, and I shall be answered.

In his lifetime, my father David had not answered my call. Would he now? Now that the best part of him was spirit, released from his earthly self?

I looked down at Pirshaz. The man ran the tip of his tongue along his thick lips and his filthy beard rubbed against my robe as he worked his jaw, but his eyes were closed, and his breathing grew deep and regular. His ardor had given way to stupor. If I moved cautiously, I could slip aside and slip a pillow under his head. I could flee the room and call the guards and this nightmare would be over.

But then, Absalom's words, spoken deceitfully to a trembling, humiliated child echoed back through the years. *You should have known this would happen. Didn't you scream? Didn't anyone hear? Right in the heart of the palace.*

Right in the heart of the palace. Again. A raging miasma enveloped me, through which emerged only the specters of men who had brought me down, each in their own way. Two brothers, each in their own nefarious way. My father, and even all-seeing Gad and Nathan who had been blind to my approaching fate. The child who quivered in fear could not have *known* what the woman trembling with rage *knew*: it would never be over. No, not like this. Never.

The man shifted his weight slightly against my body. His robe fell aside, exposing a sheathed dagger in his belt.

I set aside the lyre but forced my song to continue. A melody of mourning, of release, like the dirges the women chant to lovingly send the dead to the netherworld, pushed past the spasms of fury that threatened to close my throat.

The man did not stir.

Now . . .

My hand crept forward toward the weapon until my fingertips closed on the hilt and I slid it out in one delicate motion. I raised it, and my heart spoke again.

Lord of Hosts, remember David my father and give me the best of the power you once planted within him for justice and righteousness' sake. Help me as you helped Jael, the wife of Heber, to overcome her assailant by the strength of your will, to let sinners cease from the earth.

The intricate carvings on the dagger's bone handle dug into my hands as my fingers latched around it. A power from beyond me lifted my arms above my head, and plunged them downward, directly aimed at the soft spaces on the side of the sleeping man's chest. It slid silently inward and claimed its reward as blood spewed from the wound to soak my hands. His eyes sprang open, wide, as a death gurgle brought red foam from his mouth and nose. A nudge was enough to roll him off my lap. He landed on his back, lifeless by the time he hit the floor.

I stood over him, holding the dripping dagger, my robe spattered with the man's blood, its sweet, sickly odor permeating my nostrils as it had with Sheba's, rising as it moved through my room.

Then, finally, I spoke aloud, my song ending in a whirlwind of relief. *"So perish all your enemies. You have heard my father's voice and have saved me, this time, from disgrace. Blessed are you from everlasting to everlasting. Amen."*

And this was how it was when two of the horse master's servants came to call him for the midday meal.

They stepped over the threshold, eyes lowered, bowing dutifully. "Master, the meal . . ." one said, still looking at the floor.

I waited for him to look up. When he did, his eyes grew large, moving from me to the bloody dagger, to their lifeless master, back to me. He nudged the other man, who looked at him questioningly, then tilted his head toward me in response.

They argued in tense, hushed tones as I stood, unmoving. Finally, the second man stepped forward and kneeled over the body, touching it here and there in an ineffectual search for a sign of life. Then he looked up.

"Yes. Yes, he's dead. Do what you must," I said, impatient for what must come next. I lifted my crimsoned hands, palms facing the open-mouthed servant. I delicately dangled the dagger by the hilt between my thumb and index finger.

He rose, trembling, and took it. He walked back to his companion. More urgent though whispered consultations.

"Enough. Take me to the king's ministers." I raised my chin and pointed a finger at each of them. "Do it," I commanded. I lifted my robes and stepped over the corpse—not a murder victim but the enemy I had bested in the battle for my life. I strode toward the door and out of the room, forcing them to hastily follow me.

On the long walk through the palace corridors and courtyards to the king's council room, I kept my head high and my strides long. Breathing heavily, Pirshaz's men loped along trying to keep up. I fingered my assailant's drying blood on my hands and palms, knowing nothing but a strange calm.

When we reached the door, I stopped and waited for them to open it for me. More whispered debate. Should one of them go in first, and report what had happened? Which of them should it be? Or should they lead the blood-covered assassin-princess in right away? *Lead? Like a criminal to court? No, no, no. This would make me in charge of what came next.*

The slender wooden panels of the council room door were much heavier than they looked—it took all my strength to push it open. I stepped into the room, once more leaving the servants scrambling.

"My lords," one called to the ministers as they stumbled in breathlessly behind me.

The men who would decide my fate had turned the royal council table into a gaming board and were so intent on the action that our intrusion went unnoticed.

"My *lords.*" This time both shouted the words at once.

King Talmai's ministers finally looked up. Ten jaws dropped in unison. Five hands sent gaming pieces scattering over the row of stone-etched boards down the center of the table. As the men stood, ten chairs were pushed back so hastily, some toppled over.

The scene before me blurred around the edges and my ears roared. I shook my head to clear it. *So this is what the king's advisers do in his absence . . .*

"What is the meaning of this?" the chief minister blustered at the servants. We all stood, planted and still like a huddle of oak trees in a night forest. It seemed to me that he was more embarrassed to be caught playing games in the absence of the king than shocked by the sight of a blood-spattered royal princess in the council chamber.

"We went to call the horse master for the midday meal, I mean we . . ." began one, stumbling over the words.

That's right. Admit the man had broken into my chamber.

As the first man failed in his explanation, the other took one step forward, intent on getting to the point, looking back long enough to glare his companion into silence.

"Eved-Adad, chief minister, sir . . . we found the master of horses dying, I mean—he—he was dead when we found him and the princess . . ."

The self-appointed spokesman seemed to realize he lacked the means of telling the story and that his partner held the damning evidence. He half-turned toward the other servant, and stretched out his arm, his hand clawing the air impatiently. But the servant who had remained at my side was not to be outdone. He grabbed my elbow and brandished the dagger aloft like a prize so suddenly that the last droplets flew off in a brown drizzle.

I was as relieved as horrified when understanding dawned on the councilmen's faces. The chamberlain crossed the room toward me, his face contorted in a mixture of anger and confusion. But I held my ground, and he stopped so close to me that I could smell the beer he had been drinking with the others when we entered. "What have you done? The king's *friend*? Dead at *your* hand?" His face turned crimson and quivered. "You will be stoned to death for murder. And if your grandfather decides to save your life, he will declare you disgraced, and you will be banished from this house forever."

The blur had disappeared from the edges of the scene and the roar in my ears had lulled. "No," I said. "He will not. And no, I will not." I kept my voice low, so the men had to strain to hear and hang on my every word. "What the man you call the king's friend did to

me should not be done even to a harlot. And should one deal with a
king's daughter as with a harlot? I think not."

The king's daughter as with a harlot. Where had those words
come from? The scene before me froze. The years peeled away, and
I was back with Mara, spending the night in Shechem, the town
where Dina had been wronged. Her story had resonated with me
so powerfully because I'd had no brothers to avenge me. As the
storyteller had put it, Dina's brothers Simon and Levi, urged by
their father Jacob, had said, "Should one deal with our sister as with
a harlot?"

I had envied Dinah. I had had no brothers to rescue and avenge
me. And no father to urge them to their duty. And now, every fiber
of my being, every tie forged, every journey completed, had prepared
me for the moment when the strength of Simon and Levi would be
mine. Their spirits now came to my aid as I poured out the story of
Pirshaz's attempted attack.

The men stood motionless, stunned by my testimony. None
were prepared for my next move, not even the servant now flaccidly
holding the bloody evidence of my revenge. I turned to him and
pulled it out of his hand before he could react. The men gasped and
jumped back in horror.

The room was mine.

But I cradled the weapon gently in outstretched hands. "You
have no reason to fear me," I said softly. "I only want to show you
that, for me, this little blade was as powerful as the huge sword my
father used to behead the giant that threatened all of Israel. When
that brute you defend here as 'the king's friend' attacked me, it was
my father David I called on. From his place before the Throne of
Glory of Shaddai, I beseeched him to give me the same strength he
had had when he was no more than a young boy, to use a giant's own
weapon against him."

The council members looked at one another, and then at me, as
if I spoke in a foreign tongue. But some of them were old enough to
remember the story that had reached Geshur long before the young

upstart from Judah came to beg my mother's hand in marriage from King Talmai.

The oldest man in the room then stepped forward. I allowed him to disarm me, and he laid the dagger delicately on the council table. "Yes, Princess," the man said gently. "I remember your father. You have his fire. Our king had a soft spot in his heart for King David, and a strong alliance with him and his household despite all that happened since the day he came to take your mother away. And we all regret, deeply regret, the harm that has been done to you. Do we not?"

The elder's eyes sidled to his fellow council members, and his hand whisked the air at his side to signal them to respond until their heads bobbed silently in unison.

"But . . ." I said.

He fixed ominous eyes on me, betraying the warmth in his voice. "But we still have a killing to deal with. You have Pirshaz's blood on your hands and on the dagger with which you killed him."

I lifted my chin and fixed my gaze on him. "Pirshaz's blood is on *his* head. In the king's eyes, I will be guiltless and pure," I parried.

He paused. Had I persuaded him of the righteousness of my actions? "That may be," he finally responded. "But with the evidence we have before us, we have no choice but to confine you immediately. We will send word to your grandfather at the royal court in Jerusalem. When he returns, he will decide what to do with you."

Only when I heaved a huge sigh did I realize I had been holding my breath. They could have done nothing else. All right, this was a good thing. I would have to remain in my rooms until my grandfather returned, but my mother and the women of the palace would be with me. I would have my music, my loom, my herbs, and fresh air in my courtyard. The time would pass, and Grandfather would return. He would understand. He would realize, perhaps for the first time, that the man he had left in charge of perhaps his most important possessions was a mindless brute whose time had come.

"Send for my mother, then," I demanded. But the elder had already turned away and was speaking to the servants.

"Take her to the minister of the prison," he ordered, his voice drowning out my own command. "And keep hold of her this time," he said sharply.

The hapless servants grasped my arms awkwardly. I glared first at one, and then the other. As always, my eyes had their effect. They let go as if they had touched a burning brazier.

"*Take* her, I said," the elder repeated warningly. But the servants had had enough. Their arms dangled at their sides and they reverted to the response they knew best: eyes down, invisible.

Surely the elder would not be countermanded by kitchen servants in front of the entire council. But what would he do? I didn't have to wait long to find out.

"I will take her myself," he huffed. Then, unceremoniously and with a strength belying his small frame and wizened face, he latched one thin-skinned claw onto my elbow and steered me out the door, motioning irritably with the other for the two huge armed council room guards to follow us. At the last moment, I twisted my head to look over my shoulder, and shouted at the other men, rooted to their places. "Tell Princess Maacah," I managed, as the vulture, my old companion, settled in my chest and stole my breath away.

Was it my fate to be marched through palace halls a prisoner due to the heinous acts of men? It had been a lifetime ago and, at the same time, just yesterday. Like before—paraded, put on display, the victim of a crime against my body and soul?

No, not just like before.

This time I was victor, not victim!

But now . . . was there to be no difference—whether victor

or victim? The march through the hallways, the stony stares of courtiers and the sorrowful looks at a bloodied princess, quickly cast down, of servants who knew my powerlessness all too well.

"Tamar! Oh, my Tamar!"

My mother ran toward me, arms outstretched as if to embrace me. But instead, she stopped short and flicked her wrists upward, spreading her fingers with such power I thought I could see tongues of fire emanating from each digit. "Stop!" she commanded the elder. But he already had. My shoulder snapped back painfully as he halted. He seemed spellbound by the raised hands of his sovereign's daughter and the flash of blue-green and gold from her eyes.

"If you take one more step with the king's granddaughter, I swear I will have your head before the sun sets," she hissed.

His grip on my arms loosened. I wanted nothing more than to run into my mother's arms. He cleared his throat once, twice. I began to wonder whether my mother had bested this pompous little man.

"I—I—we—"

"Speak!" my mother ordered.

"Madam." A single word. Then a pause. He was trying to compose himself. Indeed, when he continued, he had recaptured the haughty tone for which he was famous, and his nails dug into my arm again. "Princess Tamar has committed a crime against King Talmai. She has murdered the master of the horses, the king's friend. She must be treated like any assassin. We are putting her in the hands of the minister of the prison until your father returns and can pass judgment."

The flash in my mother's eyes dimmed as she narrowed them, for the first time taking in my bloody robes.

"Mother, I had no—"

My mother raised her finger to her lips, and I stopped midsentence. She knew. In the time we had already spent together, I began to realize the source of my renowned skill at perceiving what others could not see. But this would be our secret for now.

"Be silent, my daughter." Her tone was soft, but there was no mistaking the warning. "Save your words for the king when he returns. We will face him together."

Her motherly gaze became a glare as she turned to the chief minister. "As for you. If the king's granddaughter is headed for prison, you'll take his daughter as well." She lunged at the man, who stepped back instinctively, knocking into the guards who had stood frozen in astonishment behind us since my mother first appeared.

"Why do you fear, my lord?" Maacah said sweetly. "We are your prisoners, are we not? Hold on to me now," she said, placing his free hand around her upper arm.

"March," came the order, and our strange little party moved forward. But it was neither the guard nor the minister who spoke. Maacah had given the order.

An unknown, terrible fate lay ahead. But that one word had been enough to chase away the vulture. I breathed easy. I looked over the little man's head and caught my mother's eye.

Together, we smiled.

The location of the *beit sohar* in the royal compound was no secret; the prison was the only round, bare mudbrick building in a complex of sharply cornered, finely polished plaster structures. Its soft contours belied the fear it struck in the hearts of the compound's high-ranking denizens. This was no ordinary prison. Thieves, even murderers, could hope to throw themselves on the mercy of the judges at the city gate, egged on by a curious stream of onlookers. But this prison in the royal compound was for those who had gone against the king, an offense for which there could be no forgiveness.

Day turned to dusk as we left the outside behind. A dank smell came from courtyard of the moon-shaped building, in the corner of which was a space covered with matting. A rickety wooden ladder leaned against a wall near the mat. Voices emanated from beneath, some weeping, some cackling, some chanting.

The eyes of the guard who opened the gates for us turned from heavy-hooded boredom to shock when he recognized the prisoners the chief minister had in tow. The king's daughter and granddaughter! Out of habit, he bowed before us.

"What are you doing, you fool? These are my prisoners. Call Manas," the chief minister ordered the prison guard, who scurried off to find the warden. I raised my eyes and allowed them to roam over the windows and balconies on the three levels of the prison, and back to the mats in in the corner. I was curious, but so detached I almost thought I saw myself standing on one of those balconies and looking down. *What was behind those crescent rows of wooden doors? What and who was beneath the matting?*

The warden appeared, almost running toward us.

Unlike the guard, he took in the situation right away, and stopped short of bowing to us.

"My lord, greetings. What have we here?" the warden asked diffidently, as if accepting no more than a delivery of supplies.

The chief minister didn't bother to return the greeting. "Manas," he said gruffly. "Princess Tamar has murdered the friend of the king, Pirshaz. She is to be confined here until King Talmai returns to judge and sentence her. I have granted her mother's request that she remain with her in detention."

The warden's eyes trembled as he took in the identity of his latest prisoners. They flitted from side to side, from my mother to me, to the chief minister. Then they narrowed in confusion. He knew better than to question his superior. Still, there was a decision to be made.

"I see," Manas said.

"You see nothing," Mother shot back contemptuously. "But I do see something. My daughter and I can both see into the future. Did you know that? No?" Mother rushed on as Manas cocked his head.

"Look carefully at these eyes. We won't be residing in one of these," she paused long enough to gesture grandly at the tiny windows dotting the round inner walls of the prison. "We'll be staying in your quarters, and you will bring us any of our belongings that we ask for, until the king returns."

My heart overflowed with love and admiration for the way Mother had effortlessly mustered her royal demeanor. The effect it had on the warden was immediate.

Manas looked questioningly at the chief minister for confirmation that he could give in to a prisoner's demand. Mother's bearing, and her tone, had accomplished their purpose in unnerving him; I needed no special powers of perception to see that.

But there was more here. Whatever the warden was thinking had everything to do with how we would survive, and I needed to know what that was.

The king's chief minister had already spun away on his heel, followed by the two council room guards. "Do as you like," he threw out over his shoulder, barely turning his head. "This is your realm, not mine. Just keep them here, and make sure they're alive and unharmed until the king returns."

Clearly the warden was already wondering how the king would judge him once he returned and realized the circumstances of our incarceration. But I needed to know more, and I needed to know it now.

"Well?" Mother took a bold step toward the warden, continuing to reinforce our position before he had a chance to consider the contradictions in the chief minister's orders.

"Wait, Mother," I murmured, placing my hand in hers. It was time to summon my skills. I caught her glimmering eyes widen in surprise for a moment. But when she squeezed my hand in response, I knew she understood. I locked my eyes onto our captor's before he could evade them and I reached into that place in my heart where the power resided more potent than any salve or herbal tincture—

from where the power came that sensed what drove, poisoned, and sickened others.

In the eyes of this stranger who held our fate in his hands, I saw not the cruel master of a place of punishment and humiliation, but a man, like any other. I saw confusion there, not merely because my glance had drawn him to me so completely, but confusion at his orders, to confine us in a place where men and women were punished for crimes against the kingdom, real or imagined, and at the same time to keep us safe. And I saw that his fear of failing the chief minister was dwarfed by his fear of the king if harm should come to us while in his hands. I would use that fear—and not for the first time—to save a life. But this time the life would be my own.

I blinked when I was ready to release him, and that allowed Manas to tear his eyes from mine. He shivered and sprang back to life. He motioned two guards from their stations at the inner prison door to flank us. Just as they, too, were about to acknowledge our station with a bow, he stopped them with a cold look and an imperceptible shake of his head. But he could not stop them from glancing at each other, astonished, and then at him, to make sure they had heard right: "Take them. Lock them up in my quarters. Give them whatever they ask for."

Manas's quarters extended across most of the third story of the prison. Spare but spacious. Our meals, which were brought to us morning and evening without fail, consisted not only of bread still warm from the oven, baked with fine, gritless flour, but also of fresh fruit, figs and dates, grilled fish, and even the occasional piece of meat. Clearly the menu came from the royal kitchen, not the one that served emaciated prisoners. Servants had brought my lyre and loom, and even the half-filled scrolls on which I had begun to inscribe my father's praise songs as I remembered them. They lay on a high table in one corner of the chamber with a small bowl of powdered charcoal and a vessel for water to mix it with, reed pens and a rough stone to sharpen them, all neatly laid out in a row. Sleeping mats and soft wool coverings were rolled up under a bench along one wall, which was lined with colorful cushions. The two chairs in the room were simple, but at least they had backs. They had their own colorful cushions and were even adorned with carvings. The symbols of Manas's station served well as the furnishings of our confinement.

The apartment was fronted by an expansive open space that overlooked the broad stairway down to the courtyard. This was no ordinary balcony. It was the observation post from which Manas could surveil his domain. But for us, it meant a breath of freedom. At night, when the plaster paving gleamed in the moonlight, we walked along the parapet. Weeping and chanting emerged from the tiny rows of windows of the cells below us. Who knew which courtier was confined there and for how long, for real or imagined sins against the king, or, more likely, because of some petty grievance lodged by a minor official. During the day, from that same vantage point, we could see offenders brought in daily. Most of them, we knew. No doubt victims of lightning judgments rendered in the king's absence that would allow officials access to estates and wealth, Mother said.

Their hopeless imprisonment was in bizarre counterpoint to our own confinement, especially after Manas began to visit us regularly over rich and varied midday or evening meals that would almost have put the palace kitchens to shame. Manas was not the first Geshurite we had met who claimed Israelite blood through the tribe of Manasseh, who settled this area generations ago under the great warrior Joshua. He could, he said, trace his line all the way back to Manasseh, son of Joseph, through Joseph's Egyptian wife, Asenath.

I knew the story. It was one of the many that I had been raised on at the feet of Gad and Nathan. The irony of knowing that the man whose land my people had taken at God's command had now taken us did not escape me. But we let him regale us with tales we let him believe were new to us.

One day, Mother and I picked at the bountiful delicacies laid on the table before us. As usual, we sat next to each other, our backs to the wall, across from Manas, who dominated what he probably thought was a conversation. This time, he had launched into a long chronicle about his ancestors, pausing only long enough to refill his wine goblet from the slender jug he kept within his reach. As usual, Mother and I listened, feigning interest as we had agreed to do, never knowing what the man might say that would be useful to us. "My forefather Manasseh was born in Egypt. One of his concubines was a woman of Aram, from this very region you now call home. And so it was only fitting that the great warrior Joshua gave my forefathers this region as *our* home. My forefathers lived together peacefully with the local people, and so it should come as no surprise that King David came to our city to find a wife—you, my lady."

Mother's eyes narrowed and her full lips locked in an angry line. The look was not lost on him. The garrulous warden seemed to lose his train of thought.

"I mean ... we were honored ... it was a great moment ... for our king, for your family. I mean for our family, that is ...," he sputtered. He wasn't used to us interrupting him.

Mother cut him off. "Oh yes, such an honor," she said. Her voice was bright, but I knew all she wanted was for him to stop his proud and pointed prattle—her litany of humiliation. To stop reminding her with every word that my father, her husband, the king, had taken her to seal his ties with this powerful city. And when he grew strong enough, and no longer needed her, he sent her away, back to her father's house, keeping me from her. By then, royal fortunes had been reversed. My grandfather Talmai was now in thrall to Jerusalem, so much so that he had gone all the way there to declare his loyalty to my father's son, the new king, Solomon. Of course he had, Mother had told me. And she had whispered the story that had come to her of my father's deathbed command to Solomon to rid the court of all my father's enemies.

"As for Solomon . . ." Manas began again.

Had I spoken my brother's name aloud? No, of course not. The man was simply taking up the threads of his monologue. Or was he?

"I have news."

"Well, what is it?" Mother said, with more rancor than she should have.

Ignoring Mother, Manas turned to me. "The day after you were given over into my care, the council sent runners to King Talmai at Solomon's court, to inform our king of your crime, Princess."

"Surely the council conveyed the circumstances of what you call a crime," Mother shot back angrily.

Then he looked at her menacingly. His jovial veil lifted, and his voice chilled the room. This was no longer the friendly official sharing stories of his family with two noble ladies over a meal. This was the man who ran a prison full of men and women suffering because they had threatened his king. Mother and me included.

"The council's agents informed us that when our runners reached the court in Jerusalem, they were arrested as spies. King's Solomon's men intercepted their message with word of your crime before they could deliver it to King Talmai."

Manas turned back to me. He lifted my untouched goblet and filled it from the jug. "When your brother found out you were here, nothing else mattered but his beloved older sister. An Israelite army is on its way here right now . . . just . . . for *you*," Manas said with alarming sweetness.

As he spoke, he rose and made as if to slide in next to me on the other side of the table. Mother leaped to her feet and rushed around the table to block him, awkwardly stopping him at the corner of the table before he could reach my side.

Fists clenched, she raised her arms as if to strike him, then opened her hands and lowered them to his shoulders, grasping his robe.

"What ... news ... of my ... father? What ... news?" I had never seen Mother beg before. Her knuckles whitened around the cloth of his robe with every word.

She was a strong woman and half a head taller than Manas, but when he glanced, first at her hands against his robe, then straight into her eyes, the power was all his. I no longer saw awe in his eyes. Just purpose. And so did Mother. Her fingers flew open. So did her eyes. She backed away as if she had touched a burning brazier.

What had she seen?

Deliberately, precisely, Manas brushed his robe smooth where she had grasped the fabric.

"We know nothing of the king, Madam. All we know now is that our city is about to come under attack. The reason is in this room with me." He turned to me. "It's you they want, Princess Tamar. And I'm going to give you to them."

The vulture's talons dug deep; my heart was its prey. The beating of wings trapped my breath. Had this not all happened before? Yes. For the second time in my life, a besieging army would demand a single sacrifice. But the last time, I was the negotiator, I chose the sacrifice, and in so doing saved an entire city. The power was mine. Now, a city might once again survive because of me, but I ... I was the sacrifice this time. I had been reduced to no more than a pebble moved across a gaming board.

But at least I would not meet the same fate as the rebel Sheba, whom I had condemned to death. Or would I? Would my brother Solomon, the king, have inherited that same odious suspicion that I had somehow been involved in Absalom's plot against our father?

Now where was my power? Where was my prescience? My mother's vision had not dimmed, but the eyes of my own soul were blind.

Manas's languid daily visits stopped. The key would scrape in the lock and the door would open only long enough for him to look at us, peer cursorily around the room, and lock the door again behind him. There was a new tension in the air at the prison; we could sense it even in the sidelong glances of the servants as they came and went with our meals and to empty our chamber pots.

If anything, we were better cared for than usual. The sticky summer vapors that hung over the valley of Geshur and the Sea of Chinneroth had given way to crisper days and a brighter, bluer sky. It was the Turn of the Year. In Jerusalem, the sound of trumpets would have filled the air, one of the most powerful memories of my brief childhood, and in our isolation, I thought I heard them even here. The door to the balcony overlooking the prison courtyard was kept locked. Each day, three guards entered the room, the one in charge lugging the heavy wooden key to the balcony door on his shoulder. The guard in charge would open the door, the other two would exit and take positions that would keep us from approaching the parapet. He then gestured to us that we could come out. Before the sun could move across the sky above one tower to the next in the palace compound beyond the prison, we were ordered back inside.

I chafed at this new form of confinement. And after each day's brief foray into the fresh air, more painful than if we had not been let out at all, the vulture's wings would take my breath away again. The lyre stood forlorn and silent in the corner of the room, where I had last set it weeks ago. The warp weights of a half-finished tapestry pulled impatiently at the woolen threads, stretching them hopelessly useless, but I ignored them.

I paced incessantly. "What is happening, Mother? What will happen?" I couldn't stop myself from asking every day.

"My answer won't change," Mother standing with her back to me as her hands flew over her loom. "It's the same as the one I gave you yesterday, and the day before. They're waiting for your brother's army to arrive. They need to keep us safe until then. That's all I can see."

I could see that far, of course. But my thoughts were clouded with a fear of the future beyond that, a fear I believed I had put behind me forever. As many times as I believed I had taken my fate into my own hands, the day I took the life of Pirshaz was the day I stood up against every man who had wronged me.

And so, I waited.

On the day they came for me, I had earlier dreamed I was walking through the pungent fir copse of my youth, high in the mountains near Jerusalem, seeking the nuts I once gave out to strengthen weak hearts. The crisp, comforting aroma of pine resin filled the air from flickering torches like the ones that kept the night at bay in the palaces where I grew up.

But this had been no mere dream.

I opened my eyes and looked over at Mother, her form the vaguest outline in the still-dark room. She had sat up on her mat and stared straight ahead.

"Mother . . . *Mother!*"

But she couldn't hear me over the clamor that intruded into the night. Creaking wheels, clanking armor, the shouts of men that even the stout stone walls of our confinement could not keep out. That aroma—resin from a thousand torches that lit the path of my brother's army from where they marched to the walls of Geshur. That mighty army of King Solomon, come to fetch me.

Cracks of gray light now filtered in through the slats of the locked door as I scrambled to Mother's sleeping mat and clasped her to me. We sat, wordless in the knowing. She held me to her breast, her chin resting atop my head. "Now, we wait," she said above the din. She disengaged from our embrace and rose. As if this day were no different than any other, she rolled away her sleeping mat and blanket, and motioned me to do the same. The guard would be in soon with a jug of water along with bread, olives, and figs.

But there was no sustenance that day. I paced, while Mother kept mostly to the cushioned bench against the wall and watched me, her eyes wary, occasionally looking away toward some distant place I could never go.

The cracks in the door grew bright as the day wore on, then gray again with dusk. Finally, the door rattled as the heavy wooden key turned the lock.

Manas, the man who had kept us under lock and key, pushed open the door in one swift, rough move. His small black eyes roved the chamber, landing everywhere but on us. His jaw clenched and unclenched repeatedly as if he were about to say something, until he stepped aside.

He was not alone.

The man who stepped heavily over the threshold after him looked vaguely familiar. Taller than any man I had ever seen. A silver mane spilled from beneath his helmet, still shot through with the copper strands that bound him to the mountain folk of southern Judah where my father had first reigned. It was a trait he shared with King David, my brother Absalom, and me, once, before white had wiped away the russet that recalled a tie to family and homeland.

Broad pink scars beat paths through the warrior's grit-caked beard. One emerged from the tangle and ran up his cheek, spanning the place where an eye had once been, and disappeared under his helmet. I would never forget that wound. I had treated it myself. Though I could not save the eye, I had saved his life.

"Mother," I said with a calm I didn't fully feel. She had sprung from her seat like a panther when the key turned the lock and had stepped in front of me as if that was all that was needed to shield me from the stranger. Love flooded through me to dissolve the fear.

"It's Benaiah. Benaiah, son of Jehoiada. Do you remember him?" I spoke softly. Perhaps it was I who could shield her, repeating a name from her past that would calm her and diffuse the danger in this moment.

She might remember. Benaiah had been with my father from the days of the desert. His valiant spirit and loyalty had rightly earned the title by which he was known far and wide in Judah. They had taken him through a hundred battles against men and gods. I struggled to pull a memory deep from the well of the past, from before the time of my disgrace. And hers.

"Mother, Benaiah is the man who returned from Moab at the head of his men—thousands and thousands of them—marching through the streets of Jerusalem to present the smashed altar hearths of the abominable Chemosh to the king. What a glorious day that was! Remember?"

I couldn't see her expression, but when her shoulders relaxed, relief flooded Benaiah's battle-torn face.

"*Bat Hamelech!*" he said then.

My childhood title, my native language. Those two words seemed to fell the walls of our prison as if a battering ram had smashed into them. Benaiah's next words confirmed my sense that this was a rescue. He turned to Mother and bowed respectfully. "*Gevirti.*" My lady. I had never before noticed the music in that one small honorific.

"Please," he said, gesturing gallantly toward the two carved chairs. He remained standing, as if out of respect. His damaged face worked his lips into a grimace, but the rest of his demeanor told me it was meant to be a reassuring smile. We complied, and layer upon layer of tension in the room lifted.

Then he turned to Manas. The crooked smile disappeared, and his tone went stone cold.

"Leave us," he barked at Manas, who acknowledged the order with the obsequious bow of the defeated. Our jailer backed out of the room, his head still bowed.

"You have nothing to fear from me, my princess . . . my queen," he said, turning from me to Mother, then back to me. "I have come with orders from King Solomon, your brother. He has summoned you to Jerusalem and I am to escort you there."

In the beat of silence that followed, he brought his palms together in front of his chest and raised his brows as though waiting for us to respond joyfully.

"Nothing to fear? Nothing to *fear*?" Mother shouted at him, then turned to me.

"Nothing to fear! Daughter, do you hear that? You are too young to remember how this man stood at the gate of Jerusalem with your father's other *mighty men*." She almost spat the words. "And saw off a woman forced to cede her place to another and leave her children behind."

I didn't remember Mother leaving. One day she was there, and then she wasn't. But I had Mara, and my studies, then my tasks and my place at court. My life grew up around the loss, embracing it like a tree trunk that rejuvenates, scarred, rising up from its injury. But I remembered who "another" was—Bathsheba, the mother of my brother, who came into our house and our family as the victim of a crime, but whom many called an accomplice. In my father's world, it was all too easy to turn from one to another.

"Daughter!" Mother's desperate call wrenched me from my reverie.

A shake of my head and a shiver sent the unbidden images flying. I turned to face her. To cradle her hands in mine. "I was thinking back to those days, Mother. Look at me, now," I said, drawing her gaze away from the soldier standing over us. "This is what must be. The king's will must be done. And it will be my opportunity to explain both to him and to Grandfather Talmai what happened, why I did what I did. This . . . is . . . a . . . good . . . thing," I said, rocking her hands in mine with every word.

Perhaps my gift of "sight" had been taken from me forever, but my mother's violet-green eyes could still tell me when her soul ached.

I stood and stepped between Mother and Benaiah. "What will happen to her?" I asked him calmly. "Will she accompany me to Jerusalem?" But I already knew the answer.

"No. Princess Maacah will remain in Geshur. This is her home city, after all. But your brother has given me strict instructions that she is not to be harmed. She will no longer be a prisoner; she will be safe for the rest of her life." His eyes found mine. "I pledge it."

Yes. I had his pledge. But it was only worth as much as the word of any soldier who must complete his mission at any cost. I had no choice but to nod wordlessly, as if satisfied with his answer.

He half turned his head toward Manas, who I had almost forgotten was there. Manas's head was bowed, and his shoulders slumped as if he were the prisoner now, defeated. His realm, this accused compound, had already been taken from him.

"Call for your chief minister and for my personal guards," Benaiah ordered. Manas sprang to life, pulled open the door, and gestured.

Eved-Adad had obviously been waiting outside the door with— or under—Benaiah's guards. "Madam." Slowly, almost ceremonially, he walked to Mother and bowed long and low from the waist. She looked surprised, and what was more important, hopeful. She was a mother bidding farewell to her daughter forever, but strangely, I felt more like the mother. She was my lamb and I was her shepherdess. I could hardly bear to see her go, and it took all my strength to keep my features still.

"It's back to the palace then?" she asked in a plaintive voice I didn't recognize.

Eved-Adad looked questioningly at Benaiah, and hesitated. Benaiah must have sensed the look if not seen it out of the corner of his soldier's watchful eye, but he kept his eyes fixed on us. Not his problem.

"No, no, my princess, not to the palace," answered Eved-Adad. "You are to make your home with me and my wife Shemana. You remember Shemana, yes? We've spent many a pleasant evening together with you, and there will be many more. This is what King Solomon has . . . requested," he finished, seeking, in vain, at least a nod of approval from Benaiah to back him up.

"Good-bye, Princess Maacah," Benaiah said matter-of-factly. Extending one hand to help Mother up and cupping her elbow with the other, he led Mother out of the chamber. She turned her head slightly to peer over her shoulder for a last look at me, but she said nothing, nor did I.

Never and always. The words came to me on a breeze I could neither feel nor hear as soon as she'd left the room. *Never and always.*

And I knew. I would never see my mother again, but she would always be with me.

Jerusalem

Benaiah motioned his guards to take me out.

"You won't give me time to collect my cloak and a few of my belongings? I will need warm clothing for the road now that the weather is changing." I hoped my tone contained enough of a scold to penetrate a soldier's bullheaded loyalty to his duty.

It had. He paused, then raised his hand to stop the men.

"Go ahead. But be quick about it."

Thrusting aside the curtain over the niche that held my clothing, I quickly felt through the folded garments until I reached my woolen cloak with one hand. In the same movement I tried to reach the bench where my lyre lay. Then I pulled back. No, though that instrument had saved me, I determined never to play it again. In fact, it suddenly made me sick to think of it. I turned to go to the table that held my scrolls, but Benaiah had had enough.

"Leave those. You won't be needing them," he said flatly. He nodded to the guards to take me out.

I was greeted by utter chaos as I descended the broad staircase to the main prison courtyard. It had been years since I had seen Israelites in battle dress; now the courtyard swarmed with them. Some wore the *hagora*—the broad, richly adorned belt awarded by their captain for valor in the field. A few sported bronze helmets captured in some far-from-home battle. They had flung their leather shields clumsily over their shoulders, and their short swords thumped clumsily at their sides as they carried everything they could haul out of the prison storerooms and into the main palace compound. The mat that covered the corner of the courtyard, from which sorrowful voices emerged day and night since we first came there, had been cast aside, and the last of a sorry line of people climbed the ladder out of the pit. Benaiah's army was letting my grandfather's prisoners go. My thoughts were too bruised to realize what this meant at the time, but later I was to understand all too well.

The chaotic scene repeated itself outside in the compound outside the prison. I was surrounded by four of Benaiah's own enormous bodyguards, but they could not hide the goings-on. Israelite soldiers were emptying the palace storerooms, carrying jars of wine and oil on makeshift litters. Officers shouted orders, men cursed under their burdens, and the smashing of pottery echoed in the storage chambers as the huge jars full of grain were tipped over and emptied into smaller containers. Other soldiers carried huge logs toward the palace, piling them up against the outer walls.

Benaiah's men rushed toward the gate of the palace compound, pressing in on all sides as if to conceal me. There was no need. No one paid attention to the new king's sister, even if they could catch a glimpse of her—of me—between the huge men. Courtiers and servants poured out of the palace together, decorum forgotten, running to the compound gate, like me, carrying only a few possessions: a bag, a sack, a toddler.

When we reached the city gate, the two men grabbed my forearms and squeezed me through it within the sheer force of the crowd. The veil of the woman I found myself following was nearly in my mouth. "Keep walking," one said to me. "And don't stop."

I could not, even if I had tried.

Once we reached outside, the panicked crowd thinned as people scattered in every direction. The soldiers continued their hold on me, marching me resolutely forward, across a small wooden bridge over the wetlands surrounding the city, to a rise opposite it, where Benaiah's army had camped. There they left me at a tent in the center of the camp in a well-kept enclosure with fine, stout pavilions clearly meant for senior officers. A slave woman appeared from the dim interior. Gently, she took my cloak and shawl and laid them aside. She motioned to a heap of pillows and bade me sit, moved back into the dimness for a moment, and returned with a jug of cool water.

I drained it and fell back, exhausted. When I opened my eyes again, I had no idea how much time had passed, and it took me a moment to remember where I was. I rose and wrapped myself tightly in my cloak. So did the slave woman, scrambling to stand at my elbow, just behind me, but I ignored her. I strained my ears but failed to hear any telltale sound from the outside. I walked to the tent flap and pulled it aside, greeted by a twilight sky and two guards who sprang to block the exit.

"All right, all right," I said, stepping back again so they would move aside. The smell of burning dust stung my eyes and nose like a parched eastern wind of summer. I lifted my shawl to cover my nose and mouth. The darkening heavens to the east were filled with a strange, dawn-like ochre light.

Tongues of flame undulated from the depths of the city. *The palace!*

The guards suddenly snapped to attention, as Benaiah stepped out of the shadows.

"Why?" I asked him. My throat had closed against the grit, and the single word that fought its way out was more like a croak.

"This was your brother's order, Princess. When he caught your grandfather's messengers sneaking around the palace in Jerusalem, and realized you were still alive and your mother had been here all these years, he knew King Talmai could not be trusted. These things must be done. These are the ways of kings."

The exact words my mother had said when she described her exile from Jerusalem, the only home she had known in her adult life. Now she was gone, and I stood watching her home—and mine—burn to the ground.

As for what came next—if Mother, or Mara, had been there, they would have stopped me with a glance or a soft squeeze of my hand. But they were not. I cleared my throat and plunged ahead. "The ways of kings?" The very thought was ridiculous, and I could not keep the contempt out of my voice. My grandfather could have swallowed Israel any time he wanted, if he had wanted. "The ways of my father, you mean. I did not see my brother grow to manhood, but the flames from the palace are all I need to see to know that he has taken on the ways of my father. To burn, not to build. To avenge, not to make peace. My grandfather is a kind man. He went to Jerusalem to pay his respects to the new king. That was *his* way as king. He protected me when no one else would, he welcomed his daughter, my mother, spurned by my father back to her childhood throne, and allowed her to do the same for me. He has no designs on my brother's throne." I took a breath, hoping it would quell my anger, but it only inflamed it further. "If my brother has any wisdom, he will keep Talmai safe and allow us to be reunited. He will put an end to this sorry affair."

Benaiah's own voice emerged, his words grinding against each other like stones under a wagon wheel. "You, Princess, must learn your place again, I see. Please don't try my patience any further." He paused long enough for the reality of his words to sink in. "You should sleep now. We leave for Jerusalem at dawn."

I had been commanded to sleep, which meant I stayed awake for the rest of the night. The slave woman sat against the tent wall, alternately dozing and snoring in fits and starts, which only unnerved me more, so I rolled my mat and waited for morning. The exchange I had had with my brother's general ran through my mind. It had been a mistake. I would have to win him over, and I had, if I remembered the span of my journey so many years ago, ten sunrises between there and Jerusalem to do it.

Benaiah said not one word to me when he returned. He stepped into the tent without announcing his presence from the outside—a bad sign. The slave woman stood immediately and busied herself gathering my meager belongings. At the general's signal, I rose too. Outside the tent was Benaiah's way of begrudgingly recognizing my status—a donkey, saddled and ready, which he motioned to me to mount before mounting his own and leading the way. Six guards walked in front of him, and six behind with the slave woman and another donkey laden with supplies for the journey.

The third sunrise had come and gone. We were well past Lake Chinneroth and into the mountains of Issachar and Manasseh.

Nothing I said evoked a response. I resolved to maintain my own stony silence, but inside, I wept. *Mother, what should I do? Mara, are you here for me?*

The only answer that came was infuriatingly vague. *Win him over. Win him over.*

But how?

The answer came to me that night. There were two campfires in the evenings, one for me and the slave woman, and the other— the larger—for Benaiah and his men. While the slave woman and I lay near our fire, they drank and caroused and, as they threw their scraps of food into the fire, sent sparks into the night. Benaiah's voice was loudest of them all, and the story with which he regaled his comrades held the answer to my conundrum.

"Tell it again, you say? You have all heard it a thousand times, but all right, all right, I will."

Clearly the twelve men saw this journey as a chance to catch their commander's eye, to be for him what the mighty men had been for my father, which was why their voices were murmurs and his bellowed.

Even I knew the story he told; I closed my eyes against it. It had made the rounds of the court in Jerusalem as soon as it happened.

"It was a cold day in the high mountains of Moab," he intoned. The narrative continued interminably to set a scene that everyone already knew. He had been among David's thirty closest companions, he told them, but not among the top three. Every time he told the story, he embellished one detail or another, bringing him a little closer to invading that triad, even if only in his own mind. Finally, he moved to the climax.

"I had been on another dangerous mission to carry out the will of King David. I had prevailed, killed the greatest warriors of Moab, and destroyed their temple. I was on my way back to Jerusalem with a few of my most trusted men when I stumbled and fell into a deep pit." Here, Benaiah stopped speaking. My eyes still closed, I imagined he watched the men's faces to see the effect his suspenseful pause had had, real or pretended . . . he probably didn't care. "And what should I find within it?"

The men all knew and so did I, but they waited for him to say it.

"A lion, a ferocious, roaring lion, enraged by the cold, wet snow and his inability to escape."

"What did you do, General?" one of the men asked as if on cue and without a moment's hesitation.

"Well, I grabbed that lion by the scruff of the neck and choked the life out of it. That's what I did! And that's not the only time I encountered a lion. The second time was just months ago. Surely you've all heard it?"

Once again, flattering murmurs encouraging Benaiah to tell a story that, once I heard it, I realized must have been the talk of the court.

To hear better, I continued with my pretense of sleep, but turned over and tucked my bristly field blanket over my head.

"Well, by this time, King David had died and King Solomon, long may he live and reign, had taken the throne." He paused, leaving me to wonder if he waited for any reaction at all from me, which he received none of. I continued to breathe in and out in the rhythm of one who had slipped into the world of dreams. And so, after a moment, he continued. "There was once a king who was deathly ill. His doctors told him his only hope lay in drinking the milk of a lioness. In desperation he requested assistance from our wise king, who delegated me to the task."

His voice took on an even more dramatic timbre.

"Far and wide I ranged until, down by the Jordan, I found a lion's den. I came there every day with three goats, and threw them in, and each day I crept closer to the den. Eventually the lioness became accustomed to me, her benefactor, and I was able to milk her and bring the milk to the king. And it healed him, indeed it did!"

"Most amazing!"

"No man could be braver!"

"The finest servant of two kings!"

The boisterous chatter finally died away, and I drifted off to sleep, the men's obsequious praise ringing in my ears. The next day, our party broke camp as usual. We climbed and climbed up the mountains of Samaria to the point where—for the second time in my life, I could see Mount Hermon floating far away. The mountains of my homeland lay ahead. At midday, Benaiah called a halt to let the animals rest.

And I had a plan.

"Benaiah, son of Jehoiada," I addressed him formally.

"What is it," he replied gruffly, the first words he had spoken to me since we left.

"I couldn't help overhearing your story about the lion's milk last night."

"Get those donkeys watered," he shouted at the men, drowning me out so I had to repeat myself. He inclined his head to me. "Ah, I suspected you listened in. What of it?"

"As you remember, I was a healer in my father's court. I had heard tell of the wondrous effect of the milk of a lioness, but I never believed it. Even if it were true, I would tell the sick who asked me about it, how could a mere man ever obtain it? Now I know that such a man exists, and that the healing powers of the milk are true. My brother is indeed fortunate to have you in his service, as was my father before him. And I'm fortunate to have you as my guardian on this perilous road to Jerusalem."

Finally, he looked into my eyes. I had him. Next, I told him stories of my most amazing and unlikely healings, gaining more of his trust with each one.

"I remember how gently you treated my wound, Princess," he said, touching the hideous scar across his eye as I had often noticed him doing before.

I could not help smiling when he said the scar was good for his reputation as a warrior. I thought he might have smiled too.

As the sun moved westward of its apex, Benaiah ordered us back on the road until it set. The next morning, and for the rest of the journey, Benaiah sought me out, speaking to me as though we were equals. During it all, I learned of all the happenings in court in recent years.

My father's propensity for outrageous actions had continued, he told me. He had taken a virgin named Avishag into his bed over the objections and excoriations of old Nathan the prophet.

"Will I see Nathan in Jerusalem?" I held my breath, with a prayer that Benaiah would say yes, that I would indeed see the man who, together with Gad, had saved my life. That, after all these years, he would still be there, a bridge between my past and my future.

"No, Princess," Benaiah said, his voice soft and kind. "Nathan died just last month. I told him I had been ordered to bring you back, and it may bring you some comfort that he expressed to me the hope to see you again."

I looked away to hide the tears that welled up. I would not distract this man with my own sorrow. My task now was to glean as much as I could from him about affairs of court. And so I played some more on his outsized opinion of himself. I was rewarded with the entire story of my brother's coronation in Jerusalem, while my father's fourth son, Adonijah, his rightful successor, attempted a rival coronation. Amazingly, my brother had allowed Adonijah to survive the coup. Our father never would have. But then, I learned, that Adonijah had asked my brother—through Father's wife Bathsheba no less—for permission to take Avishag, who had lain next to my father at the end to keep him warm. Granting such a request would be tantamount to taking my father's crown, and although Benaiah never said so in so many words, his self-satisfied, prideful tone when he told me that Solomon had finally ordered the death of his older half-brother, it was Benaiah who had carried out the sentence.

The stories seemed endless, but so did the road. I girded myself in these tales like impenetrable armor. By the time we had passed the peaks of Benjamin and Jerusalem came into view from the Mount of Olives, I had a clear picture of the alliances and estrangements, both temporary and permanent—the grist that fed the rumor mill of palace and marketplace—the Jerusalem court as it would be when I arrived.

I was ready.

Memories assailed me as we entered the city. The streets were still carpeted with palm fronds from the Feast of Tabernacles—a sight I had not seen since leaving home so many years before. The mountain air was bright, and the sun kissed my skin in warm greeting as I dismounted from my tired donkey and passed through the palace gates. Courtiers' fine, floor-length robes swished as they glided back and forth self-importantly on missions real and imagined, and servants rushed about. After ten days on the road, nourished mainly on bread, olives, and dried cheese remoistened with spring water, I found myself assailed by the aroma of roasting meat for the midday meal as the palace's chief steward almost ran to greet Benaiah and his men. I recognized him immediately. He knew who I was, because I was expected, but was clearly not prepared for my appearance. His mouth gaped at my mane of once-red hair now turned white and thin, my thickened body, and the aging lines on my face. Who would know me as I had been? I had left the palace in a rush, but I had taken time with me.

I would have to get used to this response.

"Welcome, my lord general," the man said. Benaiah nodded curtly but did not stop. He led the way directly to the throne room. I was still surrounded by his guards, two in front, one at each side, two behind me. After all, I was a murderer, being brought before the king. Who knows what I might do?

The crowd of courtiers parted, one stepping behind the other like a complex dance when we entered the room. In another time, the warmth in this august chamber, the affection for me, had been palpable. But now, the thing I felt most—the thing I could almost taste—was fear. No surprise there; the author of the purge so recently committed—my father—was dead, but the executioner of his will now sat upon the throne as king.

Benaiah raised his hand in a signal for his guards to stop, and they did. I felt the hands of the guards of either side of me tighten as they pulled me to a halt and the general strode forward.

Benaiah's demeanor had changed completely when he entered the room. He seemed to diminish his stride. He stopped well before reaching the man standing regally at the far end of the room, head and shoulders above everyone else, a gold crown set firmly on a rich bed of glistening, well-coifed curls.

King Solomon's robe, a rich *argaman*, was a darker shade of the colors of the throne room's walls. Coral beads were sewn at the hem, creating a pattern of waves that undulated when the king moved. A trim black beard lined the strong jaw of my brother's handsome, youthful face.

He drew himself even taller when he saw me, then nodded to Benaiah and beckoned him closer to speak words I could not make out. Then, Solomon waved me forward, not once diverting his eyes from mine.

My baby brother. The last time I'd seen him, that's what he was. All he was.

I knew what I had to do. I knew the protocol. I fell to my knees, crouched, and put my face to the ground, my hands outstretched, palms down. The smooth stone cooled my burning face. I dared not look up. Instead, I focused on the tiny pits in the flooring. When the shuffling of soft, leather shoes reached my ears, I raised my head enough to see their jewels, and their straps that disappeared under his robe. The room was so silent, it seemed to me that my own breathing echoed between the chamber's walls.

What were to be my first words? What would Mother have said? The wound of her exile to make room for this king's mother in my father's bed, the pain of the crime against me in this very house, and my own unjust exile, threatened to overwhelm my thoughts. I had to focus not on the past hurts but on surviving my present circumstances. Hadn't I learned that better than most?

And so the words burst out before I could think anymore, "Let my lord, the king, my brother, live forever!" I raised my head enough that my voice could be clearly heard, then lowered it again.

The king gasped. Then sighed. From my vantage point, I saw a forest of feet shuffling uncomfortably at sounds I imagined the people in the room had never heard their king make before. The murmuring started again, but it died down when he spoke, startling me, sending earthquakes through my heart. "My dear, dear sister! My elder sister!" He lowered himself until his bejeweled hand floated into mine. Now it was my turn to gasp as I lifted my head again. He curled his fingers, gently beckoning me, and then—as our eyes met—he lifted his chin and smiled. I took his outstretched hand and rose. A memory washed over me of the last time I had held my little brother's hand. His nursemaids had been chasing him helplessly about the room as he giggled and fled from them. His mother and our father had smiled indulgently even when his antics threatened to topple some of the elders. Finally, the king's voice had boomed, "*Solomon!* Go to your sister!"

The little boy had stopped running, turned with a jump, then ran to slip one hand in mine, the thumb of the other in his mouth. I had knelt for a moment, gently unplugging the thumb, smoothed his hair, and looked into his eyes, the color of burnished bronze.

The gasp and sigh meant he had not forgotten. Those bronze eyes still gleamed, overflowing now with warmth and curiosity. "Come, please. Sit," he invited. I looked up at the empty throne, where our father had conducted all his audiences. "No," he said, gesturing at two simple stools nearby, where older courtiers could rest as they waited their turn before the king. "Sit with me."

Benaiah, forgotten, stepped forward, his distorted features forming a frown. "My king. I regret to remind you that I have brought Princess Tamar to you as your prisoner, as you demanded, following her heinous murder of a leading official in the court of your father's ally, King Talmai. If I may, I would now inform you that the palace at Geshur has been burned, but Princess Maacah is safe, as you . . ."

Benaiah's voice faded, as Solomon tore his eyes from me to glare at his general. He still smiled, but his eyes flashed a warning at the unwanted interruption. "Yes, General. Thank you for that. And you are indeed to be commended for fulfilling your mission. You will be duly rewarded." He paused, seemingly pondering something in the distance across the room that only he could see. Was he praying? Formulating his plan or bringing it to fruition?

"Step back now," Solomon said softly.

With Benaiah out of the way, the king lowered himself carefully onto the small stool. He arranged his robes around him and smoothed the richly embroidered cloth. Now, I thought. Now the king would be forced to deliver the inevitable charge of murder, and the reunion of long-lost brother and sister would no longer matter. But, instead, Solomon leaned forward, elbows on his knees, with an informality that took me by surprise. He uttered one word then. The one I dreaded. "Why?"

Now that he sat across from me, eying me expectantly, I would have to describe the scene in the room with Pirshaz, the ugly man's incessant advances. My defense? My determination not to relive the horror of what had been done to me in this very palace so many years ago. And who had defended me then? Our brother, a man long dead and disgraced.

The circle of courtiers pressed closer. Craning their necks, straining to hear. Whispers flew from the front to the back. I couldn't take a deep breath; I panted and the scene around the edges of my eyes grew blurred.

Solomon looked at me, then looked around at the crowd. "Move back!" he barked. And then, "*Guards!*"

The king's guards, who had been standing uselessly at attention by the dais in front of the empty throne jumped to action and pushed back the crowd. Their curious faces faded behind Solomon. Now, only the two of us remained.

"Why?" he asked me again, his voice barely above a whisper.

And I wondered. How do I convey what helplessness means to an all-powerful monarch? The only image that rose to my mind was that of the great gazelle hunt. Solomon must have inherited the love of this blood sport from our father; like David had, I imagined Solomon would have returned from his forays full of stories of the thrills. Deep in the heart of the southern desert men would flush out the gazelles and drive them, shouting and waving their arms and spears, to a space built by the ancients that stretched between high walls, tapering to a point, where the killing floor was.

"If I could remind you . . ."

"Why . . . did you *flee* Jerusalem?"

The room stilled. Not the moment nor the question I had prepared for during my journey here from Geshur. But no matter how many years had passed, how many more would pass, since the day Mara and I fled the city, the bitterness of my exile was a constant taste in my mouth, an unhealed wound in my heart. And though he had caught me by surprise, I spoke without hesitation. "Do you mean, because despite what had been done to me, I was protected in the home of our brother? That I could have resumed my place in court, perhaps? Even married our brother? Is that what you mean?"

"Yes, I know what happened to you, but . . ."

I wouldn't let him finish. The plough of my memory dug deep, turning over the earth of my sorrow and my wounds, before a man who had never known a moment of uncertainty about his future. Who had been coddled and protected by men and God.

"You know what *happened to me*? Is that the way they put it here? Of course it is," I spat out. "But do you know that after *it happened*, I was accused of perpetrating it on myself? That I had been part of a conspiracy woven by Absalom, to get rid of Amnon? That I had agreed to allow that rutting pig to violate me so Absalom could convince our father that Amnon deserved to die and that he, Absalom, deserved the throne?"

Solomon's face grayed.

"What?" I asked. "That's not written in the chronicles back there?" I motioned to the wall behind the throne where wooden shelves sagged under piles of rolled parchments. "No songs were composed about it?"

His face had begun to darken. I had to tread carefully now. The king was sovereign, and I was his disgraced elder sister accused of murder. Things could go either way for me. These next moments— my next words—would either free me or send me to the darkness of death. Or worse, imprisonment.

The room had gone utterly silent; the courtiers waited for the next chapter of a saga the likes of which would make the rounds of homes and palaces in Jerusalem. I bit my lip. But of the people who could have restrained me, spoken up for me, comforted me—Mara, Gad, Nathan, Mephibosheth, Mother—none were left to me.

And so, again, I spoke.

I thought back to my days at Abel. "Of the things that I wrested from my life," I began softly, "some you will never know. But if not for King Talmai taking me in, I would not be standing here before you today. He's here, I know it; summon him, and he will speak up for me."

"King Talmai, you say?" The words were spoken as softly as mine had been, but emerged cloaked in all of my brother's threatening power. "King Talmai has been executed." My breath stole away, and Solomon continued. "It was the only fitting punishment for the man who took in our rebellious brother, then brought spies to my very household, then lied to me about knowing your whereabouts. This is a man I could never trust. I vowed I would never be in the position our father was—needing Talmai more than Talmai needed me. And so I did to him what my father commanded I do to all who betrayed him."

My mind raced ahead. Was my fate decided then as well? Did our father speak of me on his deathbed? The hideous lie about my treachery? My grandfather had also taken *me* in. I was not like my brother Absalom, but would Solomon care to know the truth? Then again, if my brother saw King Talmai as the enemy, why would he persecute me for killing one of Talmai's courtiers? So, perhaps I would be forgiven. Even rewarded?

"Good riddance to Talmai," he said, with a wave of his hand. It was so easy for him. My chance for life lay in his next words. "Which reminds me . . . why *did* you kill his chief horseman?"

My skin crawled at the lightness of his tone. I clutched the sides of the stool to steady myself.

"Did you think I did not know?" he asked. "What do you think you're doing here? When I asked King Talmai where you were, he lied and said he did not know, and all the while you were safe within his palace. He sent spies to my court with secret messages from Geshur. Did you think I did not know what you did?"

I melded my grief into a weapon of greater power than any I had ever before wielded. I stood. And when his guards stepped forward, King Solomon waved back them back.

"Listen, brother, and I will tell you why. Listen, for once, with the true, pure heart of a brother who once trusted his little hand in the hand of the older sister he loved and looked up to. Listen with all the wisdom and compassion God has obviously given you."

Silence. Silence took my place on the stool I had left, then hovered around the two of us. And then, the king said, "Speak."

I drew a deep breath and the tales rushed out. Beginning with the revenge I took on Pirshaz, for every injustice ever done to me since that long-ago day within these very walls. I filled the chamber with every intimate detail of my disgrace, not caring who, besides the king, heard.

I paced back and forth until I'd completed my sorrowful litany, breathless. Only then did I come to a standstill before my brother. My sovereign. I hadn't noticed that he, too, had stood. Until that moment, I didn't see that tears streaked his cheeks and glistened within the soft curls of his beard. His eyes were squeezed shut and his smooth young brow furrowed.

Now, I knew. I knew what the deepest pain looked like. It had been my life's work to assuage it, but that day I had caused a man to feel *my* pain. I had broken him to save my life.

He choked as he tried to speak and gave up. What he did instead was unexpected. He removed his golden crown and handed it to a nearby courtier. Then he laid one hand atop the other over his chest.

He lowered his head. Closed his eyes again.

And then, of all things, he bowed to me, long and low.

Finally, he drew himself to his full height again. What could he say to me that his gesture had not expressed? It was more than I had hoped to achieve. Much more.

Indeed, he turned away from me and searched the little knot of astonished courtiers. His eyes lit immediately on an older woman at the front of the group but a little to the side. Magnificent, beaded robes seemed to weigh her down, much too big for her wizened, bent body. He inclined his head respectfully and gestured to her to come forward. I knew who she was. He then searched the group again and called two other women forward, one younger than the other. The older woman looked vaguely familiar, but then so did half of the people in the room. Still, I could not quite place her. She was tall and regal. Luminous black eyes, lined with kohl, peered brightly at me above dark cheeks. Elaborate kohl designs covered her chin and curled around her hands and what I could see of her forearms.

There were no introductions. I was exhausted from my recitation and still speechless at my brother's response. And in any case, I didn't need them. This was Solomon's mother, Bathsheba.

"Take my sister to the women's palace and see to her comfort," he told the women, who acknowledged his command with a nod. "I will call for her when I'm ready."

We walked through the corridor to the women's quarters, which I remembered all too well. The silence weighed uncharacteristically heavily on me. "It is as if no time has passed. . ." I began, turning slightly to address the older woman, who was shepherding the rest of us from behind.

"Plenty of time has passed, my dear," the woman responded drily. "Let's save our conversation for later, shall we?"

We crossed the magnificently colonnaded courtyard that I remembered as a child. Then, I would pretend it was the Great Sea. I would sit in my big woven basket of a sailing ship and set off to see the world, becoming a character in one of the stories Gad regaled me with about the men of the tribes of Dan and Zebulon who plied the sea with their magnificent ships.

We stopped at a stout wooden door, which a waiting servant opened.

"My sitting room," the older woman said. "We will rest here while they prepare sleeping quarters for you."

I looked around the room with more curiosity than good manners would indicate. I had never been in Queen Bathsheba's quarters, where she had no doubt faced off against my father, urging him to exile my mother. Memories came flooding back of the time when this woman stood at my father's side, head held high, pretending all was well. But there was no one at court, indeed no one anywhere in Judah, who did not know how she came to be there. The innocent blood that was spilled and the crime my father had committed— against her first husband. Against her. For the first time it dawned on me how alike she and I were. Blamed for the crime of which we had been the victims.

"Come back," I heard Bathsheba say. She fluttered her hands before my eyes. "You're not the only one who reads thoughts. But now's not the time." She turned. "Bring us some fruit and wine," she ordered the waiting servant.

"It's time for introductions," she announced. "Princess Tamar," she said, turning to me and then, gesturing toward the younger woman, "meet Princess Tamar."

I was standing face to face with a younger version of myself. Willowy, the same auburn curls creeping undisciplined from beneath a finely woven, amber-colored linen veil that hung gracefully from her strong shoulders. A fine, strong face and, what was more, she had my eyes, the left glittering blue-gold, the right, green-gold.

"You have my name," I said, unnecessarily. "Why?" The young woman opened her mouth to respond, but the queen mother took the other older woman's hand and placed it gently in mine.

"And *this* . . . is *Safira*," she said, as if I would recognize the name. I had heard it before, but I could not remember when. But I realized now that this night would be spent hearing Bathsheba's story . . . and much more.

All through that night, our words swirled and darted like swallows in the evening sky. We unfurled our stories, wept at the horrors, and in the midst of it all, laughed in amazement over the victories great and small that had led us to one place: survival.

Bathsheba spoke of her helplessness as a young married woman, her husband away fighting a war for his king, while at home she fought off the incessant advances of my father. Of the murder of a husband whom she could not protect. The move to the palace as her belly grew round and full, and the quiet death of the infant half-brother I had never seen. How she came to terms with her new life and tried to do as we all had done—work every waking moment to make the best of it. Then the birth of Solomon, the toddler who had grown into the man who now held my future in his hands.

"Solomon has many fine qualities," his mother said, her voice rising in what almost sounded like despair, as if offering him to me as perspective husband rather than the judge he was to be. "As your father's soul was about to leave him, I begged him to name Solomon as his successor." In the ways of the elderly, I could tell that Bathsheba was about to launch into a long recitation of facts already known. I could not keep the impatience out of my voice.

I had had enough of bloodshed. "Yes, Benaiah told me how your son carried out my father's wishes to purge the court of all the men who had wronged him during his life by having his general kill them. Even Joab, my father's nephew and defender." My voice faded for a moment as I overcame the desire to tell the women of my time in Abel, and my fateful encounter with that very same Joab. Instead, I extended my hand toward the younger Tamar, and gently tugged until she was standing in front of us. Before Bathsheba could continue, I tried to change the course of her recitation. "Please, tell me how I come to have a namesake in the royal court?"

Young Tamar looked at Bathsheba, then at Safira, as if seeking their permission to speak.

Bathsheba went silent, then sighed with the weight of the years. "Tell her," she said.

"I am your brother Absalom's daughter," the younger woman said. Her eyes had lowered when I asked Bathsheba about her, and her mouth turned down at the corners, as if in shame.

She must have been told everything. The court leaked knowledge of others like a cracked wine vessel, staining everyone. She must have known that she was named for the aunt she thought she would never meet; the woman wronged by her father, her grandfather, her wicked uncle.

How would I respond?

She certainly did not expect me to do what I did—and neither did I. I threw my arms around her and pulled her to me. The sweet smell of henna flowers rose from her hair and reminded me of my own youth. Comfort coursed through me, sweeping away revenge. Comfort in knowing that Absalom had brought me back into his life, that he had repented by naming his daughter for me. That every day of his life he had said my name.

"Tamar . . ." Still embracing my new-found niece, I thought I heard Absalom calling. But it was the queen mother once again breaking into my reverie. "Tamar, the night is almost past." Then, turning to the other woman, she said, "Safira, tell Tamar your story."

As soon as the woman began speaking, her accent gave her away. She was not from Judah, nor from Benjamin, and every few words there was one I could not catch.

"You and I, dear Tamar, are from the same stock. I am from Moab, just like your ancestress, Ruth." The way she said the name brought back the memory of my grandmother Nitzevet and the bizarre story of how her husband Jesse spurned her because he hated his Moabite roots. Of how he had made her and my father outcasts.

Outcasts. Will it always be thus?

"I am the daughter of a Moabite shepherd whom your father David hired to care for his sheep. Even after he became king, my father said your father would come to him in the wilderness and they would pass hours together. These were your father's purest times, I realized later, once I came to court and heard the stories about him. And this is where my father learned of your father's faith in the all-seeing, all-powerful Creator of the Universe. My father begged your father to teach him the marvels of your faith."

Recognition came to me as if on a wave. "I know," I exclaimed. "I remember you at court!"

Safira jumped in surprise at my excitement. She could not know what an important part she played in bridging the years of my absence. She did not remember me, but I remembered the odd, dusty little man from the desert who was often at my father's side in the audience room, standing out among the magnificently robed courtiers and sycophants and foreign delegations. And his little girl, who as often as not ran around the room with my brother and the other children of court officials.

"Now I remember your name. It was not known in Israel," I said, wanting to draw out the moment of this beautiful story.

"No," she said wryly. "Few could pronounce it. I was always told my father had picked it out for me as the daughter of a shepherd because it means 'little goat.' When I was given to Solomon and became his chief concubine, he wanted to change it, but I refused. And so he decreed another meaning for it—in your language—*crown of flowers*. Thus, I could keep my name," she finished.

"Look." Bathsheba pointed to the windows near the ceiling. Dawn was breaking, and yet exhaustion had not overtaken any of us. The tapestries covering the walls rippled as a breeze fluttered in and stirred the air, heavy with our stories. Mine fled to the place where secret pain lives. The ghost of a shudder passed through. I felt it in the depth of my bones. And when I opened my mouth to say so, Safira and Bathsheba stopped my words by saying that the same thing was happening to them.

I was strong now. Ready to face whatever lay ahead.

No sooner had the daylight sounds of the palace begun than a servant cleared her throat outside the door to announce her presence. She opened the door carrying a jar. Behind her was another servant with a basin, and behind them, the inevitable guards.

"The king will not see you today," the guard called before the door closed.

The servants poured the water from the jug to the bowl. I splashed a little on my face, but most of it spattered on the floor as I vented my frustration. Bathsheba and Safira, however, seemed unperturbed.

"I thought Solomon would render his judgment today," I said finally.

"That is not his way," his mother answered.

"He will call for you when he is ready," Safira answered. "Until then, you are to remain in the women's palace."

Another prison? I wondered. *Or a safe haven?*

Again Bathsheba read my thoughts. "Far from a prison. We will see to it that you feel at home."

And so they did. As the days passed, we spent hours weaving in the courtyard with the other women. We played with the children, admiring their clever words and laughing at their antics. Scrolls were brought to me, and I learned the annals of the court in my father's later years, the many more wars he had fought and the realms he had acquired. I read his poems and the few of Solomon and imagined it all set to music. I missed my lyre, but the pain returned when I remembered the last time I had played it, which had been in the presence of my assailant, and so I buried the desire.

The moon waxed and waned, the winter rains began to batter the palace walls, and still I did not see the king. Bathsheba, Safira, and the other wives and concubines came and went. Each time they returned from beyond the walls of the women's palace they spoke of King Solomon and affairs of court, but I had finally stopped asking Bathsheba what his decision would be about me and when he would render it.

"He wants to tell you himself," was all she would say.

From snippets of conversation I gleaned that Solomon had sent to Geshur for more proof of my story. The palace had been burned, along with any documents, but people talked; they always did. The servants spoke of quaking officials from Geshur with whom Solomon's men returned. I could only hope I had secret allies among them who would corroborate my testimony to the king.

It rained the entire night before Solomon rendered his judgment. Thunder shook the palace walls, and through the tiny windows I watched as lightning cleaved the sky.

The world dawned gray, as if exhausted from the battering it had received the night before. When a servant opened the door for Bathsheba, the hem of her robe was soaked from the walk across the courtyard. "He'll see you today," she said, and busily directed the servants to help me dress.

Bathsheba waved the servants aside. Safira shook out the folds of my gown, and Bathsheba tucked in a few errant strands under my veil. I closed my eyes for a moment, and it was Mara's hand I felt. With her spirit beside me, I held my head high as we entered the throne room.

Solomon sat on his throne—high, crowned, straight-backed, regal. His magnificent jeweled breastplate caught a ray of morning sunlight that greeted us. Flanking the stairs to the dais were three rows of court musicians, men and women dressed in gleaming white. The young women in the first row held tambourines and bells. And on a table at the foot of the stairs, covered with a purple cloth, was an object I never thought I would want again.

A magnificently carved *asor*, its ten strings embraced by a frame of warm, rose-colored wood in a melodious design, even in silence.

Not my lyre. Not the one Mother had given me in Geshur, the one that my assailant had touched, the one that had lulled him to sleep. The one forever tainted. A new one, the wood a warm, rosy color. I became oblivious to everything else in the room as it drew me toward it. My fingers caressed the delicate carvings of a fruit-bearing vine that wound its way delicately around the edges of the sound box. They floated across the ten strings that stretched elegantly across the curved frame. The notes that emerged were alive, perfect, bitter and sweet at the same time.

I looked up at the king, who spoke. "Need you ask? It is yours. A gift from me. Because you are blessed in your wisdom and your actions." And then he stood. He looked over the heads of the singers, at courtiers who lined the walls, and said, "The judgment she rendered was righteous. I rule that she has committed no crime, and furthermore prevented a crime from being committed against her."

He walked down the five broad steps of the dais and came to my side. Taking my elbow gently, he guided me over to a row of men, each more finely garbed than the other. Behind each stood a cluster of women—their wives and concubines.

"You will be a part of my kingdom from this day forth," he said. "I want you to meet my governors."

He introduced me to each, pausing after the name to tell me the part of the country over which the man ruled. "The son of Hur, of Ephraim . . . the son of Deker, in Makaz, Shaalabim, Beth Shemesh, and Elon-beth. Hanan . . . the son of Hesed—Arruboth, Sokoh, and the land of Hepher belong to him. . . ."

Each man bowed as Solomon said his name. The men then half-turned to gesture an introduction to the women who stood behind them. This was a strange and unwanted interlude; I'd barely had the time to take in the king's judgment. I peered, hopefully unnoticed, down the line and saw there were nine more introductions to be made. Soon enough it would be over.

"And, finally," my brother said, "this is the son of Abinadab. He is responsible for the entire rich and beautiful region of Dor."

I looked into the eyes of the man my brother called the son of Abinadab. Eyes too young to belong to our father's elder brother Abinadab. Eyes too kind to belong to a man who mistreated our grandmother Nitzevet and sent her into exile. But the eyes looked familiar, and he knew it.

So did my brother. "Yes, *ahoti*, you've seen him before. He's the son of the man in whose house our beloved Ark was kept before Father brought it to Jerusalem. He came often to court as a young man, and you and he would play with me and the younger children."

I looked behind the man and saw no flock of women there. Out of the corner of my eye, I saw my brother watch me carefully. "Yes, he is the only one of my governors who has not married." I looked from the man to the king. "I believe he has been waiting for you."

I hoped I was able to keep my face expressionless, because I wasn't sure I had heard right. Not only had Solomon pardoned me, he was granting me the one thing I thought I would never have. A home with a husband. Someone I could cherish. Someone who would cherish me. And, might I dare hope it? Children.

My brother had surprised and flustered me with his out-of-place remark, so I said nothing. I felt color mount in my cheeks and wished this moment to be over. Then, thankfully, it was.

He turned to the cluster of scribes seated next to the dais, heads bent, busily recording every word spoken. Speaking slowly to ensure his words were heard precisely, he declared, "Let the court chronicles reflect clearly for all time: This woman is a heroine. She is to be praised forever."

He raised his arms and extended his hands toward me, palms down. "God be gracious to you. From this day on, I will no longer call you 'sister,' but 'daughter.' And your name will no longer be Tamar. It will be *Taphath*. And this you will be called for all the days of your life."

Before Solomon had finished speaking, I spied two men standing silently in a corner, both smiling, both nodding. Gad the Seer—my old friend and confidante—and Mephibosheth, my trusted advisor. But before I could return their smiles with one of my own, the hall went wild with cheers and applause. The girls in the choir shook their tambourines above their heads, adding to the cacophony, stealing me away.

Had I been absolved, raised to a place of honor I had not dared hope I could ever have again? And had I received a new name—if I had heard right, after the wild myrrh, the first of the spices in the incense offered at the Tent of Meeting, the freest of impurities and the sweetest smelling?

Solomon waited until quiet prevailed. "And now, you will play the lyre. Singers!" He clapped his hands in their direction, then turned back to me.

"You won't know the words, for I recently composed them. But the tune is one our father often sang before the altar in the Grand Courtyard of the palace. I heard it in my childhood, and I believe you must have in yours."

The singing began. Indeed, the words were new, but the melody so familiar my fingers picked it out immediately and I gave myself over to the rhythm of the tambourines and the song of my healing.

Elohim mishpatecha lameleth teyn.

"Give the king Thy judgments, O God, and Thy righteousness unto the king's son; That he may judge Thy people with righteousness, and Thy poor with justice. . . . Let the mountains bear peace to the people, and the hills, through righteousness. . . . For he will deliver the needy when he crieth; the poor also, and him that hath no helper. . . . He will redeem their soul from oppression and violence, and precious will their blood be in his sight. . . . That they may live, and that he may give them of the gold of Sheba. . . ."

There were other words, about the greatness of kings, but I barely heard them. The ones that entered my heart were those that bathed me in soft, fragrant myrrh—the plant of healing, protection, and of long life.

THE END

Acknowledgments

First and foremost, to Eva Marie Everson, friend, co-author, coach, and fellow traveler. To Meir Bar-Ilan, author of *The Words of Gad the Seer*, for his knowledge, encouragement, and bright spirit; Rami Arav, for enlightening explanations about Geshur; Nava Panitz-Cohen, for helpful information about Abel Bet Maacah; Matt Susnow for reading the manuscript for historical accuracy; Aaron Dov Vamosh of blessed memory, for, well, everything for over four decades; and for their encouragement, Paul and Tania Feinberg, Uri Feinberg, Maya Dubinsky, Nili Vamosh Yosef and their families; and to Riki Rothenberg and Gila Yudkin.

A special "thank you" to Blythe Daniel of the Blythe Daniel Literary Agency for her belief in this project and to all the people at Paraclete Press for your belief as well. We could not have done this without you!

Miriam Feinberg Vamosh

As always, my heartfelt *todah rabah* to Miriam Feinberg Vamosh, for trusting me to work alongside her on this project . . . not to mention our years of friendship and the love we have for each other and for Israel. What an amazing God we serve who brought us together over 20 years ago. Ah, what He knows that we cannot begin to understand!

As Miriam said, thank you, Blythe, for opening your email and taking a chance on what I think is one of the most beautiful projects I've ever seen. To Paraclete, thank you again and again.

And to my family—my husband, my children and those they married, and our grandchildren—who amaze me with their tolerance.

Eva Marie Everson

Authors' note

Ahoti, A Story of Tamar is based on a book, considered lost but mentioned in the Bible itself (1 Chronicles 29:29) that further documents the life and times of King David's daughter, Tamar, and other biblical figures. The biblical story ends with Tamar living "desolate" (2 Samuel 13:20), but the ancient document reveals so much more, taking the reader beyond a sorrowful ending to a horizon of hope.

According to a tradition among the Jews of Cochin, India, they received the book from the Jewish community of Yemen, descendants of early exiles from the Holy Land. In a fascinating chain of fateful scholarly events, a group of manuscripts, including *Words of Gad the Seer* were brought from Cochin to the University of Cambridge, U.K., by the head of the Anglican Church in India Claudius Buchanan (1766–1815) in 1809. Recently, Israeli scholar Prof. Meir Bar-Ilan took upon himself the task of resurrecting this compelling ancient work and exploring its every aspect. In 2015 he published the definitive book on the subject.

Ahoti, A Story of Tamar is the authors' adaptation of the ancient manuscript alongside Prof. Bar-Ilan's study notes, which provides a powerful modern-day significance for us all, and especially for women.

THE RAVEN, TO ANCIENT PEOPLES, represented light, wisdom, and sustenance, as well as darkness and mystery. In the same spirit, Raven Fiction reflects the whole of human experience, from the darkness of injustice, oppression, doubt, and pain to experiences of awe and wonder, hope, goodness, and beauty.

ABOUT PARACLETE PRESS

PARACLETE PRESS IS THE PUBLISHING ARM of the Cape Cod Benedictine community, the Community of Jesus. Presenting a full expression of Christian belief and practice, we reflect the ecumenical charism of the Community and its dedication to sacred music, the fine arts, and the written word.

Learn more about us at our website:
www.paracletepress.com
or phone us toll-free at 1.800.451.5006

SCAN
TO
READ
MORE

More from Raven Fiction

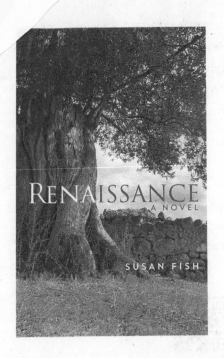